THE
DEVIL'S
SAINT

THE DEVIL'S SAINT

Dulcie Deamer

Introduction by

James Doig

RAMBLE HOUSE

2019

First American trade paperback edition

Ramble House
10329 Sheephead Drive
Vancleave MS 39565 USA

www.ramblehouse.com

Originally published:

T. Fisher Unwin, London, 1924

ISBN 13: 978-1-60543-974-7

Introduction © 2019 James Doig
Cover design © 2019 Gavin L. O'Keefe

Preparation: Gavin L. O'Keefe,
with special thanks to James Doig & Chris Mikul

The publisher has made every effort to locate the author's heirs.

CONTENTS

Dulcie Deamer, c.1920s

Dulcie Deamer: Spiritual Awakenings

James Doig

IN HER AUTOBIOGRAPHY, *The Golden Decade*, Dulcie Deamer tells the story of how the Australian occultist, Frank Bennett, a friend and star pupil of Aleister Crowley, asked her to assist him in a magic ritual to summon Pan. Bennett, who lived in a shack in Middle Harbour, Sydney, said he would build an open air altar of stones on which Deamer would recline naked; he would then cut the throat of a goat with a ceremonial sword upon which Pan would miraculously appear. Deamer declined the offer on the grounds that she was too fond of animals to allow the sacrifice of a goat. Not long afterwards Bennett died of a heart attack—Deamer left open the possibility of Satanic influence as, just before his death, Bennett said he was preparing for an experiment and had to confront and overcome certain "entities." In a 1947 article about Bennett in *Famous Detective Stories*, 'A Black Magician in Sydney,' Deamer altered the story somewhat, writing that a friend had participated in Bennett's experiment and had seen Pan appear behind the altar. Although Deamer explained the apparition as the result of hysteria, she wrote, "But there, in the bush, under the sunny Australian sky, a blood-letting mummery was carried out which belongs to Ancient Greek and Roman pagan rites, and to the frantic hysteria of the witchcraft of the Middle Ages." The episode reveals aspects of Deamer's interests and personality—a lifelong fascination with ancient beliefs and nature mysticism combined with a practical scepticism of the efficacy of magic and the occult.

Mary Elizabeth Kathleen Dulcie Deamer was born on 13 December 1890 in Christchurch, New Zealand. Her parents were George Edwin Deamer, a doctor who was always short of money, and Mable née Reader, the daughter of an army officer, who worked as a governess for a time and taught her children—Dulcie and her sister, Dorothea—at home.

A formative event in Deamer's life and thought occurred in about 1902 when the family moved to Featherston in the North Island of New Zealand. She describes the experience in a 1965 audio interview with the Australian oral history pioneer, Hazel de Berg:

When I first saw the bush—that was when we moved north to the Wairarapa Valley from Christchurch—the impact of it for me was enormous. I can't really explain what the impact was, it was so big. At once I felt absolutely at one with nature. I was simply crazy about nature. I couldn't get close enough to her. When I used to explore the hills—the woody hills, alone as I used to—I felt I was back in some earlier time. Not thinking about it but in it. This feeling was extraordinarily strong.

The beauty and raw force of nature produced a spiritual awakening in the precocious young girl that had a lasting effect on her writing and thinking. Deamer's fiction is characterised by a rare descriptive power, the ability to evoke the vitalism and magic of untouched landscape. Take the following passage from her unpublished novel, *Sacrament*:

A lovely land. Stems shot up like palest silver; other trunks were as if carved from rounded masses of lustreless garnet; veil upon veil of creepers, starred with colour, screened the rock-walled retreats of god-spirits, palms lifted motionless plumes, and tree ferns, taller than a man, and green as bright grass, crowded together where the minute humming-bird, with fiery feathers at its throat, poised like a hovering insect above spikes of tuberoses that exhaled an odour heavy and divine—intoxicating as the sacred drink made from pineapples. Great boas, mottled green and brown, coiled motionless as though entranced. With a flash of many-coloured fire the macaw spread its wings. The golden turkey strutted in the glades. The sudden hillsides were hanging-gardens of bright emerald, inlaid as with pearl and turquoise with patterns of the blue and white convolvuli. A coffer of treasure had been wrought by the creator-gods of the four corners of the world.

There is an implicit pantheism, of the presence of the divine in the beauty of the natural world, which points to an interest in the supernatural. This interest was sparked early in her life: as a seven year old, while exploring a fern-shaded gully at the end of the garden, she felt an invisible "Presence," what she later described as a "religious experience" that made an indelible impression her. A few years later, she regularly took solitary walks in the hills and gullies of the Wairarapa Valley, "powerfully drawn to touch again what I had contacted at seven."

If Deamer felt that the "Presence" was something akin to the spirit of nature, then this was another concept or entity that was drawn into her mystical philosophy. In another unpublished novel, *New Earth: A Legend of the Future*, which describes the creation of a religion built on feminine principles following the destruction of civilization, a character observes:

> "We've gone too far"—he said, "We've taken the wrong turning. We've made ourselves gods outwardly, not inwardly, and we have destroyed ourselves, and convulsed the earth, our mother. As things are, I am glad to die. I saw it coming, and I could not stop it. Something will rise out of this, but all we have known will be swept away. I am going back to the earth. Whether I shall be aware, in any mode, of anything again, I do not know. But I am glad, and ready, to sleep in the arms of Mother Earth. I have always loved her, and I have done nothing against her."

There were also more conventional supernatural manifestations in Deamer's early childhood. Her autobiography describes the appearance of ghosts and poltergeist activity at the houses at Christchurch and Featherston, and these incidents are elaborated on in a 1946 article for *Short Story Magazine*, 'Ghosts I have met.' Rumour had it that the house at Featherston had been the location of two murders, and this may have been the cause of the manifestations that "would bring that unique and horrid, eerie shock which no other kind of fear imparts." In the article Deamer claimed she had no interest in chasing the occult, but ghostly happenings followed her throughout her life.

Deamer was a voracious reader from an early age and her parents allowed her free access to their extensive library, including her father's medical works. She took a particular interest in history, archaeology, anthropology, and the works of Walter Scott and H. G. Wells, most notably Wells's short story, 'A Story of the Stone Age.' Her reading influenced her solitary explorations of the Wairarapa Valley: she would imagine herself a stone age hunter stalking and killing prey, and on one occasion she felt compelled to remove her clothes in a small glade in a sort of Palaeolithic ritual.

Her parents were also drama addicts and they encouraged a love of the theatre and acting in their eldest daughter. When Broughs'

London Comedy Company toured Christchurch in 1899, Dulcie was brought in to act in a child role in one of the Broughs' dramas. She was a great success and the experience, as she recalled in her autobiography, left her "stagestruck for life."

Thus, very early in her life, around the age of eight or nine, Deamer had been exposed to the influences that would shape the course of her life. She was soon also writing: composing poetry and a novel inspired by Prescott's *Conquest of Peru*. Perhaps the defining event occurred in 1907, when she was still sixteen, when she won a short story contest run by *The Lone Hand*, a new Australian fiction magazine modelled on *The Strand*. First prize was £30 and publication in the magazine with illustrations by Norman Lindsay, later to become one of Australia's foremost artists and writers. The story, 'As it was in the beginning,' is a Stone Age tale, clearly modelled on H. G. Wells' 'A Story of the Stone Age,' about the Strong Man who captures the Red-haired Woman from another tribe, and how the two come to respect each other as equals after they are attacked by a lion and its mate. The story was published in January 1908 and was an instant sensation; Deamer was feted in the New Zealand press as a bright literary talent.

1908 proved an eventful year for the seventeen year old girl. She continued to write and followed up 'As it was in the beginning' with three further tales of the stone age—'The First Born,' 'The Great Water,' and 'The People of the Lion-slayer'—which appeared in *The Lone Hand* in June, July and August 1908. These stories continued the story of the Strong Man and the Red-haired Woman, who are now leaders of the tribe: the death of their son, the migration of their tribe to a coastal area (including a fight with a pterodactyl), and conflict with another Neolithic tribe in which the Strong Man is mortally wounded and stabs his partner before dying. A couple more stone age stories were written for inclusion in her short story collection published the following year.

In 1908 she also became an apprentice actress with the Taylor-Carrington Dramatic Company and, chaperoned by her mother, toured New Zealand playing in a popular melodrama called *Is She Guiltless?* She also met and married thirty two year old Albert Goldberg (who had adopted the surname Goldie), a manager and publicity writer for J. C. Williamson, the great theatrical manager. It is difficult to overstate her marriage to an older, sexually experienced man: all of her novels deal with young women at the cusp of adulthood and discovering sex, worldly experience and spiritual awakening for the first time. Over the next sixteen years Deamer's life was remarkably full: she had six children (two of whom died in infancy), travelled overseas several times on theatrical tours, including to Asia, the United States and Britain, and published four novels, a collection of short stories, and a considerable amount of poetry.

The short story collection, *In the Beginning: Six Studies of the Stone Age and Other Stories Including A Daughter of the Incas A Short Novel of the Conquest of Peru*, was published in Melbourne in 1909. The short novel is *A Daughter of the Incas*, which she wrote between the ages of 13 and 16 and which constitutes more than half of the collection, is a love story involving Nahua, a fourteen year old girl who becomes a Virgin of the Sun at the high temple at the Incan capital of Cuzco, and Hernando de Soto, a conquistador during the Spanish invasion. The best story in the collection is 'Hallowe'en,' a werewolf tale in which the change from woman into wolf, achieved by magic, symbolises escape from the patriarchal strictures of married life into the freedom of a rich natural world. Deamer's opulent and sensuous style perfectly captures the magical medieval world of the story:

Hevar stole down by a field edge, her belly low in the sweet, soaked grass. A mild glow lay on the face of the field, as though the patient, hidden earth were breathing, and the breath was luminous. Twice a great owl skimmed the grass-heads with some semi-human, prick-eared, slit-eyed atomie hunched between the motionless wings.

In its 2000 words 'Hallowe'en' is packed full of this kind of intense movement and activity. There is no other comparable story in the collection and it is a shame that it was many years before Deamer reprised this imagined medieval world in *The Devil's Saint* (1924).

Her first novel, *The Suttee of Safa*, was published in 1913 by G.W. Dillingham, a New York publishing firm, where she was living at the time. Deamer described it as "melodramatic, sugary and immature," and indeed it is a passionate love story set in Delhi during the reign of Akbar, the great Moghul Emperor, in the late sixteenth century. Deamer's judgement that she would "prefer to forget I ever perpetrated *The Suttee of Safa*" is harsh: the historical detail is nicely realised and her prose is well suited to the sumptuous court life of Akbar's palace.

In 1918 she had a novel of the conquest of Mexico, *Valley of Bleeding Hearts*, serialised in *All-Story Weekly*, but it never saw separate publication. Her next book was a daring historical novel set in the time of Christ. *Revelation* (1921) is a radical take on the Passion story. It concerns Astarte, a fifteen year old dancer who arrives at the court of King Herod hoping to experience all that life has to offer; she attracts the amorous attentions of the Roman captain Valerius, which prompts the jealousy of her fellow dancer, Iris, who injects her with slow-working poison. Astarte is rescued from Valerius by David, a religious ascetic who has fallen in love her, however after a night of passion David finds her dead the next morning. She is miraculously revived by Jesus, who has arrived in Jerusalem with his disciples, and David intends to marry her much to the consternation of his mother. However, she quickly tires of domestic life and while exploring the streets of Jerusalem she is ravished by Valerius, attacked by a Jewish mob who drag her to the temple to be stoned as an adulteress, and saved by Jesus as described in St John's Gospel. When he sees Christ's suffering on the cross, he is moved to abandon his faith, but his pessimism begins to lift when he is reunited with Astarte, who has been injured in the Biblical earthquake that caused the rending of the veil in the temple. After a night together, Astarte dies and shortly afterwards David sees the resurrected Christ, his faith renewed. He becomes Stephen and establishes a Christ community in Jerusalem.

Revelation was published by T. Fisher Unwin in London and Boni & Liveright in New York and is the most common of her novels. It was well received, especially for its precise and accurate detail; the reviewer of the Australian literary journal, *The Triad*, said "the book is remarkable for its fidelity to facts of history and all we know of human nature...[Deamer] gives us a credible picture of a great period, and she makes the greatest figure in history seem more real than he has ever before seemed in a work of fiction."

The following year Deamer returned to New Testament Jerusalem with her next book, *The Street of the Gazelle* (1922). Cassandra is a captured Greek girl, enslaved by the Romans, and Evan is a galley slave who falls in love with her on board a merchant ship. He saves her from the depredations of the ship's captain and from subsequent mutineers before they are split up when the ship runs aground. Evan joins a group of pilgrims on their way to hear the preaching of John the Baptist by the river Jordan, and when they are attacked by Romans he joins a resistance movement against the Roman occupation. By chance he meets Cassandra, who has been captured by slavers and sold to a rich Roman, Philip, becoming his mistress. Evan is disgusted by this turn of events and leaves her to travel to Jerusalem to continue the resistance. Cassandra follows him there and overhears a conversation that the Romans are about to raid the hideout if the rebel group on the Street of the Gazelle. After helping Evan escape the raid, the reunited lovers die in each other's arms, after which is a curious twenty page coda in which the souls of Evan and Cassandra are given a tour of the afterlife by a Greek philosopher named Creon. The critics were cautiously positive, again praising Deamer's eye for detail and her historical accuracy, though naturally the ending puzzled most readers: "It is interesting, but it does not convince, and it exasperates as all anti-climaxes must exasperate." The self-sacrifice of lovers is common in Deamer's fiction, as is marriage by mingling of blood, which leads to a spiritual unification of souls.

In *The Devil's Saint* Deamer returned to the imagined Middle Ages of "Hallowe'en." Like *Revelation* and *The Street of the Gazelle* it was published by T. Fisher Unwin in England in 1924 and International Publishers produced an American edition the following year. After attempting to prevent a witch burning, sixteen-year-old Sidonia is accosted in a forest by a troupe of strolling players and is rescued by a knight, Gervais, the son of Count Arnold and step-son of Countess Sabina. He takes her to the city where she lives in the street of Martyrs with her mother who is a fortune-teller and presumed by the common folk to be a witch. Gervais kisses her —his "first taste of passion"—but, embarrassed by his behaviour, he leaves her on the street where she is picked up by a mysterious tall figure in a black coat and hood. Known as the Master he introduces her to a cellar tavern called the Thieves Kitchen, where he kisses her and claims her for himself. At midnight on Hallow-e'en Sidonia performs a ritual and her spirit flies off to the join the Witches' Sabbath and encounters various strange creatures:

> Moonlight, beating pinions, faces, and swift shapes—faces that had in them something of the eagle—wide golden eyes that were soulless; arched brows and noses; hair like tongues of fire; limbs flaked with golden scales or feathers. There were four—two upon either hand. Strait-standing in their air, they bore her steadfast company as the poised, they drifted —they were uncountable. Black imp-things, wickedly grinning, that whizzed and somersaulted; translucent maiden-shapes, linked hand to hand and dancing wreath-wise in the

void; bird-like creatures, sapphire-blue, white, rosy, or sable
—men's thoughts, plumaged in accordance with the emotion
that had shaped and speeded them; the naked selves of men,
women, and children, sleep-released, drifting like vapour,
dreaming, half-conscious; wandering flames, bat-thoughts,
ghosts. Overhead the full moon, an inexhaustible, round lake
of blinding silver, drenched everything in light.

This section was published separately in 1923 as 'The Devil's
Ball' in the literary magazine *Vision* and was illustrated by Norman
Lindsay.

While publicly declaring that she will reform the witch Sidonia,
Countess Sabine secretly has her produce a love philtre for Gervais.
Still unaware that Gervais was the knight who rescued her in the
forest, Sidonia performs the spell on her own behalf as a means of
gaining political power, and she despairs when she believes that
Gervais has fallen in love with her as a result of the philtre rather
than true love. Realising what has happened, Sabine orders Sidonia
to be burned as a witch; Sidonia manages to escape and is about to
commit suicide when she is rescued by Gervais. He fights for her
soul against the diabolical Master during a Black Mass in the crypt
of the cathedral; the Master is killed and is unmasked as none other
than Count Arnold who has been leading a double life. Sidonia is
captured and while she is being burned at the stake Gervais saves
her once again, the two of them miraculously unaffected by the
flames. To underline the divine sanction of their love, a massive
thunderstorm suddenly breaks and douses the flames. Sidonia re-
solves to enter a convent, believing that God "had summoned her to
enter a religious house and become a saint herself," and the novel
ends with Gervais planting a kiss on her lips, which you'd think
would hardly meet the approval of the newly ascetic Sidonia.

By the end of 1922 Deamer's peripatetic lifestyle was over and
she settled in Kings Cross in Sydney where she quickly became a
permanent and well-known member of Sydney's literary and artistic community. By that time she had split from her ineffectual
husband and left her children with her mother, who had also moved
to Sydney, to raise. One of Deamer's children, Rosemary Goldie,
who died in 2010 aged 94, was celebrated as the first woman to
serve in an executive role in the Roman Curia. In 1923 Deamer
famously attended the Sydney Artists' Ball in a leopard skin outfit
(associated with both the stone-age stories and a scene from *The
Street of the Gazelle*); she was to wear the "never-to-be-

dead-and-buried leopard skin" at subsequent balls and there is a photograph of her dancing in it with the Australian actor, Chips Rafferty, in the 1950 Artists' Ball.

Declared the "The Queen of Bohemia" by her friends Deamer embraced the Roaring Twenties with open arms, and the largest portion of her autobiography is devoted to a chapter on her life in the 1920s, "The Golden Decade." To make ends meet she focused largely in journalism and produced freelance contributions to publications like *The Woman's Mirror*, the *Bulletin*, *Aussie*, *Health and Physical Culture*, and *Adam and Eve*. In 1929 she applied successfully for an annual pension from the Commonwealth Literary Fund, which she received for the rest of her life. The pension application says that as a result of her writing she made £177 in 1926, £205 in 1927 and £198 in 1928, and lists her four children and her mother as people wholly or partly dependant on her.

Deamer continued to write poetry and she published prolifically from the 1920s to the 1940s, most of her verse being published in the *Bulletin* and *The Woman's Mirror*. A volume of her poetry, *Messalina*, was published in the Jacaranda Tree Books of Australian Verse series in 1932, and a second volume, *The Silver Branch: Twenty-Seven Poems*, in 1948. A pamphlet, *The Blue Centaur*, was published in 1953. Her poetry is steeped with the same mystical and other-worldly elements, themes and settings that characterize much of her prose, most notably the transcendental poetry of *The Silver Branch*, whose elemental images parallel the earth spirits and creatures in 'Hallowe'en' and *The Devil's Saint*. Thus, in 'The Glen of Birds':

> Seek well for Enchantment, and find her
> > In the core of a gem
> (For these hills, to clear sight, are of sapphire,
> > And I speak of them).
> Seek well for Enchantment, tread softly,
> > And see her robe's hem.

And in "The Sirens":

> Listen! their rhythmical voices
> > Where their sandstone gates arise—
> As when a temple rejoices
> > In a Mystery that lives or dies,
> > With monotonous, magical cries.

Deamer was also heavily involved in Sydney's theatre scene, particularly the experimental theatre of the 1930s, and a number of her plays were published and produced. Her "morality plays" as she called them—*Easter*, *In the Heart of a Woman*, *In the Mind of a Child* and *In the Soul of a man* were published by the Australian Theatre Society around the time of their productions at the Tom Thumb Theatre in Sydney. "That By Which Men Live" and "Victory" were dystopian futuristic plays; although they were never published, manuscripts are in the Campbell Howard Collection in the National Library of Australia.

There was a sixteen year gap between the publication of *The Devil's Saint* and her last published novel, *Holiday*, which appeared in 1940 in Australia but was not published overseas. In the meantime, in 1929 the Melbourne publisher, Frank Wilmot, had reprinted *In the Beginning* as *As it was in the Beginning*, substituting 'The Last Child' for 'The Turn of the Year.' Also, in 1932 and 1933 *Valley of Bleeding Hearts* was serialised in Australian newspapers as *The City of Blood*.

Holiday is the clearest exposition of Deamer's mystical philosophy in a published work, which explains its unusual structure and plot in which the main characters, Irene and Ezra, are transposed to different times and places, firstly in Roman Palestine, then in the City of the Carpenter (*ie.*, heaven), and finally in present day. The book traces the different stages of human consciousness, the evolution of the soul, until a spiritual "oneness" is achieved: "separateness is swallowed up in Unity—when you know that life is One, not many. And that the Soul of Unity is what we call God." As with all of her novels, the female lead is a teenage girl yearning to experience life to the full and on the verge of sexual and spiritual discovery, with physical enlightenment often leading to spiritual understanding.

Her ideas are fleshed out in more detail in her unpublished novels that survive in manuscript in the Dulcie Deamer Collection in the National Library of Australia. For example, here is a crossed out section (presumably to make the text more palatable to a potential publisher) of "Sacrament: A Novel in Three Parts":

He stood in cave temples, and in open air temples that were groves or circles or standing stones: he walked in processions that carried votive fruits and wheat, and in others that moved to make blood offerings: he knelt before Earth Goddess images, and Sun God images, and Child God images in innumerable sanctuaries, and before bloodless alters above which glowed windows of jewelled glass that displayed God the Father, in a splendour of sun-rays, and the Mother amid the lilies of the field with the Child in her arms...for his consciousness was one with that of the whole race of Adam now—Adam the sun-quickened, the earth-formed...yet he knew also that in the very flesh he had kneeled and walked, and raised his palms sunward in many of these rites, for the brief, dark spasm that was named death was a bridge between individual life experiences, even as the seed planted in darkness lifted itself in other seed planted in darkness lifted itself in other seed again into the day...there was no death: there was only the movement, in a seeming spasmodic rhythm, of unfolding life...

(Part 3, p. 71)

These themes and ideas are developed in her other unpublished novels, *New earth: A Legend of the Future* and *The Warless Land*. Deamer's personal philosophy, developed throughout her life, was obviously important to her, but she hardly mentions it in her autobiography, concentrating instead on people and events that she hoped would make the manuscript more desirable to a publisher (in fact, it wasn't published until 1998, twenty six years after she died). She wrote:

I suppose my own general attitude could be described as "basic Christianity". I know that, very early, it took its own individual road. I was quite small when I told Mother, "If I have to believe in hell, I believe that nobody goes there!" But from that time on I never discussed my "road" with Mother. What with my Stone Age researchings, "Adam and Eve" went overboard very early in the piece. But my colossal confidence in what was behind it all produced my unshakeable "something will happen" faith—which has always been justified. And from as far back as I can remember I have always *looked forward* to death, as the "next adventure" that nothing can deprive me of.

Peter Kirkpatrick, who edited *The Queen of Bohemia*, also gives her mystical philosophy short shrift, describing it as "a transcendental vitalism derived from comparative religion and, probably, theosophical sources."

Although *Holiday* was her last published novel, Deamer continued to publish poetry and even wrote a series of crime stories for the Australian pulp, *Famous Detective Stories*, in the late 1940s and early 1950s. By this time her powers were failing her and she began to be seen as an eccentric Kings Cross identity, interviewed by time to time by curious journalists like James Holledge who interviewed her for his exposé, *Inside Kings Cross* (Horwitz, 1963) —a similar fate befell the notorious artist, Rosaleen Norton, the "Witch of Kings Cross."

Deamer was forced to leave her beloved Kings Cross when she suffered a stroke in 1970 and moved to the Little Sisters of the Poor home in Randwick. She passed away peacefully on 16 August 1972. Her reputation had declined sharply from the 1940s and her death was noted in only a few newspapers. The publication of her autobiography by the University of Queensland Press in 1998 sparked renewed interest in her life and in the artistic milieu of Kings Cross in the 1920s, however it has not led to a revival of her work. This is a shame as she made a unique contribution all forms of literature and there are rare delights to be gained from her sinuous prose and mystical philosophy.

Bibliography

Dulcie Deamer by Hazel de Berg [sound recording] nla.oh-un1979556. 1965

Deamer, Dulcie, *In the Beginning: Six Studies of the Stone Age and Other Stories Including A Daughter of the Incas: A Short Novel of the Conquest of Peru* (Melbourne: Day, 1909)

——, *The Suttee of Safa: A Hindoo Romance* (New York: G.W. Dillingham, 1913)

——, *Revelation* (London: T. Fisher Unwin, 1921)

——, *The Street of the Gazelle* (London: T. Fisher Unwin, 1922)

——, *The Devil's Saint* (London: T. Fisher Unwin, 1924)

——, *As it was in the Beginning* (Melbourne: Frank Wilmot, 1929)

——, *Messalina* (Sydney: Frank Johnson, 1932)

——, *Holiday* (Sydney: Frank Johnson, 1940)

——, *The Silver Branch: Twenty-Seven Poems* (NSW: Swinburne, 1948)

Kirkpatrick, Peter (ed.), *The Queen of Bohemia: The Autobiography of Dulcie Deamer* (Brisbane: University of Queensland Press, 1998)

National Archives of Australia, A463, 1970/3727 (Dulcie Deamer – Commonwealth Literary Fund)

National Library of Australia, MSS 1539:

1539/2: *Sacrament: A Novel in Three Parts*

1539/3: *New Earth: A Legend of the Future*

1539/9: 'Anime Mundi' (a short story)

THE
DEVIL'S
SAINT

I. SIDONIA IN THE FOREST

1

THE GOLDEN FOREST of mid-autumn was as entranced and motion-less as the reflection of a maiden standing by a mirror of still water whom the spell of a wizard has transformed into a figure of gold. A blueness like the ghost of the aromatic smoke exhaled by wander-ers' forest fires dwelt in the long aisles. The deer, with their big, velvet, listening ears, stole delicately, like shadowy, graceful thoughts through a half-divine dream. The leaves were still. They were as the gold-limned wreaths of foliage that embellish the bor-ders of a holy legend written upon vellum. It was noon, but the veiled sky was whitish. There was no direct light. An autumnal trance held the world.

Sidonia took her way through the largesse of fallen leaves. She wandered, pausing often, seeming to listen for some expected sound. But there was none. She was like a person looking every-where, cautiously, for the secret of autumn, which is more myste-rious than the secret of spring, and has more power upon the soul.

Sidonia stood quite still, one hand laid over her heart. Her hand was not clean. It was shaped like a lady's but grimed like a peas-ant's. Sidonia was sixteen—an age as mystical as October's glades of gold, in the innermost of which surely the Grail is exposed for veneration on the altar of a ruined Gothic chapel—or perhaps Kundry, the lovely witch-temptress, stands clad in gilded scales, and holding a vessel filled with purple wine.

There was no sound—nothing. The raw, damp, yet incense-like smell of mould, dead fern, and dying leaves was an actual but im-palpable presence. The forest uttered yet withheld its secret. The girl stood in the midst of that perfect circle which is the eternal moment of a miracle.

Sidonia was narrow as a lad. Her short, russet petticoat was torn, and her feet were bare. A plait of black hair hung across her shoulder. Sidonia's chin was delicately cleft. Passion slept and dreamed on the sad curve of her lips. Her eyes were as dark as hidden and fathomless water in the heart of the forest. The dilation of their pupils suggested fear, exaltation, or strong excitement. If one looked fully into them they were extraordinary eyes.

Surely, in this very instant, Sacred Love, under the form of a virgin knight upon a pale, soundlessly trampling charger, would appear; or Profane Love, in the shape of a tall and evilly handsome spirit of the earth, with wan, unholy fire beneath his feet. Sidonia could not have said which she would have chosen.

No sound, no movement, nothing. A pale golden leaf dropped, flickering. The tree-roots, half-hidden by the prodigal leaf-drift, were like knotted and sleeping serpents of dark-green jade by reason of their coating of velvet moss. The golden forest—a shrine with open doors—was tenanted yet tenantless. And Sidonia waited, one hand over her heart. This was the abode of ultimate beauty—and beauty is the mask of love. Sidonia wanted love. She waited——

A faint, faint scream, heard by the spirit rather than by the ear, travelled athwart the trance of the world. There was death in the sound.

Not a leaf stirred. The forest listened.

Sidonia turned her head. The hand that had rested above her heart went out and found the coldness of a tree-trunk. She pressed her palm against the bark, that was slightly moist, as though the tree were exuding a chilly sweat.

Again came the bird-like shadow of a scream. It tingled. The girl sprang with the nervous start of a touched hare. Leafage rustled, dead wood snapped and crackled, and many leaves fell flickering as she dashed barefooted towards the death-cry. One deep excitement had been transmuted into another. No implacable arms of a lover had appeased her, but now she fled, breathless, to slake the swift, primal wonder-thirst—the thirst for delicious terror. Those in whom the sap of life is wine, not water, run always towards a hazard, not away from it. Love-hunger, when it is of the spirit as much as of the body, is one with danger-hunger. The hands of the naked soul reach towards the flames.

Sidonia ran like a boy. More and more clearly the high, tingling screams guided her. The dream-quality, impalpable as fine smoke, which had invested the forest, had vanished like smoke in air. Somewhere in this windless wilderness of trees clad in cloth of gold a sudden and savage thing was happening. What was it?

How much farther? Would she be in time? She panted with open lips, a peach-flush of quickened blood in the clear young sallowness of her face.

The screens of aureate foliage thinned out before her. Russet bracken stood more than knee-high.

"The curse of the Devil on you all! No, no! I'm a servant of God—I gossip with Him! Oh! Oh!"

That was the voice that had screamed.

Ah!

Sidonia brought up short. The shabby black bodice that sought to strangle her bosom seemed about to split. She was on the verge of a clearing, tapestried upon three sides with autumnal glories. On the fourth side there was the shaggy thatch of huts. A little smoke rose, and beyond, where the flank of the land sloped upward, were the walls, the round and pointed turrets, the steep-pitched roofs, the little scarlet pennons like forked dragons' tongues, the thin spires, fretted like stony vertebræ, of the town from which the girl had that morning come. Very far away it seemed, for the dull white noon withdrew all things to a wizard remoteness, but the distance was scarcely more than four miles—an hour on foot.

"Oh! Oh!"—a spasmodic, brainless outcry, high and thin.

Sidonia could not see the crier; she only saw men and women who elbowed each other in a close-packed group or ran to and fro like dogs on the edge of a fight. They were a rough lot—half-barbarous forest dwellers, eating goats' cheese, going nearly naked in summer, and knowing scarcely more about the business of their souls' salvation than the red foxes whose odour resembled theirs.

A little apart from the cluster two fellows were driving a stake into the earth with wooden mallets. The blows sounded dull and heavy. Tow-headed children clutching armfuls of faggots came trudging from the direction of the huts.

"The hands that hold me shall rot off at the wrist! The weaned child shall sicken and dwindle, the unborn child shall shrivel in the womb! Death on you—death on the born and the unborn!"

A pregnant woman with dishevelled, sun-bleached hair hanging on her shoulders shrieked piercingly, clapped her hands to her sides, and fell to the ground in a sort of fit. The faggot-bearing children stopped in their tracks. The grazing goats who nightly shared roof-shelter and body-warmth with their masters raised their heads. With a panicky recoiling movement the cluster of folk broke up, and Sidonia—standing petrified in the exquisite grip of the terror she had run herself out of breath to find—saw that from which the horrid voice came.

It was no clawed and feathered devil, horned and beaky, but a little tattered hag of a woman, with a wild head of ash-grey hair. She was down on the ground, bent double upon herself, her brittle wrists grasped by a couple of hairy-chested men, whose corrugated fore-heads were dashed with sweat and whose eyes were bloodshot.

"Fire! Burn the witch before she blasts us all!"—the scream of a woman who flung up her arms.

"Look! She's bewitched Meggin and the child she's quick with!"

"Fire!"

"My girl has a ringworm as big as a platter since the witch looked at her!"

"She put barrenness on my pumpkin vines!"

"My man spoke to her, and a falling tree crushed him!"

"She sends running ulcers!"

"My milch-goat dropped twin dead kids!"

"Burn her! Her eyes look crossways!"

"Light the fire! Who's afraid? The wood devils are stronger than Satan. I'll kill a white cock for them!"

"Bring fire!"

"Fire!"

Women beat their sagging, sun-browned breasts with their clenched fists. Knee-deep in the thinning bracken, Sidonia looked on with the fixed gaze of a sleep-walker.

A whimper came from the fleshless crone.

"No-o-o! Not fire—for the love of Jesus! He won't save you if you burn His mother, will He? I'm His mother. I've done nothing. I kiss the shoe of God. Not fire—it burns! Oh! Oh-oo!"

The maundering voice ended with the tremulous sound that a kicked bitch might have uttered. Two inhuman eyes with a slight cast in them, that had been blue but were now reddish, peered left right. The eyebrows above them were white and bristly.

A youth with a smoking faggot came running from the hut-cluster. Much scattered firing lay about the stake. The holders of the crone hauled her forward between them. Shrieks and screams went up, as though the mob of witch-burners were themselves licked by flame, and the woman in a fit clawed at the sere grass.

"No-o-o! Not the fire! It burns! Oh-o-o! Oh-oo-o!"

Something stirred in Sidonia that did not seem to be herself —something winged. She moved very quickly, and found herself right among the outcrying folk, close to the stake.

"Stop! You shan't burn her! She can do nothing to hurt you. She's only mad. Are you stupid as animals?"

It didn't sound like her own voice, it was so high and rapid.

A dead silence followed; everything arrested in mid-movement. Mouths that had been opened to shout remained open. The smoke from a hearth of embers in the midst of the hut-cluster hung in the air like a faint, blue-grey cord. Then a goat bleated in the fringe of the forest.

"It's a tree-maiden; I saw her come out of the trunk of an oak!"

"A wood-woman!"

Those nearest to Sidonia drew back.

There was a loud, braying laugh.

"Her! She didn't come from no oak-tree. No, sirs! She's Lame Lisa's girl—the witch's daughter."

A purple-faced pedlar with a frosty stubble of beard on jowl and cheeks shook jelly-wise with mirth. A long-haired dog, fantastically clipped to resemble a little lion with a profuse mane, sat on his haunches grinning between his master's bandy legs.

"Don't let her fool you, folks. It's just a case of witch help witch."

"A witch! Burn her along with the other!" screamed a girl of fifteen or sixteen with a child straddling her hip.

Sidonia felt like a person suddenly awakened from a vivid dream on a cold morning. Her spirit experienced a shiver. She smelt body-rankness, she saw corded muscles, she was gazed on by blood-injected eyes.

"Make her repeat a Paternoster. If she can't we'll burn her!"

A Paternoster! Sidonia could no more have recited one than she could have uttered a sentence in the tongue of the angels. She was as ignorant of prayer as a cat.

Several hands reached towards her. Oh! The fire! It was like a nightmare. Her soul screamed though her mouth was dumb. She flashed half round, dodged clutching fingers, and bolted for the golden shadow of the trees.

"Catch her! The fire for her!"

Several were in pursuit.

"Haw! Haw!" It was the rich, braying laugh of the pedlar, and the yapping of his dog was mingled with it.

Sidonia ran for her life. Behind her was—fire. The muscles of her legs trembled under her. There was a taste of blood in her mouth. Tree-roots under drifted leaves almost tripped her. Twigs slapped her across the face. She must not be caught.

Her heart was beating so that it must surely burst in another moment. She felt physically sick. Her knees were failing her. There was tall bracken about her. She dropped, and lay like a hare that listens for the hunt to go past.

Leaf-deadened tramplings came to her—nearer—someone was moving through crisp, waist-high bracken close at hand. She held in her breath. She was about to be discovered.

"Hi, boys! She's slipped us!" The speaker was within four feet of the cringing girl.

"She's changed her skin. A black fox ran in front of us as we lost her!" This voice was some distance away.

"Let's get back or we'll miss the burning, fellows."

More tramplings—receding— Sidonia released her breath in a great gasp. Every strung muscle of her went slack. She was abject, her face in the damp leaves that smelt as musty as old clothes in a chest. A series of little dry sobs shook her.

Quiet—a tranquillity like that of a shadowed pool whose mirror is unbroken by any rising fish. Sidonia lifted herself until she sat upright. The brownish-amber dusk of the forest encompassed her. The hunt had missed her; she was as safe now as an escaped rabbit. That morning she had meant only to go out a little way from the walled town to pick up firewood on the forest's fringes—the forest where there were robbers, wild boars, wolves, wells and springs that cured all diseases, hermits, tree-women crowned with oak-leaves, dwarfs, and, it was rumoured, a dragon. It had lured her, her very fears expectant and delicious. Beneath the surface of her thoughts she had hoped to meet some invincible lover—Grail-knight or pallid and handsome demon. And so she had gone deeper and deeper into the windless leaf-mists—the summer-shrouds that were more beautiful than summer.

All was still as a cathedral. She got up slowly. She must begin to go back. If she could find the way——

The deadened yet tingling rumour of a distant scream—again— Was that the smell of burning? Oh, horrible! Sidonia thrust fingers into her ears. Now she could hear nothing, but her mind still heard. That smell! Still stopping up her ears, she began to run—through bracken, leaf-drifts, mists of leaves. A dappled doe sprang up and fled off before her. Rabbits scuttled. Ahead, something pallid glimmered—the grey-white, weathered figure of a wooden Christ nailed to a tall cross where two dim wood-paths met.

Sidonia halted. She unstopped her ears. All was quiet. Not a leaf flickered. Not a leaf fell. There was only the raw incense-smell of mould, dead fern, and dying leaves.

2

THE GREYISH, WOODEN Christ was nearly life-size; the battered figure appeared fraught with infinite pain. Sidonia drew slowly near to it. She looked at the thorn-crowned head, at the iron nails through the hands and feet, at the deep wound in the side, from which not all the red colouring had been washed by rain. Her heart was sorry. Here was pain like the pain of the crone they were burning in the forest—like her own pain of fear. Pain understood pain. She was not afraid of this figure; it suffered, and had been treated unkindly. She laid her hand on the squared shaft of the cross.

"They hurt You," she said, "they killed You. But they shan't kill me! I wouldn't have hurt You like that."

Looking up at the drooping, weather-marred face of the Christ, she laid her other hand on the pierced feet of the figure. Quite similarly she would have touched the velvet muzzle of a dead deer or the blood-soiled fur of a rabbit.

There was a loud, clashing rustle of wings. A white pigeon, strayed perhaps from some dove-cote in the town, broke from the foliage behind the Calvary, fluttered a moment in the air, and then beat upward.

The girl turned her face up quickly. If it had been a seraph with eagle-feathered pinions of rose and azure she would have been delighted rather than alarmed. She was not afraid of any animal, angel, or devil, though the last two she knew only by report.

But as the commotion of the dove's wings faded a dead twig trodden by some approaching person snapped sharply.

Friend or enemy? The girl turning to face the sound, stood in the shadow of the Calvary, ready for instant flight.

The faery gold of the woodland tapestries, seeming in a manner self-luminous—for there was no light under the dull sky—was embellished with the jet and ruby of berry clusters. Twigs bearing leaves that might have been dipped in blood made a thin, sanguine mist behind the Calvary, whose shaft was seamed with emerald moss. In the gloom of gold and the red shadow of the beautiful, bloody leafage Sidonia waited. Autumnal leaves clung to her flight-loosened hair. She was pale, vital, yet still as a deer at gaze; in some fashion enigmatic as the fair yet sombre mystery that encompassed her. A plump grey squirrel ran across the wood-path, ignored the girl, and darted up the shaft of the Calvary, clinging there.

A man—a young man, naked to the waist, the hollow contours of his face softened by the down of a blonde, budding beard, his rather womanish, sensuous lips tightly compressed, his deep-set blue eyes strange flames of fire, his starved ribs flecked with blood-marks, a thorn-branch in his hand—this was what the wood-path yielded to the sight of Sidonia and of the grey squirrel.

The man advanced slowly. He lifted his head, looking up at the wooden Christ. His lips moved, his ravaged face was like the face of a person in Paradise, who is depicted clothed in embroidered robes and standing upon a sward besprent with flowers, gazing upward at the Blessed Trinity seated upon three thrones.

With a little movement—a flirt of the fine bushy tail that was like a quick shrug—the squirrel ran head first down the shaft of the cross and vanished in the crisp-red golden underbrush. The man's gaze, caught by the flicker of retreat, discovered the motionless young girl.

"Oh-h!"

It was an indrawing rather than an outletting of breath. The man's mouth remained open. He dropped the thorn-branch. He crossed himself, then made the sign of the cross in the air. Sidonia remained as she was, staring with great eyes like a doe.

"In the name of the Father, and of the Son, and of the Holy Ghost! Depart from me!"

Not a leaf loosened. Nothing moved. Sidonia stood her ground.

The young man fell to his knees in the wood-path. He beat his breast with his fists. His face was upturned, straining towards the Christ.

"Lord, deliver me! I have fled from sin into the depth of the wilderness, I chastise myself with thorns, yet Asmodeus and Ashtoreth follow me like two hounds! In spring the white May blossoms reveal the dazzling bodies of young, naked devilesses, and in autumn the falling leaves are the yellow hair of Lilith, Satan's mistress. The yellow hair falls over me as I sleep. Oh, Christ! this evil spirit has eyes more beautiful than a deer's!"

His own bloodshot blue eyes shifted from the figure on the cross to Sidonia. His face worked. He rose, took a step towards her as though drawn by cords, flung up his hands with an inarticulate cry, slewed round, and ran clumsily back upon his tracks, fleeing very audibly into the wild.

Sidonia put her hand on the cross again, as though to support herself. After about a minute she laughed a little. It was amazing to frighten instead of being frightened oneself. Something in the manner in which this mad person had looked at her reminded her of a starving dog sniffing towards a spitted capon, but afraid of the fire before which it revolved. "Eyes more beautiful than a deer's!"— that was a thing to be remembered.

What next? Wonder stood upon the right and danger on the left. Anything might issue from the dim, aureate caverns of the trees—a strayed princess trailing brocade over the leaf-drifts, or a unicorn. But in a couple of hours or less it would be dark—dark and cold as death. Already there was a chill in the tranced air like that of a tomb. It would be a night of frost.

Sidonia followed the wood-path, taking the opposite direction to that from which the anchorite had come. She followed it for a long mile, seeing nothing except rabbits, the amber dusk deepening imperceptibly under the rigid branches of the trees, above whose summits was the low, opaque sky.

A strain of music— Someone was playing in the forest. No mortal, surely. The girl cautiously approached the sound on cold and tired feet. A leaf or two flickered down on her like golden tears.

The wood-path died in a small, sere glade, beyond whose outer fringe of sapling poplars was the high-road. A youngish man, fair and rather short, stood in this open space drawing a monotonous yet piercing and plaintive air from a vielle. A lanky fellow with a tooth missing, and wearing the peaked and belled headgear of a jester, sat on the ground, alternately eating black bread and chewing a pig's trotter. A pock-pitted man sat by him cross-legged, his cap, with its peacock's feather, very much on one side. He was munching an apple, and suddenly took four more from a wallet and tossed them aloft, keeping them there with the ease of practice.

"Good lad!" said the jester, speaking with his mouth full as the playing ceased.

And then Sidonia came slowly out from the trees, looking very small and young. The fiddler saw her. He made a little bow, digni-fied but rather comical. His blue eyes, frank and smiling as a child's, looked straight into hers.

"Oh, here's company!" said the jester. "Sit down; there's plenty of room."

"Have an apple?" said the pock-pitted man. He threw one, and Sidonia caught it with a laugh.

A fallen log invited weariness, and she seated herself upon it decorously—lady-fashion. She crossed her neat ankles. She took a bite out of the apple. But all the while her eyes were on the fiddler. He had a straight nose; his fair hair had a curl in it.

"By Christ! She likes your looks, Francis," said the jester, his mouth full of pig's trotter.

Sidonia flushed a little. The fiddler, who had sat down by her, laughed shortly, like an embarrassed boy. "Do you live in the forest?" he said.

"No," said Sidonia. She hesitated. "That is —I—there's a village not far from here——"

She was afraid, suddenly, that if she told the truth someone would again point a finger at her as the witch's daughter. She desired that the fiddler should not know of this. He was youngish, pleasant-looking. As she bit circumspectly at her apple she was on the defensive.

"Where do you live?" she said.

"Everywhere."

He smiled at her.

"He's the same as us fellows," said the jester. "Picks up a living where he can find it, and if folks throw him a silver penny thanks God and goes to bed drunk."

The fiddler laughed his boyish, embarrassed laugh.

"Not drunk; my stomach won't stand strong liquor." He looked at the girl. "Do you know how far it is to the city by this road?"

"I—I think four miles," said Sidonia.

He stood up and began to wrap the vielle carefully in an old cloak.

"The night air affects the strings, and there is a frost coming. God keep you all."

His smile was as cheerful and impersonal as sunshine. It made no distinction between the girl, the jester, and the pock-pitted juggler. With another little bow he turned and left them, walking rather stiffly, as though he'd swallowed a sword, the swaddled vielle tucked under his arm. An impalpable autumnal mist, like the exhaled breath of the dying earth, subtly blurred the sight on every side. The sapling poplars were like tall, narrow flames of gold, warmthless and lightless. The banks of bracken were like cold fires.

The jester drank deeply from a leather bottle, wiped his mouth with the back of his hand, and passed the bottle to the juggler.

Sidonia, her apple eaten, sat silent on the log. She was furiously disappointed. Was she of no greater attractiveness than the man with the broken tooth or the man with pock marks? Was she something to be abandoned as lightly as an apple-core or a gnawed pig's trotter? She was enraged against the fiddler, with his straight nose and impersonal blue eyes. What a fool she had been to deny the town! Why, he would have walked with her all the way if she had spoken the truth. Four miles—and the bluish, close-pressing dusk coming down on them, frosty, and mysterious, and aromatic as a church. Her muscles, eager for movement, were all tense. But she must not get up and run after him. She had pride!

"Have a drink, girl?"

Sidonia shook her head. It was twilight already, and a twinge of panic assailed her. Four darkening miles, and her feet were tired! She could have wept.

"Must make a start soon for the town," said the jester, addressing no one in particular. "Great day to-morrow, eh, girl?"

"Yes," said Sidonia mechanically.

"All Saints' Day. And the Young Lord coming back from the wars. What's the cockerel's name?"

"Gervais."

"Very nice, too. How do they call his sire?"

"Count Arnold."

"And his dam?"

"The mother who bore him has been long dead. The Countess Sabine is his stepmother."

"Is that so? Now I know all—hic!—all the family history. Give us a kiss, sweeting."

Sidonia was brought back to earth with a cold thud. She had had experience of drunken men, and instantly stood up. The raw chill in the air was like the chill of a sepulchre.

The tall jester got to his feet almost as quickly as the chit of a girl.

"Going to leave us, eh? Without a—hic!—'By your leave,' like Francis the Fiddler. Oh, no, you're not!"

His hand gripped her. He was sinewy, unwashed, and the gap where the front tooth had been knocked out was very noticeable.

"Didn't they learn you manners at home? When a gentleman asks for a kiss you've got to give him one. You've got to give him anything he wants."

"Let me go— Please! I—I don't kiss men."

"Don't you? Well, here's a man who's going to kiss you, you—hic!—pretty brat."

"No!"

"But I say yes!"

"Here, hold on!" The thick-set juggler was upon his feet. His face had an odd, worm-eaten look, for the smallpox that had attacked him had been of the confluent variety. "I reckon I've a say in this. We share and share alike, don't we? Toss a coin for her; winner licks the honey off the bread first and loser takes what's left. That's fair enough between friends."

"Yes—hic!—fair enough. I'm a sportsman; the bastard who says I'm not's a filthy liar. Let's tie her up to a—hic!—tree, so she can't bolt while we toss for her."

Sidonia fought dumbly—fought till her hair was all about her face and half her bodice laces had burst, and the linen smock was torn right down from one shoulder. But they were two against one, and that one built for speed rather than weight. So she was dragged to a poplar, her arms bent backwards until they met behind the sapling, and her wrists secured with a knotted kerchief. She strained like a puppy trying to pull loose from his chain, and threw herself from side to side, but she could do nothing.

The blue, subtle mist—the visible breath of autumn—dimmed the raw air. The high-road beyond was surely a path only for the folk of the otherworld whose white steeds left no hoof-prints in the dust.

"Help!"

The sudden cry seemed, in some manner, a sacrilege. It shocked the pulse-deadening enchantment that held motionless leaf spray and bracken stem. It shocked its utterer even as it left her lips. It was her first appeal for succour in sixteen years of life.

"Holler away! Most folks stay indoors to-night; it's Hallow-e'en."

"That's right. It's—hic!—witch-night. Only a witch could leave us in the lurch. Unless the Devil unties those double knots for you, kid, no one—hic!—else will."

"Help!"

"Oh, shut up! Wait till you've something to yell about. You won't wait long."

"Got a coin, Jake? If the king's—hic!—head comes up she's mine first."

Silence. Twilight. Blue breath of frost and forest. Wan gold of the stirless leaf——

"The king's head! Who says I've—hic!—no luck?"

A broken tooth, hairy hands, an odour like the smell of a wet dog— Oh, better to jump into deep water with tied feet, or be burned at a stake!

"Help!"

3

A KNIGHT-ERRANT should not be self-conscious—certainly he should not be shy. But when Gervais, the sole son of Count Arnold —"The Holy Count," as they called him—saw a commotion in the leaf-drifts of the forest where two figures seemed to grapple, and cantered up with his hand on his sword-hilt prepared to champion the weaker or to judge between the combatants, and was barely able to rein in his horse before it stepped on a pair of lovers rolled shamelessly in each other's arms, he blushed as hotly as the forest couple should have done, but as the visor of his helmet was lowered no one but himself was aware of this.

He jerked hard and nervously at the bridle, pulling the horse round. This manœuvre seemed to occupy an æon of time. Sweating under his steel harness as though he had broken half a dozen spears in a tournament, he applied the spur, and the dark-brown horse plunged into a heavy gallop. But after trying to bolt for four or five bow-shots the grievance of the spur-prick weakened, and the horse eased to a sort of broken, stumbling walk, for the leaves were fet-lock deep.

The young man in the saddle raised his visor and took a deep breath. He was alone. He could have vowed wax candles to the altar of St. Michael the Deliverer for this relief. The twilight trance of the last hours of the last day of wonderful October—blue with the breath of damp and coming frost—encompassed him. Not a bird spoke. He had the bleak feeling of being a fool. This feeling is more painful than a knife-wound when one is twenty and as sensitive as a woman. But there was no badge of any kind upon the head-to-foot suit of armour that he wore, exquisitely jointed and fitted and as light to carry as steel panoply could be. When his visor was lowered he was no longer Gervais, heir of the Holy Count; his best friend could scarcely have sworn to him. Those two his horse had almost stepped upon—his inner self backed away from the mental picture, yet he was moved by what seemed a guilty interest to draw closer; a hot, bold happiness that cast off shame as though it were a fetter wallowed even in these leafy aisles. But he had been always as shy with women as some women are with men. The feeling that he was making a fool of himself deepened upon him. Yet if a cockatrice or basilisk should appear, or even an outlaw or man-slaying boar, he would be able to justify everything—or perish in the fashion proper to a Christian knight. Not that Gervais had any desire or expectation of death; quite the reverse. He always saw himself a conquerer with his foot on the dead body of the dragon. Somewhere behind him was the camp from which he had ridden out that morning—the camp of his home-returning war-companions; somewhere before him was the town that he would enter triumphantly to-morrow morning—his father's town. In the meantime he had spent five or six hours adventuring in knight-errantry, and had only succeeded in disturbing a pair of paramours. I' God's name! Was the forest as empty of violence as a sieve of water?

"Help!" A shadowy cry. Urgent; a woman's cry!

The young man sat petrified for a moment or two, as if incredulous. His heart jumped as it had done when he laid lance in rest for the first time to tilt at a mailed opponent in the lists.

With a hand that fumbled a little he lowered his visor. Under the half-instinctive spur-prick the horse blundered heavily forward again.

"Help!"

Gervais reddened the spurs in earnest this time, swept with a flame of high-strung, nervous impatience. The horse broke through thickets, crashed, wallowed, charging blindly like a wounded bull. Was he about to rescue a woman of more than mortal beauty from a serpent-headed dragon with the cold, topaz eyes of a leopard? The horse stumbled badly over a fallen tree, nearly unseating him, and he uttered a fervent and mechanical blasphemy.

"Help!"

* * * * *

Sidonia was frantic. Andromeda manacled to the cliff and face to face with the creature from the sea that was approaching to devour her was in no worse case.

He was standing in front of her, looking at her with a sort of leering solemnity, like a tipsy devil surveying a soul that has just been thrust into hell— Shreds of picture-thoughts flickered through Sidonia's head as if she were a drowning person—the glow of charcoal on a makeshift hearth of bricks; her wooden shoes, that she had abandoned to wander barefoot in the forest that wise people feared; her yellow cat—— Oh! Oh! He was going to touch her!

A sharp, wordless scream broke from the girl. There was a crashing sound, and a muffled reverberation like the thud of hoofs. The jester's hand was on Sidonia's shoulder—a soft shoulder, small-boned, and of an immaturity that was in some fashion more whetting than the full contours of a splendid wanton. With a violent movement Sidonia shrugged off the hand. Instantly and very roughly the jester caught her by both shoulders.

"Coward!" The girl's voice was crazily high-pitched. Her fluency in wild anger was the fluency of the gutter. She had courage, and was too furious now for fear.

"You slut!" said the jester thickly, and he struck her across the face.

Then, like a stroke of lightning, the flat of a sword caught him, and he went over ninepin fashion and sprawled on his back, his few wits knocked to nowhere.

Sidonia saw a knight in armour upon a foaming horse that looked black. His bare sword was in his hand and his visor was down. Perseus poising in mid-air could not have been a more astonishing sight to the rescued Andromeda.

Gervais saw a young, dark, dishevelled girl, practically naked to the waist, pinioned to a sapling poplar. He was in a blaze of fury, having seen the vagabond jester lift his hand to her. But the whole business was as vile as a pot-house brawl. His poet's soul grieved for a serpent-headed dragon with cold, topaz eyes.

The juggler had disappeared, bolting into the wilderness at first glimpse of the mounted knight. The jester sprawled on the flat of his back, his eyes half-open like a dead animal's.

Gervais sheathed his sword. Now that the rush of action was over he felt constrained, awkward. The woman must be set free, of course. She had not spoken. She was staring at him—dark eyes in a small, pale face.

He dismounted, slowly, feeling as stiff as a jointed wooden figure. The captive was still dumb. And he also. If his lips had been sealed by a spell it would not have been more impossible to speak. His hands were ungauntleted, and he fumbled for a little with the knots of the kerchief that secured the girl's wrists, finally cutting them with his dagger. She uttered a faint sound that seemed to be of relief, straightening out her arms——

A feeling of unearthliness was upon Sidonia. The knight had not spoken. Had the earth opened, and the horse that bore him—breathing flame from her nostrils—leapt forth with its rider from that magic pit? But his hands when he endeavoured to release her had touched her hands and wrists, and they were warm and human —warmer than her own. If he was flesh and blood, why—why, anything might happen. It was common knowledge how knights, riding solitary, dealt with any young wayside women they might encounter. But it would be quite a different matter to the menace of the drunken jester—almost—almost an honour.

Gervais was aware that he must say something. Courtesy demanded it.

"I trust that you have not been too grievously molested."

Was that his own voice? It came muffled, hollow, from the helmet. Shyness always made him abrupt or formal, but the voice that had just spoken did not really seem to be his own.

"No, sir—oh, no."

"Do you live close by?"

"No, sir. In—in the town."

A pause.

"Oh, he knows now how far I am from help!" said Sidonia's thought. "What—what will happen?" Nervously, and with little cold, stiff hands, she pulled the torn linen shift up over her breasts.

"The town is a long way from this place," said Gervais' thought. "It is nearly night. If I leave the girl she may be the prey of wolves. A plague on it!"

Aloud he said very formally, "You cannot return alone. I will see that you reach the town in safety."

Sidonia replied nothing. She was shivering from head to foot with cold and fatigue. Her arms were crossed tightly over her breasts. Her teeth chattered. She had been tense with fear, with rage, with hectic expectancy; now followed the reaction. The prostrate jester drew up one leg. His wide-flung hands moved, and his head. The horse snorted, lowering its head towards the ground, that had become dim as a dream, and the knight—a tall, metallic automaton —went over to it, vague in the dusk. Sidonia was so cold that she would not have cared if a prince of the otherworld had risen in a sheet of flame and claimed her as his paramour; indeed, she would have welcomed it, for both fire and love are warm.

The knight was in the saddle again. The horse moved towards her. She stood shivering, incapable of independent action. The knight bent forward, extending a hand. Mechanically she gave him hers, and in a moment was drawn right up before him. The ease of this yielded Sidonia a sharp impression of strength. But she was too chilly to be afraid; in fact, she was indifferent; even, perhaps, unconsciously disappointed. She settled herself well astride of the horse, her neat bare feet dangling, her short, torn petticoat shrugged well up, exposing calves, knees, and even a trifle more. She twisted her fingers in the horse's mane. Behind her the knight sat erect. A white, unemblazoned surcoat masked his body armour, so the chill of the steel did not strike through to her own half-clad body. On either side his rigid, metal-ensheathed arms pressed her, constricting and maintaining her in her position.

Under a touch of the knight's heel the tired horse ambled heavily towards the poplar-screened high-road, moving as though through a vapour of dreams. Now they were in the road—a wandering, phantom highway. The horse broke into a reluctant canter. Then, recognising the home-road, and spurred by old stable-thoughts, his pace quickened to a plodding gallop.

Sidonia, clung to the coarse mane. She was grievously shaken. Only the knight's arms prevented her from slipping off on one side or on the other. But her numbness was replaced by excitement. The bitter darkness of Hallow-e'en was closing down on them, and she rode through it, astride of the steed of a Dark Knight, who might be man, angel, or devil. Wraiths rose from the ground beneath the horse's hurrying hooves. They caught at the bridle with faint, elongated fingers. They swept forward, level with girth or rein or frontlet. Before the hooves an eddy of fantastic movement cast up wan arms that curved or beckoned—melting shapes, wallowing like dolphins that plunge and reappear beneath the prow of a rushing ship. Phosphorescence glowed upon vague brows—now low as the rotting and will-o'-the-wisp-haunted trunks of fallen trees, now high as the first blurred, golden sparkle of the frosty stars. Sidonia was not afraid. She sagged back upon the steadfastness of the knight, leaning more fully against his breast. She was safe. How wonderful was this ride—this horse and his master! She became more and more convinced that an armed male angel—St. Michael, perhaps, whose effigy she had once seen on a banner—had come to her assistance. Such things were surely reported of angels, and angels did not seek women for the purposes of love, as men and devils did. So it was certainly an angel who had delivered her from the drunken jester, and was carrying her home at a gallop.

Gervais was tired, and at the start had been rather annoyed, though sorry for the girl, of course. But it was novel to ride with a woman in his arms. She was small and young—innocent, doubtless. A gradual inner warmth overspread him. The girl between his arms was silent. He himself could not speak. The curdled darkness of the autumn night enveloped them. There was nothing but the thud of the hoof-strokes and the pounding forward motion of the horse. This mutual silence seemed to merge and blend. It became, in the consciousness of the young man, an intimacy almost like that of marriage. He sat rigid in the saddle, glowing inwardly with an ir-rational rose-red flame that increased in heat. The pale bosom of the girl, as he had seen it, came again and again before the eyes of his mind. She was pure as a candle of white wax upon an altar. The sense-warmth that had come out of nowhere was playing the very deuce with him.

Ashamed of his own thoughts, he felt unworthy to sustain her between his arms.

"Yes, this is certainly an angel," said Sidonia's inner self. "He says nothing, he does nothing, and he is taking me home." It was very wonderful— But did angels never love? She knew scarcely anything about them. There was something lacking in the adventure —the flesh and blood ardour that delights and terrifies. Subcon-sciously she experienced a twinge of envy, visioning the girls who had been the half-willing prey of strange lords in inlaid armour mounted upon tall stallions. Yet heaven had provided her with a rescuer steadfast as a pillar of steel.

They were leaving the forest, for the unseen road had begun, gently, to slope upward. The horse slackened to a trot. Out of the cauldron of the mists the full moon was rising—very large, and of a rose-gold hue. The witchery of the night became tinged with opal-escence. Tenuous sylph-shapes thronged and floated—alluring, carrying the promise of unhuman and nameless delights like nectar in a dim vase of pearl. Menace had been replaced by the glamour of magic.

Very soon they would be at the open door in the walls of the town, and then the knight would set her upon the ground, and he and his horse would instantly vanish. Sidonia was saddened by this thought.

Slowly the moon rose. The horse had fallen into a walk. Gervais was on fire, despite the outer cold. Through a long silence the girl had lain between his arms—where, as yet, no woman had rested. He wanted to disarm, to press her strongly against his breast, to hold her to him with all the strength that he had. He was divided between the shame and the sweetness of desire—both absolutely new.

Out of the mist, with which was mingled the strengthening au-reate luminance of the moon, the walls of the town took shape— high and dark, with upshouldering buttress-towers and broken, battlemented tops. Here and there, through some high-placed arrow-slit, a hint of light showed. Slowly the horse with its double burden drew nearer. Very far off a wolf howled, but under the glamour of the moon there was no terror in the sound. A rumour of wood-smoke, like the after-taste of incense, touched the nostrils lightly—given off by brush fires kindled by hut-dwelling herds-men. But Sidonia had forgotten the smoke of the witch-fire that had drifted to her through the forest——

The door of the walled town to which the forest road led up was a deep archway fanged above with the downward-pointing iron spikes of a double portcullis. A pair of cressets flamed fitfully on either side of the inner end of the tunnel-arch. Right up to the archway came the burdened horse. Now the teeth of the first port-cullis were almost overhead. There was a halt—a pause. Sidonia quailed inwardly, fearing that this was the end.

"In which street do you live?" said the strange and hollow voice from the closed helmet.

"In—in the Street of the Martyrs, sir."

Sidonia felt that she was shamed. She had named a laneway of vile reputation. And as a matter of fact it was only a stepping-stone to her own abject lodging. It was no street to be mentioned to an angel.

The horse moved forward again. The light of the cressets fell across Sidonia's eyes, momentarily dazzling her. A voice chal-lenged. Without answering, the knight, drawing in the reins with one hand, raised his visor. There was a startled exclamation. The horse, heel-struck, reared a trifle on sliding hooves, then blundered into the murk ahead, that was lighted rarely by beams from shutter chinks or the glow-worm yellow of some little votive lamp before a wall-shrine dedicated to miracle-working saint, or Mother of the Infant God, or wounded Christ.

Sidonia's heart beat quickly with pleasure and bewilderment. Now indeed she knew that an angel had rescued her. The watchman at the gate had challenged them, but when the unknown knight, without uttering a syllable, lifted his visor, they had allowed him instantly to pass. Doubtless they had been blinded by his unhuman beauty. She was no longer conscious of the numbness of her bare, dangling legs and feet, or of her hands that still determinedly gripped two tufts of the horse's mane.

The streets they followed seemed deserted; it was the supper hour, and most folks were within doors. Hanging signs thrust out towards them like fantastic branches; dim gargoyles cave head downward; the small flames of the little votive lamps sweetly illuminated the painted brows and breasts of carved saints who held palm branches, croziers, or the emblems of their torture and death.

With a sureness as of familiarity, the knight guided his stallion, which walked at a foot's pace. Another miracle! The ways of the town were evidently as well known to the angel as to Sidonia herself. They entered the Street of the Martyrs. It was narrow as a coffin and smelt of decaying things. Here the darkness was unleavened, though above the faint, mellow light of the moon touched the gabled roofs.

The horse halted. There was a motionless pause. Then, slowly, the knight dismounted. Sidonia leaned sideways towards him. His face was only a pale oval to her. He slipped his hands under her armpits and lifted her to the ground.

The moment had come; the miracle was at an end. He was about to leave her—to vanish utterly. Sidonia's numbed and stiffened legs would scarcely support her upright. She clutched at the knight's hands and fell on her knees. Feverishly she covered his hands with kisses. She drew down his hands and pressed them against her breast. Fear of being severed too quickly from him made her brave.

Gervais was as staggered as though he had been dealt a blow. He drew the girl quickly to her feet, his ensteeled arm supporting her. Her head was thrown back. Dimly he perceived that her large, dark eyes regarded him as if he were the giver of her life or death. His desire to know her mouth overwhelmed him like an irresistible adversary. A feeling of fire went through him. Without speaking a word, he bent to her and touched her lips. They were cold, soft, gently curved. His own lips dwelt on them. It was a new paradise. His arm that held her tightened. Instinctively he pressed more closely on the lips that were under his, and they yielded, parting a trifle beneath the pressure.

He shuddered, and raised his head. The girl caught her breath in a sob. She began to tremble from head to foot.

It was Gervais' first taste of passion. He was both hot and cold now. The shrinking and self-conscious poet warred with the just-born man. God! Was he capable of plundering a virgin like any rank man-at-arms? The girl's sob struck him like a fist. He released her, turned, groped for the stirrup, and in a moment was in the saddle. There was a slipping of hooves on the cobblestones and then a quick, loud clatter down the laneway—Sidonia stood on the cobbles with the mellow moon bathing the peaked roofs high above. The nectared chalice had been snatched from her. She was destitute.

II. HALLOWE'EN

1

A COBBLED LANE with decrepit houses of lath and plaster, three and four stories high, seeming to lean towards each other across it; an October moon, frosty yet mellow, steeping their thatched gables in a witching glamour; and in the lane, like someone fallen to the bottom of a mountain cleft, the waif Sidonia, down upon the bitter stones, her face streaming with tears that were the only warmth in a lifeless world.

The vanishing sound of the horse-hoofs had been caught up into silence. There was nothing now—nothing! The tears that were like scalding water ran over her face. She felt as empty as a tube from hunger; her half-naked, miserable little body cried out with fatigue; she had been hunted through the forest like a black cat—and abandoned by the angel who had kissed her.

That was the core of the matter—the very crown and apex of her despair. To be caught up to the threshold of heaven and then dashed, like Lucifer, down into the depths; to have the heart burst into dazzling blossoms, and then be plucked from the breast and trodden under the hooves of a retreating horse! Sidonia was too wretched for further life. Gooseflesh, chilblains, hunger, other folks' outworn garments, when the vivid soul lusted for brocade and hanging sleeves of silk; drunken men, sluts, love-longings, and the thwarted spring-quickenings of the body; black bread, blacker looks from the many who more than half believed that Satan himself had fathered her in actual fact; children, caught indoors as she passed by, flung stones, oaths, the dregs of the flagon— The chill of the cobblestones burned her as though she were upon a bed of coals. She moaned, but the will to raise herself was wanting. Life held nothing.

The thought of the devil occurred to her. It was a thin ray of hope.

"Oh, Satan——"

45

She spoke within herself. She was becoming numb, and death seemed increasingly preferable. The hazy moonlight, like a luminous semi-substance rising from an alchemist's crucible, dwelt upon the steep-pitched roofs of thatch. A cat, black as the ace of spades, took its sinuous way from a shutterless garret window. Its fixed and lambent eyes were baleful as those of a basilisk, and it had an air of unholy purpose. A step sounded. In the foul and obscure lane, deserted partly through fear of the witch-night, someone was approaching.

A tallish figure, dark as the murk that filled the cleft between the houses, took form and presence. A black cloak fell to the heels; a black hood, cut to a long, down-dangling, fantastic point like a monkey's tail, shadowed the face. Coming to where the girl lay on her side, the figure paused. It stopped, seeming to examine her, then lifted her with apparent ease.

"Oh——" Sidonia uttered a faint sound.

"Poor, cold little slut," said a deep and richly modulated voice—a man's voice. "We'll soon see whether you're worth warming."

They turned aside from the lane, passing under an arch. Here there was a smell as if the carcass of a dog had been left to lie in the cold and fetid shadows. Beyond was a court or yard, with the superstructure of a well rising like a little gallows in the midst. Past the well went the tall man in black, and on, and down a flight of steps, and through a heavy, half-open door into a red glow of light.

Sidonia became aware that life, not death, was claiming her— had flung hot arms about her. She was warm—heavenly warm. Flame-red beat through her closed eyelids. She lifted them, and looked straight into the flames of a great fire. It blazed on a stone hearth, and a suspended pot bubbled, giving out the fragrance of simmering meat and onions. A cup was set to the girl's lips, and she drank down a quantity of hot, spiced wine. The fire caressed her without and the liquid within. She turned her head to discover where she was.

A big, low-vaulted room with torch-blackened walls and roof; tables, benches, filthy trodden straw upon the floor, a number of people, and beside her, supporting her, a young woman whose loose auburn hair was chapleted with silver tinsel flowers. Opposite stood a black-cloaked and hooded man, wearing a black mask.

"Where am I?" she asked, drawing away from the auburn-haired young woman and sitting up straight upon the wooden stool.

"This is the Thieves' Kitchen."

Oh! Now Sidonia knew. The cellar-tavern that went by that name was not thirty steps from her own refuge. It was a rendezvous of prostitutes, pickpockets, strolling players, and sons of Cain; a place of brawls, knife-fights, and crude laughter. She had often wished to enter it.

The masked man spoke.

"I think you were worth thawing out—or you will be. What is your name?"

The deep and rich voice of him carried power, like a clenched fist resting upon the arm of a throne.

"Sidonia, sir."

The auburn-haired young woman made a feline forward movement.

"I know her—I've seen her. She's Lame Lisa's daughter. You shan't pick a dirty little slut of a girl out of the gutter and put her before me—God's death! you shan't! I'll spoil her! I'll show you!"

She had flung out her two hands palm upward, the fingers in-curved like claws. Her voice rose shrill as a harridan's. Her fury had come as suddenly as a storm in August.

The masked man took a step towards her, and, without speaking a word, he struck the girl a smashing blow in the face. She dropped instantly, all in a heap. One hand went to her bruised cheek, and she moaned.

"Catherine!" said the masked man, raising his voice.

Out of the fitfully-lit chaos of tables, benches, straw-litter, and seated figures beyond the hearth-glare a dishevelled dark woman came slowly.

"Catherine, give the young lady seated upon the three-legged stool something to eat."

His intonation was ironic. He turned and sat down himself upon a bench, playing with a red-coated monkey that crept out from beneath it. The background was the confused and general noise of the Thieves' Kitchen. No one had paid any attention to the screaming voice of the splendid, auburn-haired vixen, or to the blow that had muted her. She nursed her cheek, making low sounds that were like a dog growling in his sleep.

Catherine filled a wooden bowl from the stew-pot and gave it to Sidonia with a piece of bread.

"Who is he?" asked the witch's daughter in a low voice, looking towards the masked man. She had been too hungry to care much what happened before the food was given to her, and now the pleasure of eating robbed her of any qualms. The spiced wine, too, had assisted to translate her into a region of confidence. Her head swam a little from it.

"He's the Master."

"Is that his name?"

"They all call him that."

"Does he live here?"

"No—no one knows where he lives."

Sidonia, warmed by the meat and onion stew, considered this.

"Is she his woman?" She indicated the sloven beauty with the marred face.

"He has favoured Sylvane for a month. Sylvane was angry because she feared that he would now favour you."

At this Sidonia looked quickly at the masked man—the Master. He was teasing the coated key, which showed its teeth at him in a scowl that was both human and animal. His long hands were beautiful. The inordinately lengthy point of a his hood fell over one shoulder and dripped nearly to the floor. He was finely built, and the fire-red drenched his black habiliments. The horrid pain of loss returned upon the girl. The young man beneath whose lips her own lips had parted like a breaking seal had been caught back to Heaven (a locality vaguer than dreamland). Why should perfect happiness be so short—like sudden light when a door is opened, like a mouthful of wine swallowed? Her whole self rebelled. She was mad for the thrill of flesh and spirit that had visited her and fled like summer lightning.

The dark young woman, Catherine, had lapsed right down beside the three-legged stool, in the glare of the hearth. Her eyes were tired, and looked older than her age, and as though they had been fixed too often in the glaze of passion. Her drooping mouth was like the Virgin's in a representation of the burial of Christ. Her soul brooded motherwise on the thought of her man—a bully and gambler who relied upon the earnings of her prostitution to recoup his losses at play. Her life had not been frustrated: she loved like a dog.

Through the continuous babble of the Thieves' Kitchen cut a sharp, lilting strain. Francis the Fiddler, risen up in the pulsing torch and hearth light, was playing with a sort of fury. His face was intent, with rather the look of a serious boy.

"Make room!"

"Now we'll see who's too drunk to dance!"

Tables and benches were thrust back. A fat man fell to the floor and wallowed there, retching his heart out. Couples began to shuffle and stamp and jog together, their feet scuffling on the straw that was as foul as the underfoot of a kennel. The Master stood up, lifting the gibbering monkey to his shoulder, where it clung. Sylvane bestirred herself. She was upon her feet again. She drew close to the Master, her tarnished blue and silver dress, with hanging sleeves, cut low like a great lady's. He did not look at her. She caught his arm.

"Go to hell!" he said curtly.

Sylvane threw back her tawny head and laughed.

"Come here, sweeting!" called someone from the flickering welter of the crowded, torch-lit cellar, and then she was dancing with a hairy ruffian who wore rings in his ears.

Sidonia, the empty food-bowl beside her, had turned away from the open hearth, watching the rout. Francis the Fiddler, who stood upon a bench, was plain to see. Her eyes dwelt on him. He was of a pleasant appearance, but had she really panted to walk the length of the road with him? It seemed impossible! Oh, the lips of her celestial knight—firm, yet hesitant! She was abandoned—an outcast of heaven and earth—yet she had been brought in out of the night and given spiced wine and meat and onions. She glanced at the Master, standing tall and black, with the monkey clinging to his shoulder. Perhaps hell was kind. She had always known that it was warm.

More couples were dancing. Overset pewter mugs spilled dregs of beer and harsh wine upon the slatternly floor. A brown bear with a ring through its nose sat upright on its haunches with absurd gravity. No one heeded the stout drunkard, who still retched hoarsely at intervals. Two men, facing each other as they straddled a bench, were throwing dice, and Catherine, raising herself up with the effort of a woman of twice her age, went slowly to them, skirting the dancers. The younger of the men, having made his throw—a high one—leant back a little. He was blonde, shaven, and had the air of a gentleman. Catherine leaned over him. Her loose hair fell about him. Then he bent forward again.

"Fetch me a mug of beer, Kate. Be quick, you dawdling fool!"

The crazy, screeching music spurred the body like the crack of a devil's whip. Perspiration glistened on the pale face of the fiddler, but his expression was still one of intent and boyish gravity. He might have been a sexless child exhibiting a difficult accomplishment—a creature below or above the level of human excess. The jostling and shuffling dancers became more abandoned. The men hugged their women to them like bears smothering their victims. Here a couple of lads danced together with lewd movements, and another—one of a troupe of vagabond actors—had rigged himself out in female petticoats and was dancing with the bearded bear-leader. A second actor, wearing sable tights white-painted in imitation of the bony frame of a skeleton, and with his face hidden by a grinning death-mask, leapt into the fun, prancing, and rattling a couple of drumsticks upon the parchment of a small drum slung before him.

"The Dance of Death!" said a man's resonant voice. "Get up, my girl; we'll tread it."

Sidonia, sitting as spellbound upon her three-legged stool as if she were watching the seethe of movement in an ante-room of hell, looked up and saw that the Master was standing over her. Was—was he about to dance with her? She rose——

It was feverish—mad and amazing. She was held sternly up to the firm body of the tall masked man, and, so held, they threaded slowly the slackening jostle of coupled rogues, wantons, and shameless, smooth-faced actor-lads. There was high laughter, outcries, and the loud rattle of the drumsticks. The impersonator of death, his skull-mask white and ghastly, leapt up and down as though he were hung on wires.

"Eat, drink, and be merry, for to-morrow you die."

Hoarse voices of protest rose: "Oh, shut your trap!" "No monk's talk here!" "Have a drink yourself, old worm-feeder!"

The string music ceased; only the blatant rat-tat of the mock-skeleton's drum continued.

Sidonia found herself again by the wide and glowing hearth, down whose cavernous chimney a bleated deviless astride of a broomstick could have flown with ease. The Master was with her, and she swallowed more spiced wine, then sat again upon the stool while he drew up a bench and sat by her. Her head was spinning, but pleasantly. Several of the torches had burnt down, and the cellar was in more than half darkness. The skeleton still pranced, and a third actor, very drunk and arrayed in a long gown and false whiskers, announced that he was God the Father, and that a miracle-play entitled *The Creation of the World* was about to commence. A beggar on crutches, with one foot drawn right up by some shrinkage of the muscles, applauded this, and poured out several gold pieces, offering to buy drinks for the whole troupe. But the actor in the long gown tripped and fell heavily, and all was drowned in laughter.

"Sidonia," said the masked man.

"Yes, sir."

"Live while you may. Eat life, and drink it. Are you afraid of damnation?"

Was she? Her head swam. Red fire, meat and onions, dancing, noise, the excellent proportions and rich voice of the Devil——

"No!" she said decidedly.

"Are you afraid of me, Sidonia?"

She felt his fingers on her bare arm. They slid from elbow to wrist. They were tense. A tingling went over the girl. Her heart suddenly was racing. Something within her crouched down and shivered, and something else strained forward like a hound on a leash. She was scared and eager. She turned her face and looked up into the hood-shadowed eyes of the masked man. Was he the Devil?

"Take your hands off her, the little gutter-rat! D'you call her a woman? Look at me! God's death! you *shall* look at me!"

Sylvane, the auburn-haired, truculently drunk, stood full in the hearth-light.

"Look at me!"

Raising her two hands, she tore her low bodice right apart.

"Am I not beautiful?"

"Get out of my sight," said the masked man. "Nothing is beautiful when it is undesired. Go back to your bear-leader and get drunk with him."

"Undesired! Oh, Christ, that's funny! Me! I don't care how you've treated your other women —your other fancies—but don't think you can throw me over for a gutter-thing, a piece of dirt, a ——"

"How dare you!"

Sidonia was on her feet, furious. The flat of her quick hand caught the other a stinging slap on the face.

"Curse you!" screeched Sylvane.

"Haw! Haw! Three to one on the dark 'un!"

"I'll take you!"

"Keep it up, girls!"

Sidonia was striking cat-like. Quicksilver seemed to run in her veins—cold yet hot—and her body was a thing without weight. Her hair was clutched at; she clutched in turn at the tawny dishevelment of the other, mixed with silver tinsel flowers. She tugged with her full strength. Sylvane screamed like a peacock. The breath that came from between her painted lips was rank with wine. They clinched, bosom to bosom. Sylvane was half an inch taller, heavier (she was three years Sidonia's elder), but very drunk. With another scream she fell backward, measuring her length. Sidonia was uppermost. The fall barely jarred her. Another of the same breed as Sylvane would have thumped her inert adversary's head against the floor until dragged off, but Sidonia disengaged herself, and got up unsteadily. Her hair and her wretched clothing both looked as though she had been dragged through a hedge. She was in tatters, but felt exalted, loose-jointed, and wonderfully free.

"What did I tell you? I always pick 'em, dog fight or woman fight."

Even Catherine's man, the blonde gambler with the handsome priest-like face, had risen to his feet. But the Master had not moved. He was laughing in a silent, inward way. Sidonia, upborne by spiced wine and the sense of victory, felt affronted. Satan himself should not laugh at her. She had pride!

Her hands fumbled at her bodice strings, trying to draw them tighter. Her shoulders were naked, but her streaming hair partly clothed them. Sylvane still lay her length, unheeded now by anyone save Catherine. Going past her, Sidonia took her way between benches, stools, tables, and the prostrate bodies of the sleeping or drunken. A thick and smoky darkness closed round her, but here was the half-open door.

A hand gripped her shoulder, and she almost screamed.

"Sidonia," said the rich voice of a man.

"Oh!"

"A little cat with claws, eh? Put up your face."

"No, I won't!"

She was enclosed by arms of iron—constricted. There was no possibility even of movement. She had a faint impulse to call on God, but what was the use? She was Lame Lisa's daughter—an outcast. God was an old man dressed like a bishop who sat on a gilt chair and was haughty and sonorous—she had seen Him represented like this in the open-air miracle-plays at Easter. Her face was lifted now—instinctively, for she sought to breathe. There was no escape. A hypnotic numbness seemed to check the pulse of her heart——

The Master's mouth found hers. The spirit of her winced desperately, and then became passive, like a thing suddenly killed. Strength—that was the first sensation she received—strength, sealing her mouth, pressing her body—a sheath of steel about her. Cold strength; lawless strength; the pang-like thrill of abandonment went through her; liberty, wild as the night wind that shreds the flying clouds, hot as levin; all fetters broken, a mad laughter uttered with flung back head, riot, dead shame— Strength that upholds and crushes her physical being had cried out for. It satiated her—almost soothed. Something within her leaned upon it with a long sigh. Yet, deep down, the centre of her soul withheld itself, contracting under the contact like a sensitive plant. Her lips did not part and answer as they had done under the ups of the angel. But something within her desired that they should part. Ah! demon lover!

"You are mine, Sidonia."

There was no answer. The deep, low voice had an iron certainty.

"You shall eat and drink life—little, frail thing. You know the Church of St. Saviour?"

A pause.

"Yes."

"To-morrow is the Feast of All Saints; the following day is the Feast of All Souls. On the night of that day, an hour after sunset, you will enter the church and go towards the Chapel of Resurrection. To the right of this chapel is a doorway and a flight of descending steps. Go down them until you come to a closed door. Knock twice and then once at this, and you will be admitted."

"Yes," said the hushed, automatic voice of Sidonia.

"You will not forget. And you will come. In the Church of St. Saviour they worship death; in the crypt we worship life. Put up your face to me."

Ah, demon lover! Satan! Oh, God! But He was an old man, and angry, and she wanted the fire of life—even if it seared, even if it stopped the breath.

"You are mine, Sidonia."

She was released. Where was he? The broad chink of the partly-opened door showed wanly because of the moonlight that was without. She—she must go home. Her head felt light and she was trembling. She sidled through the door-opening and climbed the stone steps that led up to the level of the cobbled yard. Oh! the bitter cold! She crossed her arms over her breast. Moonlight like a benediction possessed the yard. She walked out into this clarity —naked-footed, naked-legged, with black hair streaming over naked shoulders. She walked stiffly, cold-struck. Heaven and Hell—a young knight in armour and a masked man in sable raiment. She—she was sealed to the Master, was she not? Heaven had abandoned her; she was too poor, too tattered and outcast for Heaven. Oh, why had the angel left her in the Street of the Martyrs? Now—on the night of the Feast of All Souls—she would become the paramour of the Devil. It was, of course, a strange distinction— a lifting up. Adventure! No girl of her acquaintance—daughter of taverner, rag-picker, scavenger, or charcoal-seller—could lay claim to such a thing. But oh! why had the knight from Heaven left her in the Street of the Martyrs? Her head swam——

"Saints preserve us"—a loud cry close at hand. There was a clatter of a dropped lantern and of panicky, slipping feet upon the cobbles.

"A witch! Oh, Lord, deliver me!"

Someone, belated, had glimpsed the stark, strange little figure of Sidonia, with its bare, crossed arms and streaming hair, beneath the moon. Imagination had done the rest, and the fellow would have a tale as long as his arm to tell—of a nude maiden with a black cat squatting on her shoulder and a broomstick at her feet.

Hearing the outcry, the thought of Hallow-e'en recurred to Sidonia's brain, confused by wine, fevered by hectic stimuli, and numbed by the shock of cold. It was the witch-night. But how could a witch fly naked through such a rigour of frost? Perhaps, nearer to the lightsome moon, the air was mild. How wonderful to fly astride of a goat—no, of a dark horse with wings—and perhaps find Heaven.

She had crossed the width of the yard, and now came to where, behind the several wooden posts that supported upper stories of lath and plaster, a row of half-sheltered horses were tethered. There was a clean but acrid smell. At one end of the shallow open stable a ladder led upward to a trapdoor. Climbing this ladder slowly, the girl thrust up the heavy, hinged square of wood with her free hand. She had come home.

2

"WELL, AND HOW'S the business of knight-errantry? What luck, Gervais?"

"A blank, eh? But why look so glum about it?"

"I—oh—er—nothing."

Silence.

One small lamp burned in the stone-walled cell of the forest monastery. The cell was cold as a tomb and bare as a picked bone. On the hard pallet, above whose head hung a crucifix, Gervais sat, leaning back against the naked wall. On a stool facing him sat the young man who had spoken first—boyish, tanned, his fair hair crisply curling.

"Oh, brace up, man! What's the girl's name?"

Gervais, who had been looking down at his own folded arms, lifted his face quickly—almost with a start.

"The—the girl?"

"Of course, what's her name?"

"I don't— What the devil are you talking about, Hugh?"

Hugh laughed.

"Come on—confess, Gervais I'm an easy-going priest."

"Confess what?"

"The whole affair, my boy. You haven't spoken three words since you dismounted, and you've lost your appetite. I know the symptoms. You hardened saints are always hit the hardest in the finish."

(He was about the same age as the other—twenty—but spoke from wide experience, cheerfully. As a matter of fact his affairs of the heart had started at sixteen.)

Gervais was leaning slightly forward now. He was beautifully built—less boyish in the whole set of him than the other, and with an unconscious quality of gravity—of dignity—investing him like a close, invisible garment. The dark head, too, was beautiful, and the rather pale face, with its perfectly cut mouth of a priest, or a poet, its unaggressive strength of jaw, its brow of an idealist, and its strange eyes between grey-blue and violet—the lover's colour; eyes that looked quickly at one and then away, as though lost in abstraction or embarrassment.

"I'm not a saint. I tell you again. Hugh, I've nothing to confess."

The voice was abrupt—odd.

"Oh, all right. A wink's as good as a nod to a blind horse. Shall we talk about dragons? I heard a good tale yesterday of a knight —Sir Something or other—who tackled one with trained mastiffs. He schooled the dogs by teaching them to worry a dummy dragon, I thought it a fine idea,"

"Yes. Where did this happen?"

"Oh, in some country on the borders of Christendom, of course. Nothing worth while ever happens in one's own country—except love adventures. One of these days I'm going travelling. I want to hunt unicorns and cameleopards, and see the people with three eyes and the dwarfs with two heads. Will you come with me?"

"You know I will."

"You don't sound very enthusiastic to-night. She must be a fine girl."

Gervais stood up.

"I think I'll sleep, Hugh. I've been in the saddle half the day, and it's dulled my head."

"Exactly. I'm sleepy myself. Good-night!"

"Good-night."

The door of the guest-cell closed. Gervais was alone. In the environs of the forest monastery his men-at-arms were encamped. To-morrow—All Saints' Day—he would ride at their head into his father's town—the town which he had entered at moonrise with a bare-legged girl before him and without any flourish of trumpets. Only the guard at the gate knew of this premature and unheralded incoming, and at his outgoing he had bribed them to keep their mouths shut. What a cold, feverish ride back that had been! Interminably long, yet so packed with indecision, desire, shame, and exaltation that it had seemed to endure for scarcely more than a moment of time. A cataclysm had occurred; the heavens had opened, the earth had trembled! Gervais had kissed a nameless scrap of a girl, and had found, in that instant, that she was more desirable than his soul's salvation. In fact, his hazy notions of the bliss of the redeemed melted like mist in sun before this new, foreshadowed bliss. He was on fire. It was like the shock of birth or death—and as universal an experience, though he did not realise it. But his case was an exceptionally severe one, for he had the mind of a poet and the bodily chastity of an anchorite.

He measured the breadth of the guest-cell—a matter of a few paces—turned, and measured it again. Sleep was absurd. (And, anyway, the bed looked singularly hard, even to a young man who had slept on the ground rolled in a cloak.) God! that kiss! What a heaven dwelt upon the lips of women—no, of one woman only. (He was as sure of this as of the truths of religion, though he had never accumulated an atom of proof. It was a blind and binding faith.) And he had been about to rifle the casket—to break profanely the sacramental bread. He was aghast at himself, yet uplifted into a hot, strange pride. A glowing, rose-hued vapour filled the guest-cell. Hugh, with his talk of casual loves, dragons, and unicorns—why, he had seemed to be speaking from an unbridgeable distance. He had been as irrelevant as a dog scratching itself before the altar during Mass. As well lay bare this fevered, miraculous tumult to him as speak of sacraments to a stable boy. All his desires rose from the earth, but this had fallen like lightning from heaven. (Gervais' condition was extremely serious.) The Street of the Martyrs! To-morrow, when the cheering was over, and the High Mass, he would go to this street and see her, and speak to her. Oh, what an eternity to wait! Why had he left her this night—there, in the gut of the lane, between the tall, decrepit houses? An emotion of shame that was vivid as a girl's answered this, but this very shame itself had a shivering, arrowy sweetness. He would kneel at her feet and ask pardon for—for——— Oh, he would kiss her hands and beg leave to be her knight, her servant. And then——— Abruptly he went down on his knees by the narrow, ascetic pallet. His eyes were on the black wall-crucifix, with its white figure, Black and white—ebony and ivory—like the hair and shoulders of the girl who had kissed his hands and then his lips.

"Lord Christ, I pledge myself as a Christian knight to the service of this woman, in life and in death."

He sunk his face between his hands as he had done when he watched beside his armour in the Church of St. Saviour all through the night of vigil before he received the accolade.

3

"I SEE A long life—yes, a long life."

"Oh, good!"

"S'sh!"

"The heart rules the head."

A giggle.

"S'sh, Margaret, you mustn't!"

"Mustn't what? It's my fortune, Anne. You're scared to have yours told, aren't you?"

"Oh, be quiet; we're spoiling everything. I want to hear. Please go on, ma'am."

A single lantern hanging by a cord from the low rafters contended with the obscurity that smelt of stables, dried balsamic herbs, mice, and tom cats. The closeness of the place was such that one could have cut the air with a knife. Charcoal embers glowed like celestial rose-leaves on a hearth of bricks. A pumpkin suspended from the rafters showed large, wan, and vague. It might have been a livid incubus, devilishly buoyant, stationary beneath the roof, listening and seeing without eyes or ears. Under the lantern a woman sat on a stool, holding the open hand of a dark girl who knelt by her. A fair girl pressed close. Before the hearth a yellow cat couched, humped up, its forepaws tucked in under its broad white chest.

"There is trouble through the heart."

Another giggle.

"Shall I be married, ma'am?"

This from Margaret.

"There are two marriages."

"Oh-h!"

"Oh-h!"

"How soon, ma'am?"

"Not yet—no, not yet. There's trouble first. Tears. I see a fair man. Young——"

"She's not looking at your hand now, Margaret!" said Anne, speaking into the other's ear.

They waited, breathless.

"I see a sword. Spurs. He's a man of rank—a knight. He brings trouble. I see pain. Ah! it is his bastard of whom you will be brought to bed."

"Oh-h!"

The two girls pressed together, nudging each other, shot through and through with the delicious confusion that is avid for a further shock.

"But after suffering comes happiness. The child will be a fine boy, and an honest man weds you within a year of his weaning."

There was a deep sigh of escaping breath—held unconsciously. Margaret had already had her money's worth. She seemed to go limp, like a pricked bladder that collapses upon itself.

The witch was a big-boned woman with a patchwork bed-covering drawn round her shoulders. Her crisp, plentiful hair, prematurely grey shot, fell about her rather long face, that was still haunted by an ashen ghost of beauty. The mouth was small, prim, prettily set—a travesty of the Madonna-mouth; in other words, the mouth of a fool. The face was drawn, waxen-yellow. The lightish eyes of the witch were like those of a vain and simple child which has been struck a heavy blow.

"Oh! God's mercy!"—a sharp squeal from Anne.

"Oh!"—an involuntary echo from Margaret.

Anne was on her feet, both hands clutching her petticoats about her knees. A huge black cat stalked past her, ignoring her. It sniffed at the fur of the somnolent yellow cat, recoiled, hissed venomously, and then, deliberately, began to wash itself.

"It—it rubbed against me! gasped Anne. "I thought——"

She had thought that it was the Devil, but stopped short of saying so out of consideration for her hostess—and for her own skin. The most careful courtesy is called for when one is dealing with a witch. The black cat certainly had a devilish look. Perhaps it was a familiar, and might take the shape of a spotted calf or a green monkey when no one was about.

Margaret had risen too.

"Thank you, ma'am. A good-night to you."

"A good-night to you," said the witch, in as ordinary and Christian a manner as any honest woman, even with a touch of the *grande dame*.

Holding to each other as though they were drowning, the two girls picked their way to the farther end of the long, low loft—for it was no more than that. Their hearts were hammering. Every creaking, tiptoed step that carried them farther into the dark added to their dreads. The homely odour of tom cats became the fetid devil-smell. The pumpkin was a floating phantom. They were in expectation of long tentacles cast round their ankles or bat-wings beating about their heads. Hallow-e'en is both the best and the worst night to pay a visit to a witch.

After timeless, nightmare moments they found and raised the trap-door, and with innumerable pains and terrors descended the vertical ladder into the open stable that was below. The trap-door, clumsily lowered, fell into place with a heavy bang.

The witch, sitting forward on her stool with her drawn face set towards the charcoal hearth, chafed between her palms the silver coin Margaret had given her. It seemed to warm her, though her lightish eyes of a child were a thousand miles away. What a life had been that of this big-boned, clairvoyant fool! A tall, rather weakly, handsome girl of good blood, she had been turned out into the street by relatives terrified at the rappings that followed her, and the satanic movement of tables, stools, and settles. An alchemist and his wife had offered shelter, and then, stripped naked in the innermost chamber of his laboratories, she had submitted to hypnotism in order that materialisation might follow upon her trance, and the true "philosopher's stone"—the living, speaking, palpable, if transient eidolon—be obtained. But the end of these stupendous experiments of secret science was banal, fleshly disaster, for the alchemist —dark, dynamic, of Southern blood—seduced his guest, and the bitter wife, threatening to denounce him to the townsfolk as a black magician if he demurred, drove out the girl and her girl child. Then had followed wretched wandering, and final refuge in the hut of a lonely woman suspected of witchcraft. Here years had passed. The woman died, and her hut-mate inherited her reputation and a number of unintelligible formula written on parchment in ink and blood, together with recipes for love-philtres, febrifuges, slow poisons, and for draughts to allay colic. Lisa, the outcast, and her girl might have remained here until the cows came home, but a hue and cry was raised, the poor novice witch was forced to attempt the ordeal of the white-hot ploughshares, and then fled limping, for from that day she was Lame Lisa. Now, for a matter of twelve months, the four walls of a loft had been her boundaries. She abode in it like a crippled rabbit in a burrow. Folk came to her—always at night and always timid as mice. She sold them the various mixtures of the recipes, and told their good or bad fortune, and supplied them with little images of wax that could be melted over a slow fire if the death of an enemy was desired, or heart-pierced with a rose-thorn to procure the love of some indifferent person. Almost as abject in her manner of living as a leper, lame, pain-aged, nocturnal, and afflicted with an unreasoning love of cats, she was solaced by a sense of stateliness and importance. But always her heart was the heart of a small animal that has been hunted.

Time passed. Both cats drowsed, humped up with bristling fur. The witch—like Atrepos cloaked in patchwork, or a sordid Sibyl— hung forward on her stool. The prim mouth, with its downward droop, was pursed; the uncombed, grey-shot hair was all about the eyes of her.

A sound told that the trap-door had been lifted—and then lowered. Someone approached slowly, on bare feet. The cats dreamed on. Sidonia came right up to the hearth and knelt down, and held her palms to the warmth of the embers.

"Oh! Sometimes my daughter comes home to her mother."

The tired voice of the witch was peevish. She did not seem to see that the girl's hair was in disorder, her chemise in ribbons, her bodice-lacings broken, and her legs briar-torn.

Sidonia did not answer. She put back the black locks from her eyes, feeling the giddiness of partial intoxication. She endured her mother just as she endured the chief circumstances of her life. In the abyss of her soul resentment at the usage of her dam was smouldering fire. But in some oblique way this very feeling increased the distaste that was normal with her. The two of them were as incompatible as oil and water, and mother, with her daytime dozings and her muttering aberrations, was little better than a lay figure, anyhow.

"Put this with the others." The witch extended her long, lady-like hand with the coin in the narrow palm of it.

Sidonia took the coin, moved one of the outer hearth-bricks, and placed the piece of money cheek by jowl with two or three others that lay there. She put back the brick, and the mental images of a cabbage, a loaf of rye bread, and a sheep's heart—luxurious purchases—flitted through her confused mind.

The witch's head drooped farther forward; she was just a mound of patchwork surmounted by a tangle of greying hair. A crutch lay on the floor beside her. Subconsciously Sidonia remembered the day of the white-hot ploughshares. It was the impetus of that memory that had carried her forward into the mob of forest folk and lifted her breathless voice on behalf of the withered lunatic palsied with spite and terror. Yet her mother was to her only a circumstance to be endured.

In the stillness a sharp crack sounded, as though flooring or rafter had been rapped smartly with a stick. The girl took no notice. Such uncaused sounds had followed them ever since she could remember. Her head was clearer. She sat between the drowsing cats, hugging her knees. The stifling, half-warmed air of the loft was grateful to her, relaxing her body, but her brain was on fire. Sealed to the Master, deserted by the angel! Freedom, passionate life! Oh, to fly on a black horse with wings! And this was the Eve of All Hallows—the night when the upper air was populous. It must be midnight now. What was the method?

Set against the wall of the loft, between the hearth and the heap of rags that was a bed, was an antique wooden chest. It had been there for no one knew how long, and now contained the dubious wares of Lame Lisa's trade. (But Sidonia never thought of her mother as a witch, though she trafficked in witch-goods. Dark power, night-flying, and mad abandonments—these were the stigmata of Satan's real servants.) Drawing back a little from the hearth, the girl got up and moved quietly to this chest. The older woman, sunk in one of the long, hypnotic stupors that were habitual to her, was as stirless as the two cats. Once again the sharp, causeless raps sounded.

Sidonia knelt down and lifted the broken-hinged lid of the chest. She was impelled to all her actions—something had laid hold upon her. Within her, inside of the last six hours, there had been a breaking down, a letting free—a mysterious, seething alchemy of passionate emotions. She was above—or below—herself. Automatic. Overstimulated. Quick and mentally fearless she had always been, for she was her father's daughter.

A balsamic smell arose from the depths of the chest. Bundles of dried herbs half filled it, and among them a withered, grotesquely human-shaped mandrake-root—said to have been dragged, uttering dreadful screams, from the ground beneath a murderer's gibbet by a black dog, which had immediately died. The dim, oily light of the single lantern scarcely illuminated the chest's entrails. Sidonia groped, encountering glass phials, salve pots, and a dried toad. Ah! here were the scrolls of parchment!

Rap-rap! A quick, loud double-knocking so perceptibly jarred the time-blackened crosspiece above the girl's head that it was a wonder no dust was shaken down.

Ten years earlier her mother had taught Sidonia to read and write, but these words seemed senseless. Oh! they were the names of demons of the air! How fortunate! They were long and difficult. Sidonia repeated them carefully—"Typhurgus, Aplestus, Philokreus, Miastor." Kneeling erect, she scanned the scrolls hurriedly. There were diagrams, zodiacal signs, rhymed couplets, and the names of Chaldean, Syro-Phœnician, Egyptian, and classical gods and goddesses, together with those of Biblical and Talmudic angels and demons. It was as incomprehensible as the babble of a delirious person. (Indeed, the last owner of the formulæ, which had passed through many hands, had understood them scarcely better than a parrot.) Disappointed, the girl replaced them. But she had memorised the names of the four demons of the air. Perhaps that would be enough. Yet she hankered after something more concrete—some salve, such as she vaguely remembered having heard spoken of in connection with witch-flying. Groping again in the chest, she fished up a little pot containing a dark and sticky substance with a vile smell. That smell in itself was diabolic; it satisfied her. She closed the chest and went softly back and stood by the hearth.

It was the midnight of Hallow-e'en.

The thought of a broom occurred to Sidonia, but it was unattractive. She blew out the sickly flame of the lantern, and the loft was in darkness save for the faint pink phosphorescence of the hearth and the greenish floor of the loft. She continued to repeat the invocation, but now her voice was withdrawn into her mind; it was there that she spoke.

A shower of raps reverberated upon the rafter's, the walls, even the flooring.

"We are with you. We will help you," said another voice, that was outside herself and yet spoke also in her mind. "Trust yourself. Lie back in our hands."

A flush of pleasure, and then a sensuous rapture of relaxation such as overcomes a person sinking into the yield of a feather bed, suffused Sidonia's mind and soul. She no longer saw, she no longer felt. She had been drawing inward and inward towards the centre of herself, and now there was nothing but utter rest, and soft darkness like black wool.

The dim figure of the naked girl that had stood for a number of seconds rigid as a figure of wood or a person hypnotised gave at the knees and fell suddenly to the floor, lying crumpled before the chilling hearth. The yellow cat, disturbed by the thump of the fall, started awake, stood up, stretched, and settled down again. The black cat slept on. The strengthless, diffused ray of livid moonlight was the only creature that moved in the loft.

* * * * *

"Up! Up! Look, little sister!"

Sidonia opened her eyes, which she seemed only to have closed for a minute.

Oh!

Moonlight, wide feathered pinions, height, hurtling speed—and company. The shock was as though a pail of cold water had been flung over her. She nearly lost her balance off the back of the winged sable horse whose sides her thighs gripped, and she caught at the mane to steady herself as she had done when the angel's stallion began to gallop.

"Don't fall, little sister! If you fall, and are afraid, you will instantly return."

"Where—where?" Sidonia did not know who it was that had spoken to her, nor why she questioned. Her mind whirled; it was like a swarm of gyrating silver sparks.

A wonderful wild laugh answered her. It was unhuman, beautiful, terrible. There was the whoop of the wind in it, the chime of water, the scarlet of fire, the sonorousness of earth. It enraptured and infected her. All of herself leapt towards it like child to parent. Fear was gone like a feather in a storm. Releasing the sable mane, she flung up her arms and laughed, as might a person who was insane with happiness. Her body, borne dizzily upward, seemed itself light as a wing; she could race on the air, she could run with the winds! Her hair streamed about her like a mermaid's in the swirl of the tide.

Moonlight, beating pinions, faces, and swift shapes—faces that had in them something of the eagle—wide golden eyes that were soulless; arched brows and noses; hair like tongues of fire; limbs flaked with golden scales or feathers. There were four—two upon either hand. Straight-standing in the air, they bore her steadfast company as the black horse rose. Oh, but the others! They darted like swallows, they circled, they poised, they drifted—they were uncountable. Black imp-things, wickedly grinning, that whizzed and somersaulted; translucent maiden-shapes, linked hand to hand and dancing wreath-wise in the void; bird-like creatures, sapphire-blue, white, rosy, or sable—men's thoughts, plumaged in accordance with the emotion that had shaped and speeded them; the naked selves of men, women, and children, sleep-released, drifting like vapour, dreaming, half-conscious; wandering flames, bat-thoughts, ghosts. Overhead the full moon, an inexhaustible, round lake of blinding silver, drenched everything in light.

Sidonia looked down. The town was a patch of darkness from which the needle-points of a couple of moon-touched spires rose. She had no giddiness, just as she had no sensation of cold. But she wanted to descend—to sweep low above the roofs that had witnessed her sad, trudging fatigues. Like a bolt from a cross-bow aimed at the zenith the black horse, with his mighty raven-feathered wings, still hurtled upward.

"You shall fly down, little sister. Speak to the horse which your desire has shaped for you."

It was one of the four beautiful demons who spoke.

"Down, down!" breathed Sidonia, leaning forward and again twisting her hands in the lavish blue-black mane. The mad upward rush instantaneously ceased. The horse hung for a second on pulseless wings, and then plunged earthward down the dizzy lapis-lazuli precipice of the night.

It was heart-stopping—a swoop of utter horror if a grain of fear remained. But Sidonia shrieked with the pure joy of it.

Oh, the wind of the cloven air!

Now the shingled roofs rushed up to meet them, and the church spires were like cross-tipped javelins thrown at them from the earth. Now they swept with a train of attendant sylphs, spectres, and globular, will-o'-the-wisp-like flames over the gables and the winding clefts of the streets. Weathercocks crowed shrilly at them. Gargoyles yelped like dogs. A stone griffin clasping a stone coat of arms between its claws hissed out fire and lashed its forked tail, unable to join the flight. Cats clinging to thatch or shingles glowered with flattened ears. But one—a black were-cat—leapt into the air with a mew of joy and followed the fleeing rout. The figures of saints enshrined in niches along the front of the cathedral glowed with a soft bluish light. The were-cat sheered widely away from them, its fur bristling, its swollen tail as stiff as a ramrod. But Sidonia felt only the innocent interest of a kitten in church. She was elemental, and therefore in perfect accord with Typhurgus, Aplestus, Philokreus, and Miastor, who might harry the soul that feared them in sheer sport, but were the strong playmates of their own kind, and would fawn like gentle and puzzled hounds at the passage of an angel or a discarnate saint.

A nude, red-haired young woman astride of a bearded he-goat, whose horns she gripped, came hurtling over the roofs. She waved to Sidonia, and in a moment was flying with her. Her green eyes were elfish, and had an irresistible sidelong shine. Her mouth, wide and laughing, was of a ripe animal fullness.

"You're new!" said she. "I often fly, but I haven't seen you before. Do you live in this town?"

"Yes," said Sidonia. "Near the Street of the Martyrs."

"How funny! My father is the head of the Goldsmiths' Guild, and we have a house that faces the Church of St. Saviour. Yet you and I are really good friends, because we do the same thing."

They smiled unreservedly at each other.

"How did you learn to fly?" asked Sidonia.

"Oh, I heard a wandering friar preach a sermon in the marketplace against witchcraft. He described the devils, the broomstick rides, and the wild times they had at the witches' Sabbath. It all sounded so exciting, and I was feeling so dull, that I thought I'd try to do what they did—just for fun! So I stripped naked at midnight and called on all the devils I could think of—and now it's easy."

There was something infectious in the sidelong twinkle of her. She was bubbling with life-joy, and utterly candid. But several of the creatures that followed her were unpalatable. There was a hog, a leering faun with furry ears, and a thick-lipped beast thing with a woman's body and the hindquarters of a dog.

"Up! Up! Let's see the world, and then dance with the others at the Devil's ball!" cried the red-haired daughter of the godly master goldsmith.

"Let's see the world!" echoed Sidonia. She was wild with the excitement of speed and freedom.

The winged horse and the he-goat, with their clinging riders, shot upward. The unhindered moon drenched them with its arctic silver. Forests unrolled below them like the undulations of a sable cloak; rivers resembled dropped, shimmering girdles; mountains lifted their snowfields like peaked canopies of blue-white satin, and the blue shadows of the fliers flitted across the printless snow. Continually they were joined by others—solitary beldames with thinly streaming white hair whizzing on broomsticks, young girls riding sows or goats, and a sprinkling of renegade monks, and of students of the forbidden sciences, mounted on hay-forks, staves, or black dogs. One man—an aged wizard—rode a dragon with peacock-coloured scales.

The company was mixed indeed—but scarcely more so than that of the Thieves' Kitchen. Sidonia was so interested that she wanted to look two ways at once. The red-haired girl cried shrilly to this or that one, with whom it seemed that she was acquainted.

Now the moonlit sea glittered beneath them. Huge sable shapes towered and weltered, spasmodically shutting out the moon—cloud-giants. A hurricane wind arose; thunder bellowed, lightning glared, and to the right and left of them the thunderous torches of volcanoes painted the rolling vapours with auburn light.

"The earth wakes, little sister! The earth is alive as we are!" cried the demons of the air, and they darted hither and thither like summer swallows through the chaos of storm and speed.

"Yes!" shrieked Sidonia.

Everything lived; everything was in motion. How could one be afraid of that of which one was part?

Higher and higher rose the blast of the hurricane. The moon was gone. Sidonia, clinging to her horse's mane, was whirled like a grain of dust through a roaring blackness that had swallowed witches; wizards, neophytes, were-cats, and all the strung-out train of following devils created by gross, malicious, or hateful thoughts. Then sudden silence, motionlessness that was dizzying—a gradual greenish light, grateful and limpid. Sidonia saw that she was astride of a smooth tree-trunk, sunk in grass, and that as she lay forward upon it, it was two tufts of grass that her hands clutched.

She sat up straight. Great trees surrounded her. Water fell in crystal sheets from cool cavern mouths. Everywhere there was movement—goat-legged fauns peeped; a young female centaur trotted close, her mare's body cream-white. Here were play-fellows! But the light was dimming, the tree-shapes became obscure. An intense red flame shot up and pulsated, nearly blinding her. Red! She had always loved it. It was, after all, a better colour than green. It was excitement.

Oh! what a blare of sound! Mewing, yelping, howling, screaming, laughing, grunting, neighing, whooping. Sheets of fierce fire beat upward—a breathless conflagration—and against the scarlet dark shapes pranced, mingled, or were swept pell-mell by veering currents of the maddest confusion.

Someone caught at her arm. By the fiery light Sidonia saw that it was the daughter of the master goldsmith.

"The Devil's ball! Dance with us at the Devil's ball!" she screamed, her voice barely audible above the babel.

Hogs capered upon their hind legs. There were horned and beaked things, scaled things, bloated things smooth as slugs, obscene things with the shrivelled breasts of a hag, things with the heads of skulls, cocks, baboons, or dogs. Stripped girls danced with man-shaped devils. Shaven-headed monks—glimpsed for a moment between the red-lit eddies of the dance—parodied the sacred rites of Christendom with the assistance of grotesque acolytes, long-tailed and cloven-hoofed. Flutes made of dead men's bones were being played upon, with bagpipes and drums. White arms embraced the metallically glistening bodies of tall demon-husbands. The whistling flames that streamed up like broad banners illuminated a cauldron of chaos.

Sidonia was amazed. The noise deafened her; the glare dazzled her. She was horrified yet attracted. Something urged her to plunge into the fantastic debauch and mix herself with it—her starving hunger for excitement, perhaps. Shrinkingly, like a bather stepping into water, she made a slight forward movement. Oh! they were all round her—they surged and jostled. Feelers touched her, whiskers tickled, sleek fur rubbed. She had no feeling of kinship with these monstrosities. She shuddered, with arms crossed over her bosom.

"Dance! Take a partner!" came the high-pitched, laughing voice of the red-haired girl. She herself had been grappled by a shaggy satyr, and they reeled together.

"You shall dance with me, Sidonia."

Whose voice was that?

The tangle of creatures parted, and the Master was before her—as close as he had stood in the Thieves' Kitchen.

He was masked. He was all in black. Red-lit, the height and the proportions of him seemed more splendid than those of a man.

"Are you afraid, Sidonia?"

"No," she said.

He caught her to him. Together they moved through the seethe of hell. Premonitions of abandonment thrilled through the girl's body. They seemed to be descending. The furnace-glow was above them. Below was a sullen flame the colour of dragons' blood. Thick tentacles reached, and appeared to beckon, but Sidonia, with closed eyes, embraced the Master.

"Mine! Mine!"

His—— Yes; but she was suffocating! Strangling smoke, carrying a filthy and breath-catching odour, enveloped them. Her flesh encountered the touch of tentacles, slimy as snails. The quick grunt of hogs came from every side, Surely a herd surrounded them! An unhuman, leathery hand was laid on her—the hand of an ape. She must have air; she must escape from the circle of foul, fawning things that were symbolic of pollution. She strove ineffectually, all her muscles relaxed, exhaustion having replaced excitement. The arms that held her were of iron. Her shoulder smarted where it had been abused by the bared teeth of a kiss with mercy.

"Give me air! Let me go!"

"Never, Sidonia." And he laughed.

She still struggled, loathing and fear seated in her soul. And then despair! She was lost. And she had half hoped to fly on her winged horse to Heaven, and find the celestial knight who had kissed her lips.

* * * * *

In the loft where the livid moonlight moved imperceptibly the yellow tom cat, disturbed a minute or two before by the collapse of a girl's stripped body, had just begun to dose comfortably with his front paws tucked in beneath his chest. The girl, lying upon her back, twitched, shuddered, moaned. Then there was the sound of a long, relaxing sigh, and her breathing became regular. The mother of the girl, patchwork-shrouded, drowsed upon the three-legged stool. The pallid pumpkin hung from the rafters. The pot containing the noisome unguent for the cure of warts had rolled into a corner. It was about ten minutes past the hour of midnight.

4

ANNE AND MARGARET—safe home from their witch-bearding adventure—had just climbed into bed. They had not removed their linen shifts, for it was very cold, and they hugged each other beneath the coverlets, whispering, and uttering smothered giggles.

The moonlight entered through a lozenged window and fingered coldly the silver tassels at the four corners of a velvet cushion on a bench at the bed's foot, for Anne and Margaret were favoured waiting-maids in the service of the Countess Sabine, and lived softly and well.

"Oh-h, Meg! A fair knight! Who is he?"

Convulsive giggling. And then—"Don't! It was all nonsense, Anne!"

"But the witch said so!"

"S-sh! Don't!"

A pause.

"It can't be the Young Lord—he's dark. And he never speaks to a woman, anyway. None of the girls can understand it; he's not a priest."

"Perhaps he's a saint."

"Oh, God forbid! Isn't one saint enough?"

"You mean the Count?"

"Of course. I wouldn't care to be in the Countess' shoes. Would you?"

"She's nearly a saint herself, Anne. She's always in church."

"I know. But I wouldn't give a penny for a husband who locked himself in every night and wrestled with devils."

More smothered giggling, and another pause.

"But the Count hasn't always been a saint, has he?"

"Goodness, no! He was quite a devil himself until ten years ago. I heard all about it last week."

"Was he—was he very wicked?"

"Oh, he was terrible!"

They snuggled closer, mutually enjoying themselves.

"Tell me!"

"He was Godless—a blasphemer—and, they say, a wizard."

"Yes—yes"

"He ruined every girl he set his eyes on—scores and scores."

"Oh, Mother of God!"

"He kept a stuffed crocodile in his chamber—that's how they knew he was a wizard. No Christian would want a devilish thing like that. They say it's there still."

"But, Anne, why did he become a saint?"

"A wonderful monk converted him. He preached a sermon on death and judgment in the Church of St. Saviour, and everyone wept, and some made vows of pilgrimage, and others threw all their jewels into the poor box. The Count had a sort of fit, they say, and fell like a dead man at the monk's feet. When he came to himself he was like a lamb of God. He's been a saint ever since."

"How wonderful!" sighed Margaret, burrowing deeper into the feathers. The end of the story had moved her so sweetly that she could have shed tears—like the kneeling penitents in the Church of St. Saviour. "And does he wrestle with devils now, Anne?"

"Every night," said Anne firmly. "Hundreds of times he has had to replace the crucifix in his chamber because the devils break it."

A longer pause.

"Anne, can you think of any knight who has fair hair?"

"Oh, for shame! I can't think; I'm sleepy. Let's visit the witch again on St. Andrew's night—I'll have my fortune told."

* * * * *

With a sigh the Countess Sabine woke and raised herself a little, looking with misted eyes at the moonlight that anointed the foot of her carved and canopied bed, which was approached by three shallow steps as though it were an altar. Her soft and sloping shoulders were bare. Her auburn hair was gathered into a silken net. She was thirty years of age, but might at that moment have passed easily for twenty.

She sighed gently again and let herself lapse back into the hollow of her feather pillows. A caressing dream, like an amber cloud, still surrounded her. She was relaxed in a bland enjoyment of it. It had left a honied taste in her mouth. There had been kisses—of hands and lips; love—— Who was the lover? With a smooth inevitableness—like that of spring or sunrise—she became aware that her dream had concerned Gervais, her stepson. There was no jar—no shrinking backward. She lay tranquil, basking emotionally. It was as though something that had been folded budwise had opened its petals. That was all.

Sabine had never known the sensation of shame. She had no regrets, no conflicts. She took life as she found it, and said her prayers, and did her best, always, to get what she wanted. In this her attitude towards life was fundamentally the same as that of a cloistered ascetic; the difference lay in the fact that Sabine and the ascetic wanted totally different things. All conscious existence struggles for that which promises it the most happiness. But ideals of happiness vary as widely as living beings. The saint and the sinner act under the dictation of the same impulse, but one is the elder brother of the other.

"God helps those who help themselves," might have been Sabine's motto. Her God was an easy-going person—a sort of benevolent uncle, half panderer, half slightly-deaf trustee of all delights. She prayed much, and with great fervour.

On either side of the wide bed-chamber there was a closed door. Behind that on the left the waiting-maids, Anne and Margaret, slept within call. Behind that on the right was the chamber of Arnold the Count. It was fast-locked. Every night, from sunset till sunrise, it was fast-locked. A faint noise came through its oaken thickness, as though something had fallen or had been cast down. Was the Holy Count striving with devils, spiked and hoofed?

Sabine did not seem to have heard. Hers was the indifference of custom. And in any case she had no curiosity concerning matters which did not directly affect her desires. For thirteen years she had been a wife; for ten years out of that thirteen the Count had been a saint; she accepted it as she accepted summer and winter, and conformed herself to it. But beneath the surface the sleepy current of her nature slid on through a primal darkness, harbouring strange, swift, eyeless things.

Gervais. To-morrow was the day of his return. A satisfaction that was almost spiritual suffused her. She recalled that it was the Eve of All Hallows—the night when women sought by means of white magic to discover the identity of future lovers. Her love-dream had, of course, been a foreshadowing of its own fulfilment.

She turned luxuriously on to her side, her unclad body sunk deeply between the billows of a feather mattress, and in a minute was asleep. The moonlight strayed among the raised fleurs-de-lys of seed pearls with which the white velvet coverlet was encrusted, and englamoured the carvings of the wooden bed-posts.

It was about the hour of midnight.

* * * * *

The locked chamber of Arnold, the Holy Count, was empty save for two faint, attenuated fingers of the moon that had been thrust inward. It was a large room. The stuffed carcass of a young crocodile, about six feet long, was suspended beneath the ceiling, upon which, on a ground of dark blue, had been painted the signs of the Zodiac. Tapestry depicting scenes from the Passion of Christ masked the walls. The bed was monastic. On a table set between the two narrow windows were books, a skull with a peacock's feather drawn between its teeth—symbol of life's vanity—and a small crucifix. Shelves supported more books, an hourglass, a spirally-carved ivory fragment, said to be portion of a unicorn's horn and possessing the property of detecting poison in liquids, a penitent's scourge, and several rolled-up charts of the heavens and of the countries of the earth.

Lifelessness—vacancy. Had the Count, on this most enigmatical night of all nights of the year, been dematerialised by demoniac agency, or caught up bodily into some seventh heaven, like the Apostle Paul?

A slight scraping sound, a rustle like that of dead leaves. At the back of the chamber the tapestries were parted, and some person, emerging from a hidden and secret entrance, came slowly forward into the ashen twilight of the room.

It was the Master.

Behind him the tapestries were again in place. He extended his arms, stretching mightily. He yawned. Moving to the table, he appeared to contemplate, by the light of the moon, the objects that were upon it. Suddenly he lifted the crucifix, weighed it a moment in his hand, and tossed it against the farther wall. He stretched and yawned again. Evidently the need of sleep was heavy upon him. Turning to the ascetic pallet, he reeled slightly, then fell across it like a person utterly exhausted. In a few moments the deep and regular breathing of a profound sleeper set a faint pulse of life in the bleakness of the chamber.

Already the Master was in the red-lit whirlpool of the Devil's ball.

Hour succeeded hour. The moon set. A bitter darkness was upon the world. After a blind æon had passed the darkness became mixed with a struggling grey, and a cock crew. The figure that had fallen upon the strait bed in sleep sudden as that of a drunkard stirred. It raised itself. It stood up. In the comfortless, neutral dusk that precedes the day it stripped itself to the skin, laid away the habiliments in a chest, enwrapped its nakedness in a linen sheet, and lay down again upon the bed beneath the coverings.

The greyness lightened. Far and near cock answered cock. A blotch like blood trembled upon the arras above the bed's head, which faced the narrow, eastward-looking windows. A tardy sun, incarnadined, was rising from the redly-sweltering mists. It was the morning of the Feast of All Saints.

Upon his hard, monkish bed the Count Arnold still slept. The head of him—his black hair lightened with a thread or two of silver —was nobly moulded. His face, expressionless in sleep was pale as a death-mask, strong, endowed with a beauty that was both sardonic and poignant. The rather too perfect lips, that were neither masculine nor feminine, were close-set, but there was an elusive quirk to them—the merest shadow of a trait, as though as angel sneered or a devil pitied. One could not have said whether they were best fitted to kiss the relics of some saint or the mouth of some shameless sinner. They were an enigma—like the riddle of good and evil.

Trembling sun-spots were multiplied upon the arras, becoming more golden than ruddy. They illuminated the pictured Calvary, glorifying impartially both the good and the bad thief, who, in any case, were both at one in their mutual, grotesquely portrayed agony. A random sunray touched the brows of the sleeping Count, and his eyes unclosed. They blinked, narrowed, and he frowned involuntarily, then sat upright in his bed, bearing some resemblance, sheet-swathed as he was, to a dead man who raises himself in his coffin at the voice of God.

His consciousness was serene. It was like a sheet of virgin parchment. Ever since the occasion, ten years before, when he had fallen as though struck by lightning at the feet of the passionate monk, his day-self had walked blameless and detached, knowing nothing of his night-self—the old Adam—which prowled the city, debauching the ignorant, spurring the depraved, and perpetrating blasphemies as deadly as any attributed to the Devil in person. In every man there is, perhaps, a fiend married to an angel, but at the moment of the Count's seizure this union had been broken, and angel and demon—the light and darkness of him—dominated their host by turns. Yet whereas the angel was ignorant of the fiend, the fiend retained some scornful knowledge of the angel. So the day-self of Arnold was passionless as a discarnate spirit and his night-self shod with the fires of hell. He had evaded the locked struggle which is the destiny of the human hybrid of heaven and earth, but had split his soul from head to heel in doing so.

With the oncoming of the hour of sunset, punctually, a deep-seated psychic uneasiness gripped the Count, and with it fear—a fear that was formless and incommunicable. Like a poisoned animal that seeks to be alone he would enter his chamber and lock the door. In the morning he always woke in his bed, feeling spiritually purged, and as though a weight had been lifted. But in the room itself there were often traces of strange occupancy.

Now his peculiar grey eyes, tinged with the hue of violets, noted the shattered crucifix upon the floor. Inwardly he shuddered. As always, his mind recoiled from the mystery. It was something to be passed by with averted head—something to be mentioned to no one—something to be forgotten.

A subdued, mellifluous ringing of church bells began abruptly in the waking town. The sound mingled with the level warm gold of the sunshine. It was a glorious autumnal morning and a feast-day. Ignoring the outrage offered to the crucifix, the Count rose, donned the usual garments of his dignity, and kissed the relic of the Holy Cross which was enclosed in a jewel of crystal suspended about his neck by a gold chain. He was indeed of a good height; stately, unusual, and giving out a simplicity so perfect that it was twin to the subtlest deception.

Thatched attic roofs on which grass blades sprouted, shingled gables, fretted spires, peaked turrets, battlemented walls, caught the glad morning-light. The steady and soft pealing of the church bells continued. It was as though from every belfry circle upon circle of flying seraphs radiated towards the boundaries of the world, their shining wings becoming fainter and fainter as the widening sounds diminished. Evil was vanquished; in the sequence of the eternal, ever-recurring cycle the archangel, Michael, trod Lucifer underfoot.

III. ENTER THE YOUNG LORD

1

BELLS—STEADILY, SWEETLY ringing. Church bells.

"Ouch!" said Sidonia's consciousness as it reasserted itself, for her body was in a miserable plight. Why was she lying on the floor? And what was this warm oppression that crushed her chest? Only the black cat, Gib, humped up and crooning himself to sleep.

But why? Ah! she remembered! Her determination to fly. The names of the aerial demons.

"Ouch!"

She sat up, clasping the cat to her bare breast as she did so to prevent it from scoring her with its claws. It purred louder than ever, remaining quiescent in her cradling arms. Tib, the yellow cat, was her favourite; Gib had never previously manifested such a preference for her. There was something strange in it.

A ray of morning sunlight, blurred by the lead-set lozenges of crude glass through which it struck, penetrated into the loft. It lightened, yet intensified, the deep-brown dusk. Close at hand a sweet-throated bell was ringing, and all the bells of the city swung with it. It was a feast-day.

The gooseflesh was out all over Sidonia's body. She was half paralysed with cold, and also with a sort of bewilderment, and could only sit and hug the warm and strangely complaisant cat. Her thighs ached, as might those of a person who had gripped a barebacked horse (in the flesh or in the spirit—or in both). Her shoulder smarted, for there was a mark upon it as if teeth had broken the skin. She bore various bruises, but whether gained during the day or night she could not have said.

Her memory only carried her definitely to the midnight stripping, invocation, and anointing. But she lad a confused sense of subsequent adventure, delight, horror, and excitement. She felt both ashamed and proud. And beneath both emotions was the feeling of loss. The celestial knight had left her in the Street of Martyrs. He was in Heaven—a region higher than twenty church steeples placed

76

upon another. What was the use of thinking angels? She was pledged to an assignation with the Master. The Master—— It seemed to her that she was already his.

At some hour during the night Lame Lisa must have, partially roused from her self-induced semi-hypnotic stupor, for she lay now on the litter of rags, with the patchwork coverlet drawn over her—an indistinguishable, mounded shape, quite naturally asleep. She habitually slept through the day, eating only at sunset, and then scarcely enough to keep a cat alive.

To all intents and purposes, throughout the greater part of the twenty-four hours Sidonia was alone.

Gravely, joyfully, the many church bells sounded—christened bells, each bearing a name that was holy and potent; each adequate to banish evil as far as its voice might carry. Sidonia, the unchristened child of an outcast, huddled, as it were, at the feet of these tall and gracious spirits of the blessed chimes, cradling the black cat. She liked the sound. It went over and past her like water, leaving nothing.

Witchcraft or no witchcraft—night-flying or night-dreaming —one's body must be clothed, and food eaten, and more food bought. So Sidonia put the cat out of her arms and lifted her stiff, shivering self up. Her garments—a beggar's choice!—lay where she had abandoned them the night before. Presently she was combing out her hair with a wooden comb, and plaiting it. The yellow cat rubbed against her ankles, uttering little purring cries that were like monosyllables. The black cat sat in the sunbeam licking its fur. From below came the stamp of horses and the growling voices of men.

Sidonia dipped the corner of a cloth in a pitcher of water and cleansed her face. From under the loose hearth-brick she took one of the silver pieces. It was her intention to obtain a drink of warm milk from a neighbour who kept a pair of milch goats. Then she would break her fast with rye bread, see the spectacle of the Young Lord's victorious entrance, purchase a further supply of food, and return to the loft. She threw an ancient cloak round her shoulders. It shrouded her, providing an illusion of sombre decency. Lifting the big yellow cat, she kissed and hugged him.

"Tib shall have goat's milk, and a mouse of sheep's heart. His mother will fetch it for him. Tib must be a good boy until his mother comes back."

Tib was not a good boy, and Sidonia knew it. When, at nights, he vanished on disreputable errands, she became anxious, for where most folk saw only a yellow tom cat with a dirty white chest and a torn ear, who uttered sounds like a dying child or a lost soul, and was, perhaps, a satanic messenger as well, Sidonia saw a prodigal son.

She glanced into the dusk where the witch, her mother, slept. It never seemed to the girl that Lisa was the mother of her flesh and blood, still less of the self within the flesh that felt and thought. They were like strangers brought together by circumstance and bound by long mutual dependence, for while Lisa earned the illicit silver coins Sidonia stood between her and the world.

She would like to have plaited a coloured riband into her hair, as it was a festival day, but she had nothing. They were poorer than church mice.

Slowly, and rather stiffly, Sidonia, the little pariah who had eaten of the tree of the knowledge of good and evil, descended from the loft that housed the witch, the witch's cats (a pair of sinister, furry familiars, if gossip could be credited), and the lonely sunbeam.

2

"HE'S COMING!"

"No—not yet!"

"Yes! They're letting out the doves from the cages."

"I can't see anything. I wish I were taller!"

"I'll lift you up, girl."

"No, you won't! What do you think I am?"

"Something a man could eat even if he wasn't hungry."

"Oh! The idea!"

"There are the trumpets!"

"Who are you shoving? I'm as good as you are."

"God bless the Young Lord!"

A hundred voices spoke at once. Toes were trodden on, elbows were dug into ribs, the plump arms of girls were slyly pinched by perfect strangers, smooth-faced or bearded; small, sunny-headed children, bare as grubs save for brief shirts, were hoisted on to shoulders, hard red berries, dropped mischievously from windows, caused heads to turn, hands were waved, sparrows twittered, the sun shone as mellowly as though it were August instead of November —though the shadowed places were raw and damp, and the clash of bells in the two grey towers of the Church of St. Saviour just across the little square set all the air a-quiver.

Between the fair stone houses, from whose upper windows hung rich and sombre carpet strips brought by adventurous merchants from the Orient lands of the phœnix and the Demon of Cathay, one glimpsed russet and amber foliage. Where the principal street of the town entered the cobbled market-place before the church a stage had been erected, whereon a blonde, long-haired lad, impersonating a chief of the Heavenly Host, waited to present a gilded branch —symbol of victory—to the Young Lord. He appeared ill at ease in the shapeless linen robe, that resembled a nightshirt several sizes too big for him. At the front of the stage sat a double row of very young girls, with chaplets of autumn berries, and their hands clasped nervously in their silken laps—ready to sing in chorus. Overhead, the joyous chaos of sound that rushed out, pell-mell, from the twin belfries of St. Saviour went tumbling and sparkling over the roofs and the chimney mouths, over the apple-trees and the tall and shivering poplars of gardens, over sprouting thatch and battlemented wall, over field and fallow and rutted wagon-track, until it sank, like water into moss, into the listening silence of the golden wildwood, where man adventured at his peril, and where a stag might lift his crested head, wondering with wide ears whether that were indeed a sound that fell like a leaf through the air and was at rest.

A victory—even though it had been gained in the lands beyond the forest that were dream-blue with distance—was no slight matter. For defeat might bring in its wake—perhaps a month later, perhaps two, perhaps three—the rumble of ox-drawn war-engines approaching on the forest roads, the toss of many-coloured helmet plumes, the blue and red and gold quarterings of hostile shields, the disorderly march of singing men-at-arms blackened with the smoke of burning huts and sanguined with the blood of the butchered out-dwelling folk. Then arrow flights, battering-rams, and the scaling-ladders of assault. And then—if God was blind and deaf—a catastrophe dreadful as the Last Day—weltering streets, shrieking women, sacked houses, altar treasures scattered on the steps of the churches, wine running in the gutters. Slaughter, rape, sacrilege, drunkenness, and despair. So the townspeople displayed their treasure of carpets and tapestries, and wore their holiday clothes, and rang the church bells to give welcome and honour to the Young Lord.

Several white doves, with eyes that seemed dark-bright as jet, were released simultaneously from their wooden cages and fluttered confusedly upward, their noisy wings making a sound like the brushing rustle of stiff brocades.

"He's coming!"

Behind the crowd, in the gut of a laneway, a young ragged girl stood. Insignificant; singular only in her poverty when all the world was dressed for a festival. But Sidonia was accustomed to her rags and her inconsequence, which she shared with sparrows and stray dogs. She was aware only that she wanted to see. The released doves fluttered high overhead in the crisp yet sunny air; down where the girl stood there was nothing but dirty house walls and intent backs.

Oh! A silver cry of trumpets, sharp athwart the golden tumult of the bells.

Sidonia found herself on the tip-toes of her bare feet, between a tall fellow and a short one, trying to see over the starched white linen headgear that had a Sunday air. The tall fellow, shuffling in closer, trod inadvertently upon her, and she uttered a squeal.

"Sorry, sister"; and a long, rough-shaven face peered round, its amiable leer betraying a broken tooth. The leer changed to a dropped jaw. The face, in its sudden dismay, became ludicrous.

"Christ save us!"

The tall vagabond, his jester's bells tinkling, backed away like a scared horse.

"Oh! Oh! There's Devil's work here!"

People faced round, startled, staring. Half a dozen young lads agog for excitement—tousled, freckled, out-at-elbows—seemed to have sprung up from the ground.

"That girl's in league with Satan! I met her last night in the forest, and she called up the Devil, and he rose from hell on a dark stallion and knocked me silly. I can show the marks, folks!"

He was ghastly under the grime, and visibly sweating. His black-nailed forefinger shook as he pointed it at the girl.

"It's true. It's true as the Gospels! I saw it—I was there myself. She's a witch!"

The stocky, pock-marked juggler was spluttering with earnestness and excitement. He began crossing himself as hurriedly as if he were catching flies.

Sidonia had taken several steps back the instant she recognised the jester. She remained stiffly at gaze, one hand clutching the black cloak whose tatters parodied the scalloped fringes of state trappings.

"She's the witch's daughter!" piped a boy's voice. "Hell-cat! Devil's brat!"

The shrill sing-song was in the key of the puerile gutter-raillery of children.

"Hell-cat! Devil's brat!" A dozen ragamuffins joined in at the top of their voices.

A semicircle of hostile eyes regarded the ragged, bare-footed girl as if she were a toad exposed by the overturning of a stone. Several women crossed themselves. Sidonia was pale. Her face, framed by the two long, dark plaits, had a frozen look. Her unique eyes were fixed, expressionless. The clamouring bells and the freed doves were in a world of sunshine high above the muddy trench of the lane.

A clot of dirt, badly aimed, splattered against a wall behind the girl. A rotten egg, culled from the lane's refuse, struck her, fouling the wretched cloak that was wrapped closely about her.

"Hell-cat! Devil's brat!"

The stink of the rotten egg was in Sidonia's nostrils. Ignominy, attack; the accusation of the reeking, mongrel fellow who had tried to rape her. And she—— Yes! she was Satan's paramour! Fury, and a hot, twisted pride, swept through her, and she trembled. What were these men and women with their holiday clothes and their blank faces, these yelping lads and malicious children, compared with her, who was the Devil's mistress? She could call on demons; she could ride the night wind and wake with stiffened thighs; the power of hell overshadowed her with its glooms and splendours; she had known the lips of Satan, and he was with her. All this was presented to her with the instantaneousness of a glare of lightning. Throwing off the filth-splashed cloak with a shrinking and abrupt movement that seemed to come right on the heels of the last outcry, she flung up her hand.

"You! How dare you! Who have I injured—who have I hurt? Answer that, you sons of bastards! Oh! Cowards! Curs!"

She was shaking as though the sweep of the passion that poured through her was too great for its channel. Her eyes—always extraordinary by reason of the dilation of the pupils—seemed about to dart actual levin. She appeared suddenly taller by at least an inch.

There was a breath-caught hush under the golden torrent of bell-music that poured on and on in lovely, clamorous indifference.

"Bring holy water!" said a woman in a sharp, frightened voice. Immediately came a truculent outburst from the hobblede-hoys—"Stone her! Duck her!"

Several missiles struck the wall. There was the surge of a forward movement like the clustered half-rush of a little pack that is eager but afraid.

The semi-naked girl, her sallow body and straight, sun-stained limbs revealed through a dozen rents and hanging tatters, stood like a spear planted in the ground—a spear that quivers. She lifted her thin, bramble-scratched arms. Her eyes seemed to see everyone yet no one.

"Stop! I tell you you cannot come any nearer! You cannot! I'm stronger than you are—than all of you! Not one of you can hurt me; you can't take another step forward! You can't!"

Her head tilted back, and she laughed as though it was the best joke in the world. It was a ringing, rising laugh—unbridled. Her arms had dropped. The tingling sureness that possessed Sidonia was similar to the confidence that had gripped her when she invoked the demons of the air, only twenty times more intense. Her faith was shadowless. She was triumphant—inviolate. It was the wild joy of it that prompted her to laugh. They could do nothing—nothing!

The irresolute forward lunge had been halted by her cry of "Stop!" Boys and youths, some with stones in their hands, stood awkward, their face muscles relaxed, their mouths a little open. When she began to laugh their jaws dropped still further; the eyes of the other watchers became fish-like for roundness, and the jester covered his face with his dirty, trembling hands. But one lad—a brutal-jawed youngster with his hair over his eyes—made a movement as if to advance, the blood-lust being upon him. Abruptly he uttered a scream, falling back as though he had trodden on something white-hot, for all those in the lane, believing implicitly in the strength of witches drawn from the incalculable might of Satan, were as fully aware within themselves that they *could* not go forward as Sidonia was confident of her power to forbid them. So a barrier of faith and fear, invisible as glass, separated the wretched little waif of sixteen from the tradesmen, the 'prentices, the riff-raff, and the respectable wives and daughters, who would all have piously watched her burn to death and then have gone home to a good dinner.

Unconscious of cold—scarcely conscious of time and place—Sidonia moved slowly backward, retreating from the half-circle of faces that were so comically afraid. She walked on air, not on mud and partly-frozen filth. An archway opening into a paved yard was upon her right; without knowing why she turned aside and passed beneath it.

The yard was empty save for some hens and a cock with a silver hackle. Horse-stalls opened upon it, and one heavy door that stood ajar. Sidonia went across to this door like a sleep-walker, and pushed it inward, and entered the house to which it gave access. She had no hesitation or any anxiety; she was lifted above self-consciousness.

Behind, in the lane, twenty people were talking at once, and several boys had already approached the threshold of the archway, nosing about like eager yet timid dogs on a blood-scent.

"Come back. Come back this minute!" screamed the mother of one of them. "Do you want to feel the claws of Satan?"

The silver-hackled cock, arrogant in the deserted, dung-sprinkled little yard, clapped his wings against his sides and uttered a hoarse crow. Those who were nearest retreated with the jumpy haste of panic, and so overwrought were all nerves by ghostly fears that one woman, turning green-white, fainted, slumping down into the muck like a dropped sack of rags.

Meanwhile Sidonia, automatically pushing the iron-bound door to behind her, went a few steps forward into the twilight of a rich man's deserted kitchen, and paused. Onions and smoked hams hung from the ceiling beams. There were scattered vegetable parings, unscoured pots, an idle spit, and drippings of blood and of melted fat. But they were unreal. They might vanish at any moment, revealing—what? Sidonia knew yet did not know. The Unseen brushed lightly against her, yet her eyes were held. She tingled, hardly aware of her limbs. She was numb, feather-light; expectant, incurious, concerned more with the emotional thoughts that swam like clouds into the sphere of her mind than with anything else. Onions, hams, cooking-pots—they had no real existence. At any moment they might break like the rondure of a bubble in which all manner of objects are reflected for a long instant.

At the threshold of the archway one hardy spirit, braving hell, craned his neck forward, verifying the emptiness of the homely horse-yard, the cracks between whose paving-stones ran with yellowish liquid and whose abundant droppings furnished occupation for the speckled hens.

"She's not there!" he announced hoarsely.

Immediately he was joined by others. They viewed the hens, the cock, the stable litter, and the shut door. Evidently the witch-girl had transported herself elsewhere, slipping through the fingers of christened men like water through a sieve. The house itself stood outside their speculation. It pertained to pious and wealthy folk; even devils must respect such a combination.

Shrilling across the babel of the hallowed bells the silver-tongued trumpets of victory spoke for the second time.

"He's coming!" And then, out of the clamorous distance, "God bless the Young Lord!"

What was a vanished witch? A fled nightmare, a cobweb of the soul! Here was the tide of life running like a sparkling river, with a hero to be acclaimed riding down the current of it. The gazers melted from the arched doorway of the horse-yard. Even the woman who had fainted—drawn to her feet now by friends—turned her head feebly in the direction of the street, her velvet dress one long smear of dirt.

Beneath the hams and the garlands of onions, in the twilight that smelt of cabbage water and of burnt fat and sugar, Sidonia stood stiffly, breathing with the rhythm of a deep sleeper, her arms hanging at her sides. How close was reality about her! She had a feeling of the nearness of fire—banners of flame that beat upward, and dark figures moving swiftly against the fierce scarlet. Was it a memory—a memory from last night? Past and present were knotted together in some way. Or was it that reality was timeless? The Master—he was here too. All the passion of her wanted his arms again. Had she been his—and afraid? Now a flame burned in her that was as scarlet as those she saw without seeing. The knees of her being weakened in a fiery languor. She felt the presence of satyr-things—of sportive, rearing centaurs. Vague vistas opened, wherein, amid flaring, trampled blossoms, the cloven-footed swine couched with the leopards of cruel and beautiful abandonment.

Crying trumpets—the muffled sound of them—came to her like far-off voices dropping from a height. She would climb that height; she would see over the heads of the people—the shadowy, strengthless people who had thought to hurt her. Half in the real and half in the unreal world, she moved towards a staircase that turned upon itself, its stone steps vanishing into partial darkness.

It was no effort to her to mount it. At moments the stone walls closed in on her; at other moments they receded. If the servants had not run out into the street sight-seeing it is hard to say what they would have made of Sidonia, but the bewilderment would have been all on their side; she herself was either above or below the ordinary considerations of five-sense life.

The staircase ended in a doorway masked by tapestry. Voices were audible. This was evidently the principal room of the house, where meals were served, guests entertained, and the young un-married girls exhibited their skill with musical instruments to rela-tives or politely attentive friends. Sidonia parted the tapestries and walked out, bare-footed, on to the rush-strewn floor as composedly as the Mother of God treading the golden pavement of Heaven.

The room had both breadth and length. Two windows looked down upon the street. Unbroken tapestries of knights and ladies, grouped with horses, hawks, and greyhounds, left nothing of the naked walls visible. Deer-skins were laid upon the rushes; there were carved seats and an embroidery frame. Over one of the seats lay a cloak of velvet embossed with silver fleurs-de-lys. A table bore chessmen, roses, a basket of embroidery wools, and an hour-glass from which the sand had just run out. Two women and a girl, their plump, satin-covered backs turned to the room, leaned from the opened double window. The other window, narrower, and set somewhat apart, was open too.

Sidonia, the uninvited guest, noticed the faint smell of the roses and the sombre harmony of the tapestries. These things were good; her senses demanded such things. But they were nothing to the beauties of the real world, though terrors were entwined with them like serpents. She made no endeavour to move without noise, and paused by the disordered table to take a rose from the medley that had been spilt upon it. The three women, pressed together, leaned out over the street.

"Oh-h!" gurgled the young one, laughing at something.

Sidonia, passing close, went to the window that no one had occupied and leant on the broad stone sill. The hinged square of leaded glass lozenges, that was set widely open, screened her partially from the three other gazers, if they should look towards her. But they were as unconscious of her as of the presence of the good and bad angels with which the atmosphere was said to teem.

The cobbled street, that widened out into the market about fifty yards farther on, was in confusion as a few soldiers with pikes tried to maintain a clear passage. Immediately beneath Sidonia's window a shivering little monkey, wearing a coat and a cap with a feather, perched on the shoulder of a gipsy-looking man, extended its tiny, leathery hand as if to implore alms. People shrank from it with shrill laughter. To them it had the look of a changeling. It was the same monkey that had crept from under the bench in the Thieves' Kitchen the night before. Another face from the same hell-sink, bearded and starveling, was turned skyward, for with his back to the house wall sat the beggar with the contracted leg, who had poured out gold pieces and offered to buy drink for all the rascally actors.

"Charity, for the love of Christ!" His high-pitched, almost infantile voice ascended thinly. From time to time coins were dropped into his hollow palm. A dozen pikemen, three abreast, appeared in the street, clearing a forcible passage. People were jammed up against the house walls, breathless but animated. Someone who had trodden accidentally upon the lame beggar gave him three pieces of silver, and joy was regnant. Voices chanting in unison mingled now with the clash of bells—the sweet, approaching strains of the Te Deum.

"The shrine—— The shrine——" A hushed utterance like a wind through leaves was upon the lips of everyone.

The lame beggar was trying to rise with the aid of crutches. There was the suggestion of panic in his hasty efforts. He managed to lift himself up, but was immediately wedged between the bodies of the crushed sight-seers.

"Let me by, kind people. I am very ill."

His childish voice rose, cracked as a penny whistle.

"The sight of the saint may heal you," said a stout woman, who was likewise unable to budge.

A muffled sound came from the beggar. That was precisely what he was afraid of. He earned an easy living lame; he would have to sweat like a labourer if he were sound. The thought of work turned him sick. The oncoming shrine, with its power to perform a malicious miracle, inspired him with hate and terror. But it was impossible to move.

Sidonia sat now sideways upon the window-sill, leaning well forward. A sense of reality with regard to what she saw and heard and felt was returning to her. Yet no fear of any kind was mixed with it. Her fury of rage against her defilers and attackers had swept her mind and spirit like a great wave, and the passionate core of her had been laid naked. The gate which she herself had opened into that other world which lay so near was being drawn to as the forces ebbed a little, but, once opened, it could not be entirely closed.

She felt perfectly confident, and filled with a sort of contemptuous hate for the men and women in the street. It seemed to her that she should always be lifted above them as she was now.

Nearer and nearer came the beautiful male chant of the Te Deum. Sandalled monks in black and white robes appeared, bearing painted church banners with gold and silver fringes. Before them was carried a tall gilt crucifix. They were all singing. Sidonia understood no Latin, but to ordinary church-attending folk it was as familiar as their neighbour's conversation. The feeling of expectancy was becoming breathless. Joyful, hallowed, and glorious things were happening.

Now came acolytes strewing dried rose-petals and swinging silver thuribles, from whose perforations gushed the smoke of incense. An exotic odour, like the palpable savour of prayer, overlaid the odours of the street. People were going down upon their knees and uncovering their heads, for the shrine was coming.

More acolytes—two by two—bore great candles of yellow wax, guttering wildly or displaying blackened, wind-extinguished wicks. Holy water was sprinkled right and left upon the people by a priest in the golden vestments of thanksgiving, who dipped a miniature broom of bound twigs into a silver vessel shaped exactly like a bucket.

And then the shrine itself, carried on poles—a long, narrow coffer of enamelled goldsmith's work with sides of glass. It enclosed the uncorrupted body of the city's saint—a bishop dead over a century before. He lay in his robes of office, the mitre upon his head, that was supported by a white satin pillow, a golden crozier set with crystal and amethysts laid beside him. The sunken profile of a withered, yellowish face was visible, and two folded hands, shrunk to strange, brittle-looking claws of the hue of parchment.

Every head was bent as at the elevation of the Host. Quite a number discerned the odour of lilies that was said to emanate from the dead flesh miraculously isolated from corruption. Hearts were uplifted, and clarified as with a heavenly dew. A pang of delicious and softening emotion struck through the soul of the crowd.

Immediately below the wide-set windows of the house of wealth there was a smothered groan. The crippled beggar, his crutches still under his armpits, stood now upon two feet instead of one. At the moment of the shrine's passage a convulsive shudder had taken him—a shudder of fear and faith. The contracted sinews had relaxed as the might of the dead saint—combated by his terrified will and abetted by his terrified belief—touched him like the finger of God. The whites of his eyes showed and the teeth chattered in his head.

"A miracle!" exclaimed someone hoarsely, for the shrine had passed.

"A miracle! A miracle!"

"Glory to God, and to his saints!"

The beggar was clapped upon the back by a dozen hands. Tears streamed from the eyes of men and women. He remained mute, shivering. Inwardly he was as impotently furious as a trapped rat. His livelihood had been filched from him. He would have to work.

A blare of trumpets—right under the watching casements, as it seemed. And here were the trumpeters—scarlet-clad youths on horseback.

"The Young Lord!"

Every head craned forward, every throat uttered a cry. For the moment even the welcome of the church bells was inaudible.

"Gervais! Gervais!"

A tall horse, its white housings embroidered with silver fleurs-de-lys, leaving nothing visible save its onyx-dark eyes seen through eye-holes and its massive hooves and bearded fetlocks, came slowly, stepping upon the thrown roses that were already partly trodden into the slush between the oozy and unevenly set cobblestones. More liberated pigeons fluttered skyward. Flowers fell from above. There was a confusion of beating wings, tossed roses, and waving hands. Men and women, mixed with the pikemen who were unable to hold them back, pressed round the caparisoned horse. The street seethed like milk that is about to boil over.

The rider of the horse, in complete armour, but bareheaded, sat him beautifully, gathering up the gold-embossed crimson bridle in one ungauntleted hand. His face was set like a mask, with a little frown between the brows. He seemed aloof, grave to severity; cold as a young hermit-saint, and proud. The truth of it was that Gervais was suffering abominably from self-consciousness. He hated crowds.

"God bless the Young Lord!"

"Back! Back!" shouted the pikemen, but no one obeyed them. The big horse whose white and silver housings almost swept the ground had been brought to a standstill.

Sidonia was leaning even farther forward. Her black hair, which had come unplaited, hung downward like a dishevelled veil. She gazed with all her eyes at the horse and rider. This was the Young Lord—the heir of the Holy Count, the deliverer of the town, and the chiefest person within the circuit of its walls.

Suddenly the face of the ensteeled rider lifted, and his head turned as if at a spoken word. Looking sharply upward, his embarrassed violet-grey eyes encountered the eyes of Sidonia—deer-dark, widened in an unconscious, consuming stare.

Outwardly no flash of illumination dazzled the onlookers; Gervais simply looked upward, sitting rigid upon the halted horse. He saw dark eyes that were poignant, loose-tressed hair, a pallid young face, and a young bosom breaking through shredded raiment. He saw the girl of last night—the girl who was mixed with his blood, with his soul, as it seemed; the girl whom he desired and prostrated himself before, as before his God; the beggar-girl who had given him the fire of life.

Sidonia saw—the Young Lord. As far as her knowledge went she had never set eyes on him before. If anyone had told her that she had known his mouth and the embrace of his arms she would have looked blankly at them. To the best of her belief only two people had kissed her—Satan and an angel. The lifted face was of a startling uniqueness. It was austere, yet ardent; with straight, chaste brows, yet exquisitely lipped; arrogant yet with something also of the quick, nervous shrinking of a woman or a child. The gaze of the violet-grey eyes was like the quivering grip of a hand. They uttered something, but she could not understand it, though it went like a slight shock through all her body. Like someone answering automatically when suddenly spoken to, she put her hand on the rose she had taken, and that lay beside her on the wide stone sill, and flung it quickly outward to the young man upon the stallion hooded in white and silver, to whom girls waved and men shouted and mothers held up their infants as to St. Michael, the dragon-conqueror, himself.

Gervais caught the thrown rose. In the instant of the catch his eyes were averted from the face of the out-leaning girl, and at the same moment the big, hairy-fetlocked horse moved forward again.

"Long live the Young Lord!"

The halt had been a matter of moments only—an eddy of acclamation, an upward look, a thrown red flower. Already the panoplied stallion was a couple of spears' lengths past the window, and another mounted knight, his visor raised, was in his wake. The bells clamoured, the people cried out, and heavy horseshoes tripped against cobblestones.

Gervais, the dark rose crushed in his closed hand, was carried forward by the tall, slow-footed, shouldering horse. Before, he had been self-conscious, a prey to the nervous anxieties of a shy man who has not outgrown his boyhood; now he was like a person who has met the Holy Virgin face to face in the middle of a marketplace, and who is divided between dismay at his own inability to grasp the full wonder of the momentary vision, and an intoxication of the spirit that confuses thought.

3

THE MOMENT SIDONIA had thrown the rose she drew herself back, and her feet found the rush-strewn floor. She stood a little aside from the window, her face turned from it, one hand on the cold sill.

A light had broken upon her. It illuminated an amazing land-scape. She stared at it, her hand gripping the stone of the window-sill. Gervais, the Young Lord. There was power in her now—the wonderful power of hell. She would be lifted above all these people, and all their eyes would be upon her; she would have everything of which she had dreamed—for, by the power of hell, she was to be-come the paramour of the Young Lord.

She knew this certainly without a tremor of doubt. Her heart was beating with excitement. It was natural and fitting that Satan's mistress should be also a seducer, and so attain the luxuries of the world—pictured hangings, sleek fabrics, spiced foods, serving-maids, and a feather bed. The gaze of the Young Lord had held hers as if she were a vision. The power of hell was behind her—in her. It was most wonderful.

The half-dozen or so of mounted knights with red, blue, or green-dyed ostrich plumes tumbling from their helmets had gone by, and now the men-at-arms were passing, three abreast, the heads of their long, backward sloping lances barbed with berry clusters, fern, or evergreen leaves. But the street was forgotten by Sidonia, shaken by the heavy beating of her heart. She did not think of the Young Lord as a man; he was an effigy—a symbol—a symbol of breathless triumph.

Leaving the window, she moved out into the room. The two women and the girl still surveyed the street. When the Young Lord's horse had halted they had been too busy waving their hands and throwing roses (kisses also) to observe the dark rose that he had caught as quickly as a schoolboy. When you are sure that the room behind you is untenanted you don't notice trifles.

Sidonia looked at the beautiful cloak of sky-blue velvet that was cast over the seat near the table. The silver fleurs-de-lys with which it was powdered reminded her of the fleurs-de-lys on the white housings of the Young Lord's stallion. She needed a cloak herself. It was cold, and the rotten egg had ruined the miserable black one she had discarded in the lane. Quite naturally, and without any thought of before or after, she put her hands on the sleek velvet. It felt like a magic moss, inconceivably short and fine, or like the supple spoil of some lovely animal from the regions where beasts were scarlet and azure and human-folk as black as the flue of a chimney. She lifted it up and put it about her shoulders, snuggling into it. It fastened with twin placques of silver a little below the throat, and fell to within half an inch of the ground, concealing her superbly from bare shoulders to bare feet. It was warm as a shroud of fur; it seemed, in some inevitable way, to be as much hers as her own skin. And yet, preposterously, it was not hers. She must ask leave.

"May I have this cloak?"

Her raised voice was clear as a child's.

The three people at the larger window jumped as if they had been pricked, and all turned instantly. The plumpest woman squealed; the eldest ejaculated "God save us!"; the youngest, a girl of about Sidonia's age, kept her large, ripe, pulpy-lipped mouth shut. She had green eyes, and her dark-red hair was caught in a silken net. Had those rounded thighs—masked now by a narrow white gown—straddled a he-goat? Had those salient though covered breasts been exposed to the midnight wind, and those cat-coloured eyes gleamed sidelong with unchristened laughter?

Sidonia looked at the red-haired girl and the girl looked back at her.

"I know you," each said to the other without speaking.

"May I wear this cloak?" said Sidonia again aloud.

"Yes—oh, yes," said the red-haired girl quickly, speaking while the other two were still speechless.

Sidonia inclined her head a little. She did not really feel any gratitude, though of course she should have done so. The cloak seemed to be naturally hers—a compensation for the outrage of the rotten egg, and an earnest of her new dignities. Turning away, she passed out from the chamber as unhurriedly as she had entered it, her carriage very erect, her small, soiled feet making scarcely any sound.

"What—who was she? What have you done? My new cloak!" gasped the plump woman.

The red-haired girl—a clever minx—could think quickly at a pinch.

"Didn't you see the light—the crown of light?"

"What!"

"Oh, mother! We've had a saint from Heaven in the house—perhaps, even, the Mother of God herself—and you never knew it!"

"What do you mean? What are you talking about, Violane?"

"The saint, mother—the saint with the light round her head, who appeared from nowhere and asked for your cloak. Didn't you smell spices?"

"She—she certainly came from nowhere, and I thought she looked strange. There is a smell here—like spices——"

There was. It was the after-taste of the church-incense that had fumigated the street.

"But—but why should a saint want my cloak, Violane?"

"Perhaps to take it to some poor soul dying of cold, mother. Saints do such things, don't they? Someone a hundred miles away. Oh! we are blessed!"

She clasped her hands together, not certain whether it would be better to break into sobs or to fall on her knees. But tears were difficult, so she knelt suddenly.

"Violane was always pious, wasn't she, from a little thing?" her mother was saying to her grandmother an hour later. "She has a wonderful nature. I hope she doesn't take the veil, though. Seeing visions—— I didn't see the light, but I smelt the spices. I wonder which saint it was. The cloak was a new one. What an honour——"

It had been an anxious moment for Violane, the cat-eyed little pagan, when she turned quickly and recognised Sidonia. Not that she remembered her in the ordinary daytime sense of the word—it was just a rush of instinctive, formless certainties. Her quick, animal-like mind, always on the alert to guard her day-life from her night-life, simply followed the path of least resistance in dealing with this vague danger. She would, at that moment, have given Sidonia a papal tiara set with precious stones if she had asked for it, and to explain her as a heavenly apparition had seemed the best way to silence any outcry over the sky-blue cloak. One thing had suggested another. Now the intrusion from her night-life had safely withdrawn, taking her mother's new cloak with it, and she herself was in the odour of reflected sanctity. In twenty-four hours the whole town would be talking of the vision.

4

IN THE CHURCH of St. Saviour High Mass was being sung. Soldiers and townspeople mingled in the market-place before the edifice. There was chaff, love-making, and the exhibition of half-healed war scars.

The church had taken nearly two hundred years to build. It was the composite soul of generations dead, incarnate, and unborn solidified like a wave frozen in the act of breaking. Awe, aspiration, simplicity, scourged virtues, squirming lusts, fears grovelling like hysterical women, hopes like tall, spear-shaped lilies, beauties like handfuls of jewels, ugliness, wisdom, puerility, cruelty with fetters and fire and mercy with an alabaster box of ointment, fixed and made permanent as the carved rocks of mountains. It was wonderful, and beautiful, and strange, and it inspired fear—even horror. A horde of stone devils leaned, grinning, from its parapets. They sank their chins between their scaly palms; they protruded their tongues; they gnawed gleefully at the petrified cadavers of sinners like dogs gnawing bones. Even the terminals of the leaden waterspouts were evil, wide-mouthed creatures with close-folded batpinions. All these things were where they were because entrance into the building was impossible to them—or so it was hoped. The excommunicated but vigorous lusts of the christened workers in stone and metal had given them their shapes. They were leeringly gross, rapacious, grotesque. Effigies of bishops, saints, angels, and sanctified kings occupied rows of niches. In tangles of stone foliage stags leapt, and dogs, and hares. Even lions, monkeys, and wild boars were represented. A feeling of the fellowship of all clave to the edifice like the living tendrils of a gold-green vine; the morning stars sang together when men rejoiced; stags, boars, and bears could be subdued by the loving sermon of a saint, and even the snail on the dock leaf knew when a man of God passed by. Yet in the solemn glooms beneath the pointed arches lurked the shadow of ghostly Judgment, terrible as the rack and searing-irons of mortal tribunals, and once a year a cat—the witch-animal—was placed in a sack and hurled to its death from the summit of one of the church towers.

Now, within the walls of the church, the roll of the organ was like a mellow and thunderous voice catching up all souls into a region of sonorous joy, where, for a space at least, they became simple and great, and heard the footsteps of God, even though they could understand nothing of Him.

But the God of each differs from the God of the other, and one man's highest ends where another's lowest begins. So the Countess Sabine, gratefully stimulated by the soft, deep, tremendous sound to which the very stones vibrated, felt that her stepson's love was assured to her, and the lips of her inner self moved in a half-articulate promise of refined waxen candles and perfumed oils to the church's shrine. The sentiment that stirred her was the most religious of which she was capable—which is not saying much, but, then, she had not made herself. She felt soothed, uplifted.

Count Arnold, his eyes cast down, his hands folded, was absorbed in prayer.

Gervais, rigid in his panoply of armour, looked fixedly upward, as though the Holy Ghost had appeared to him. The beggar-girl was uplifted before him like a transfigured saint. Her outstretched hands were filled with roses; lilies were beneath her naked feet. He worshipped her, and in doing so it seemed to him that he was worshipping God.

"*Gloria in excelsis Deo*——" proclaimed the sweet male voices of the choir as the organ ceased.

"*Laus Deo!*" exclaimed the soul of Gervais. His heart swelled with praise. Never before had he felt so moved to adoration of the Maker of all things.

"*Et in terra pax hominibus!*"

The Countess Sabine lifted her eyes of forget-me-not blue to the high altar, above which was a three-fold altar-piece whose central panel depicted the hoary-bearded Creator judging the just and the unjust. She felt sure that Gervais would soon become her lover. God was benevolent, and she had promised the candles and the perfumed oil.

"*Lumen de lumine! Deum verum de Deo Vero!*"

A pregnant woman far back in the dim body of the church began to weep softly from pure joy. Her unborn child was coming towards her, running over blossoms that were like stars. Angels attended it. Heaven was about her, and in spite of the glory it was as dear and homely as a plot of parsley by a kitchen door.

"*Et incarnatus est*——"

The voices of the choir, blended into one beautiful and sonorous voice, deepened to a note of wondering awe. The shadowy length and breadth and height of the fretted stone cavern, where broken sunset lights dropped downward like dew from circular windows that were a mosaic of violet and ruby and amber glass, seemed to be waiting.

"Et homo factus est——"

Every head was lowered. The carved beasts in the foliage niches should have bent their stone knees, if that had been possible, for heaven had become one with earth, and lowest was merged sweetly into highest. The beggar felt himself exalted, and the man of substance put on humility—if only for the moment. Nursing mothers and women with children clutching at their gowns were aware of the mantle of God's Mother. Hearts callous as the palm of a smith's hand felt the prick of sensibility. Pain was lightened, the sting of death was half withdrawn. A young woman who had been seduced by her lover melted into a storm of repentant sobs, her hands pressed over her face, and just across the dusky threshold of the main portal a little mongrel dog, feeling the general hush, lifted its sad brown eyes and greyish muzzle, as if a master had spoken to it by its name.

But outside, the sculptured devils, perched upon every vantage-point, barked mutely, grinned, and leered, and gnawed their provender of damned souls. They and their chattels were beyond the scope of mercy. And beneath them, looking up towards them, was the witch's daughter—the reputed Devil's child—Sidonia.

Her skirts wetted, as it were, by the welter of coarse, genial life that frothed up to the very threshold of the church, she was yet entirely alone. Men-at-arms stared at her, women looked—and looked again. But no one had spoken, no one had let or hindered her. Some seemed in doubt as to whether she was or was not an apparition. The cloak of celestial blue robed her from narrow shoulders to naked heels. Her head was held as erect as a princess's, and she had the look of a person wrapt in a cloud. If she had displayed tatters she would probably have been molested, even pelted, but the rich cloak ensured reverence. And then it seemed, too, that she might vanish into thin air at a touch.

She looked up towards the outward-leaning devils. Were they really her associates? They were very hideous, though of a horrible cheerfulness. It could not be a bad thing to have creatures of that sort siding with one; everybody was afraid of them. One needed friends. The warmth of the cloak was delicious. It was exquisite not to be shivering. The curious confidence that filled her was unreflecting, and her breathing was calm and even. She was destined to seduce the Young Lord and be lifted up above all the townspeople.

A profound undertone of sound—solemn, like subdued thunder—appeared to dimly shake the towering stones. It rolled out like a volume of slow, dark water from the principal portal of the church. Lofty was this portal, and the inward-opening double-doors of iron-bound oak were set wide. Dusky it was also, as the entrance to a cavern, and a double row of saints guarded it. A blind man, half-naked, was seated at the side of it, and next him a dreadful, earth-coloured beggar-woman, partly devoured by a cancer. The man's palm was upturned for alms; a wooden rosary was between the fingers of the woman, and her dog-like eyes were tranquil. The organ-note rolled past them and over them with soft thunders, and tramplings, and the drone of wings.

Sidonia had never entered the great church. The stone saints did not appear unfriendly; they were a blandly expressionless company, enwreathed with gracious foliage wherein little forest animals lurked. She slowly mounted the three shallow steps, stood a moment, and then, like a person who under some obscure compulsion enters a place of danger, went forward into the heavy and cavernous gloom. So great was her confidence in the strong arm of Satan that a mere automatic impulse of curiosity had led her into the mysterious citadel of God.

The drone of the organ sank in dying vibrations like dark water into dark moss. Chill. Awe. A close-huddled assemblage that yet gave one a feeling of solitude, for it was intent upon other matters—a dim, tense, curiously immobile mass. Yet it was compact of a variety of little sounds and movements—breathy whispers as beads were fumbled, snuffles, a stifled sob, the whine of an infant squirming to find the breast. But the silence was a reality; it pressed downward like the weight of a hand.

Sidonia lifted her eyes. The vague, springing columns resembled branching trees that had been petrified by a spell. Sunset light was sprinkled high above—violet, ruby, and amber. She withdrew her gaze and looked straight forward athwart the dusk that filled the womb of the cavern. There was a nest of lights—the starry yellow of scores of clustered candle flames. It was a galaxy, soft and glittering. It was the high altar. This was the House of God, so God could not be all that she had thought Him. In its own way it was beautiful as the heart of a gloomy pine-wood, as night, as morning and evening. And no hurt had come to her since she softly entered.

Yet if the followers of God were to be believed, He was her natural enemy.

Everyone was kneeling; no one stood erect. With the instinct of the animal which identifies itself with its surroundings in order to avoid notice, Sidonia also went down upon her knees. Not that she was nervous or doubtful, but, in the hunted, instincts act automatically.

Like the voices of a regiment of male spirits somewhere in middle space the voices of the full choir broke across the cold and murky hush, that was flavoured with incense as heavily as a pine-wood with resin. It was a proclamation of wandering triumph, of reverent joy. Dim faces were upturned, whispering lips moved faster. It reached an apex, then folded its wings and dropped plummet-wise into silence. A bell tingled—little but clear. Sidonia thought of the bells hanging from the necks of sheep straying in the forest.

The heads of all were bowed, as in a sudden panic of humility. They struck their breasts with their doubled fists. Within a few feet of Sidonia a cloaked girl with dishevelled hair, who had been weeping with hands pressed over her face, cast herself forward upon the stone floor and remained so. The expectant tension in the gloom was painful. Something of tremendous importance was about to happen. The festival babble of the market-place, though audible just beyond the dark threshold, was robbed of significance; it broke like spray against a rock. The smell of close-packed bodies, of incense, and of the hide of the little mongrel dog, not a foot away from her, were mingled in the nostrils of Sidonia as she knelt among the other kneelers, waiting, with a sudden quickening of subconscious fear, for the climax.

Again the bell tingled. Though little sounding, like a sheep bell, it had a golden quality. The scores and scores of bodies, bent down upon themselves, were immobile. What terrifying event was about to dazzle and stun the five senses?

For the third time the bell rang, louder and longer, and Sidonia, stiffly erect upon her knees, looked towards the far-off galaxy of candle flames with eyes that were afraid to blink. Whatever God had in store for her, she was not going to betray to Him that she quailed.

As the sacring-bell ceased to tingle through the straining silence a united cry of praise and triumph leapt from the lips of the choir. The organ woke with a crashing thunder-roll. The darkness broke in a beating of shining wings; chariots of flame ascended, in which

stood seraphs blowing through trumpets of gold; the deep foundations of the earth trembled with joy, and the weight that had pressed
down upon all hearts was rolled away like a great stone—or so it
seemed. Heads lifted, an outbreak of coughs in various keys cleared
tightened throats, noses were blown, the little dog violently
scratched itself and Satan's mistress trembling under a nervous
reaction, burst into helpless tears.

As she knelt, sobbing, she tried ineffectively to wipe her wet
face with the edge of the velvet cloak. Something had broken down
within her. She was no longer a semi-automaton; she was Sidonia,
the daughter of Lame Lisa, naked to all the winds of the world. The
music triumphed and thundered, seeming to lighten the darkness.
The girl who had cast herself prone lifted herself painfully up until
she sat back on her heels, her dim face raised. No one took the least
notice of Sidonia, there on the fringe of the obscure, huddled
throng. She looked upward again to where a great, fretted rose of
violet glass gloomed like the night that is the holy, inner soul of
light. Below it were a row of niches, in each of which a pictured
figure glowed in crimson and blue and emerald and dusky orange.
One of these was a man in armour, with surcoat and pennoned
lance—St. Michael or St. George. It instantly brought back the
memory of her angel to the girl, and the quick pain in her breast was
so sharp that she thought her heart was breaking into two pieces.
She pictured him in Heaven, where the houses were built of pure
gold, the trees never lost their leaves, the brooks ran wine and
honey, and it was always summer. (A friar had once preached to
this effect in the open market when she was on the skirts of the
crowd.) He had quite forgotten her, of course. She was sealed to
Satan now, and destined to subjugate the Young Lord. But it was all
the fault of the angel! She hated him, and loved him, and would
have wallowed on the ground before him and embraced his feet.

Her tears had ceased. She was uneasily conscious of the glory of
her cloak, and of the manner in which she had acquired it. How was
she going to reach her mother's den wearing this mantle of wonder?
People would naturally suppose that she had stolen it.

The tide of music sank. A man's voice intoning three unintelligible words came faint and small across the herd of kneelers:

"Ite missa est——"

Everyone was getting to their feet. There were groans and
grunts. The great doorway was already choked with the first out-
flow. Hands were being dipped in the stoup of holy water, and
brows, breasts, and shoulders signed. Mothers moistened their

children's fingers. All faces wore a refreshed look, as though they were turned to the lusty world of the flesh with renewed eager-ness—a confident and childish zest.

The outer light fell across Sidonia's eyes, bright and keen. The sounds and sights of life rushed up, as it were, to meet her. They frightened her. Her spirit was shivering like a kitten that has been worried by dogs. Everything was hostile. Her heart cried out for the witch's loft, with its make shift hearth and her yellow cat. She was so utterly alone.

She sidled, keeping close to the uptowering stonework. Behind an outjutting buttress was a little shadowed cul-de-sac. Refuging there, one seemed half a hundred miles from the mob that frothed about the portal flanked by bland saints.

"It is! It's Lisa's girl!"

"No, I think not. Never mind, anyway."

"Never mind! Let the little slut go as if she'd never put a hand on me! You may be half a corpse already, Catherine, but, by God! I'm not."

The tall, auburn-haired wanton was at no pains to modulate her voice. Beside her, Catherine showed slovenly and haggard by day-light. The swarthy bear-leader was with them, and Catherine's man. The bold, projecting buttress screened the aristocracy of the Thieves' Kitchen from the townsfolk crowding to see the great people leave the church, whose steps had been strewn with spicy herbs and roses.

Shadowed by the buttress, Sidonia stood against the grey church wall.

"Oh, it's the witch's daughter all right!"

Sidonia caught back her breath, as though she had trodden on something pointed or knocked the corner of her elbow.

"I may be, but—but I am not a strumpet," she said in a sharpened voice that quivered.

There was no drink in her now. She faced Sylvane bleakly, and little cold shivers went over her.

"Oh!"—a sound from the wanton that contained all the violence of a dozen vile words. And then she was upon the girl like venge-ance itself.

"No! No!" gasped Catherine, who looked suddenly as deadly sick as though she were going to faint. "Stop her! Take her off!"

She turned her face first to the bear-leader and then to the gam-bler, twisting her hands together.

The bear-leader uttered a grunt that was a laugh.

"Let them fight it out," said Catherine's man. "They're both sober this morning. It's an even go."

Sidonia had raised an arm, instinctively, to defend her eyes. She was cuffed, pummelled, kicked on the shins, and had her hair dragged—all in a moment. Sylvane, the tawny-tressed young fury, was like a cataclysm—an act of God. But the younger girl was game. She struck back, clutched hair in her turn, and used her nails. The devils jutting from the parapets above laughed down on the tussle impartially; it reminded them of home.

Sidonia was getting the worst of it. Weight and height will tell. She was breathless, trembling, and her lip was bleeding. Sylvane had a scored cheek and had been struck in the eye. She laid hold of Sidonia's velvet cloak, and with a wrench tore it loose and away from her. Uttering animal-like, snarling sounds, she clutched at the girl's poor wreck of a front-lacing bodice, at her tattered chemise, at the rotten stuff of her petticoat. There was a ripping and tearing. In a few strenuous, panting moments Sidonia was stripped as bare as an ungloved hand.

"Ho! Ho!" grunted the bear-leader, and Catherine's man threw back his head and laughed like a schoolboy.

Sylvane seized her adversary by the shoulders and shook her till her teeth rattled.

"I'll teach you to throw dirt at me, you dirty little witch-brat!"

But she reckoned without the spirit that informed her opponent's lizard-slender body. Sidonia jerked free and hit out, man-like, with a clenched fist. She caught the other fairly in the face, and Sylvane staggered, dark blood running from both her nostrils.

"Good for you, little 'un!" said the bear-leader, who played no favourites in a straight-out dog, man, or woman fight.

Sidonia glanced towards him dazedly, and on the instant became aware that she was as naked as a young crow.

Convulsively her thin, crossed arms covered her bosom. She pressed knee to knee, bending down upon herself. The devils gloated, the two men grinned, and Sylvane, frightened by the bleeding of her nose, tried to staunch it with the corner of her lifted petticoat, standing squarely meanwhile upon the stripped girl's garments.

"Don't look so scared, sweeting," rumbled the bear-leader, "Your uncle will look after you," and he moved forward.

This was monstrous! It resembled that sort of shameful dream from which one wakens with a gasp and a feeling of unbounded relief. If this hairy man should lay even a finger on her Sidonia felt that she must die! Flight alone remained—flight from the night-mare, from unendurable contacts. Everything was gone except her horror of the bear-leader. Still with her crossed arms pressed against her breast, and bending nearly double, she darted sideways. She must escape! Her limbs trembled, and a blackness swam before her eyes. Nothing was real save horror, and a deathly sickness. The world span like a teetotum, and she fell forward on her face.

"Oh! Mother of God!" said the Countess Sabine—much as if a mouse had run suddenly before her. She stopped short, for a young girl, mother-naked, had appeared as if from nowhere, lurched, and fallen face downward right at her feet. The Count, and her stepson, Gervais, who were immediately behind her, stopped also. Nobody seemed to know quite what to do or say.

Sabine, resplendent in cloth of silver and flesh-coloured velvet edged with ermine, her hair drawn back from her brows and caught in a silver net, looked down at the girl with a faint interest. The Count had instantly averted his eyes, for he practised a continence as rigid as that of the strictest forest hermit, and Gervais, who had seen nothing but a streak of flesh that darted and fell, felt the re-luctant blood stain his face, as though it were the body of his sacred girl that lay on the cobblestones under the thin sunshine. He stared fixedly over the heads of those immediately in front of him, looking as arrogant as a prince of hell. The holiday-makers—noisy enough a moment before—gazed fish-eyed.

A dark young woman, shabby and sick-looking, emerged as the prostrate girl had done from nowhere in particular. She carried a cloak of sky-blue velvet, and without paying attention to anyone dropped straight down on her knees beside the girl and laid the mantle over her.

"My good woman, what's the meaning of this?" said Sabine sharply. (She was the first to find speech, but actually the affair had been a matter of seconds only.)

Catherine lifted dark, filmed eyes to her.

"The poor little thing has fainted," she said simply. "I couldn't let her lie bare on the cold stones."

"Fetch back that cloak, Kate, you slut!" The unmodulated voice of a young shrew, unpleasant as a peacock's, seemed to shock even the gargoyles high above. Next moment Sylvane—blind to every-thing save the loss of the mantle—broke out into the open, her nostrils bloody, her splendid hair a scandal, and the whites of her hard, sapphire eyes as bloodshot as a drunken man's.

Blue eye encountered blue eye, the one pair pale, forget-me-not coloured; the other mineral-hued, hot and dangerous. Scattered auburn hair was matched by smooth auburn hair gathered into a silver net. (It was evident that Arnold the Count favoured the same type of colouring both as man and devil.)

Under the calm, feline gaze of Sabine, assured and sumptuous in her velvet and cloth of silver, Sylvane wilted. Something in her aspect suggested the outlawed animal unexpectedly cornered. But she had not lost her tongue.

"That girl's a witch-brat, lady! Her mother's a witch! She tried to tear my eyes out two minutes ago. She's Lame Lisa's daughter, and the Devil was her father!

"A witch!" The word passed like a winged breath from mouth to mouth. People fell back a step or two. The Count, austere, sallow, magnificent, came a pace forward, as if about to speak, but Sabine stretched out her hand, speaking first.

"You accuse this girl—this child—of grave things, but mercy is greater than justice, as God is greater than Satan. This is a day of thanksgiving for the victories and health of my dear stepson, your master, therefore I will take this wretched girl under my protection, and by the help of Heaven endeavour to win her to a Christian life."

It was well spoken, and with a gentle and cultured intonation. Sabine was always utterly sincere. She was, at this moment, the gracious benefactress—a deputy of Divine Mercy. (That was consciously. Unconsciously her buried self had said quickly "If the girl is a witch and the daughter of a witch she can procure love-charms that will bind Gervais and fire his indifference. Probably she has fallen at your feet as a direct answer to a prayer. Keep her.")

An admiring murmur came from the townsfolk. Their Count was a saint, their Countess a pattern. Sylvane stared dumbly, drawing the back of her hand across her nostrils, where the blood had dried.

"The Countess' will is my will. Mercy is greater than justice, and this should be for us a day of mercy, for God has given us triumph."

The Count's utterance was measured and resonant; it would have graced a bishop.

Again came the hushed, admiring murmur. Sylvane moved back a step, her truculence tucking its tail between its legs. She was overawed. The Holy Count had looked past her—over her—as though she were a broomstick. He never allowed his eyes to rest seeingly upon women.

A tall young man-at-arms lifted the lax body of the witch-girl, carrying her like a baby. Sabine moved serenely forward again, her inner self purring softly, at peace with all the world. The Count followed her, and Gervais. People pressed forward to kiss the Count's hands or to touch him furtively. Several cried out that they were cured of muscular pains, or even of partial deafness or blindness. It was common knowledge that beneath his ermine-furred raiment he wore always a hair-shirt. Handfuls of silver were scattered right and left as a general largesse, occasioning yells, shrieks, and wild scrambles. But Gervais, walking like a person in a dream, paid no attention. He was considering how he should absent himself in order to go to the Street of the Martyrs. Half a dozen paces behind him the young man-at-arms, looking very sheepish, carried the Countess' protégé, whose nudity was wrapped rather haphazardly in the blue velvet cloak sprinkled with silver fleurs-de-lys. He half expected his burden to change into a black hare, struggle with him, and leap to the ground, and cold sensations ran up his spine. Sidonia herself, returning to semi-consciousness, had a confused feeling that she was in the arms of her angel.

IV. THE LOVE-PHILTRE

1

"I HAVE DIED, and I have reached Heaven," said Sidonia within herself. Her body was sunk in the billowy embraces of a feather bed. As she lifted half-reluctant eyelashes the glimmering square of a little window was right before her, a heart-shaped pane glowing like a ruby set in the centre of its semi-translucent lozenges.

A sudden sprinkle of chilly water wetted her forehead, sending a shudder through her. No, this was not Heaven. She sat up as quickly as she could, discovering an arras-hung chamber, a four-post bed (which held her), and two girls looking at her as if they were afraid that she might bite them. They were Anne and Margaret.

"Who put that water on me?" asked Sidonia rather sharply. It is not pleasant to be roused from a dream of Heaven by a cold shock.

"It—it was not holy water," explained Anne, stammering. "We had to bring you out of your faint."

Sidonia looked at her without comprehension.

"Will you please get up now and dress? The Countess is waiting for you." Margaret was even more nervous than Anne. When the girl, sitting up in the bed—which was her bed and Anne's—turned her shadowy eyes upon her she experienced a queer, panicky feeling, and a sensation as if her stomach were sinking. They were unlike any eyes her own had previously encountered. Their big-pupilled gloom was luminous; they had a tearless animal poignancy; they seemed to look straight through her at—inconceivable scenes. Margaret's courage fluttered in her throat; if she had come face to face with Beelzebub she would probably have dropped him a curtsey first and screamed afterwards.

"The Countess? What are you talking about? Where am I?" said Sidonia.

Anne and Margaret looked at her, both at a loss.

"You—you fainted at the Countess' feet just as she was coming out of church," said Anne diffidently. "And she—she had you brought here. She wants to talk with you." (It is scarcely possible to tell a witch-girl that she has been adopted for the purpose of conversion. To say the least it is impolite, and might even be dangerous.)

Sidonia wrinkled her brows. She remembered now—— Why should the Countess—the wife of the Holy. Count—have interested herself in her? The answer came like a flash of incandescence—it was hell's work! Hell, that had taken her under its dark wings of power, that had lifted her up to be Satan's mistress, that had commissioned her to enthral and subjugate the Young Lord. Some obscure and unthwartable plan was being carried out, and she was at the heart of it—moved here or there, like a white chess-piece over a sable board. Pride rushed back into her, and elation. All was well. She felt confident, and the strange glow in her was next door to actual happiness.

"I will get dressed," she said, and she did not show any surprise now.

They laid out for her a shift of fine linen, a dark-blue gown with hanging sleeves, silk hose with pretty, buckled garters and narrow, pointed blue and silver shoes of strong, soft stuff.

Sidonia concealed her excitement, but with difficulty. This was Heaven indeed! She had never in her life worn hose or possessed garters, and the dress fitted her like a clinging sheath. Enscabbarded in this demure yet revealing fashion, her body seemed supple as a serpent.

Nothing further was uttered in the bed-chamber of Anne and Margaret. The silence was peculiar—even unearthly. Sidonia was absorbed—held in a sort of rapture by the caress of the clean linen, the fit and cling of the dress, the pressure of the garters, and her certainty of Satanic favour and guidance. The other two girls were embarrassed—in a sense overawed. Lame Lisa's daughter had brought with her a breath of wildness, of nameless, alien things. The unknown cave to her, close as her own olive skin. Still without anything said on either side a door was opened for her, and she went through it into the chamber of the Countess Sabine.

Light entered through two lancet windows. The floor was rush-strewn, but a strip of carpet was laid down before the carved chair on which the Countess sat. The canopied bed bulked large and shrine-like; one felt that it should be an altar for reverent and elaborate rites. A book of devotion lay in Sabine's lap. She was looking placidly straight before her, her face as smooth as a damsel's of fourteen, her small, pulpy mouth rather prim in its set, and delicately coloured like a fruit.

Sidonia came a little way forward, and paused. The room was sumptuous beyond her dreams. Here, also, the kennel-like atmosphere held a certain grateful degree of warmth.

"Sit down by me, child," said the Countess Sabine pleasantly.

Without speaking Sidonia trod the miraculous carpet, that felt like forest moss, and lowered her small self until she sat, with neatly gathered up legs, upon a great brocaded cushion near the Countess' footstool.

"What is your name, child?"

"Sidonia."

"Are you a witch?"

The question, with its flavour of burning faggots and dark tribunals, might have been "Have you slept well?" or "Do you like the weather?"

Sidonia was looking up at the Countess with her unreadable eyes. After a little waiting pause she said quite simply, "Yes."

She believed absolutely in the truth of the word she had uttered.

"Your mother is a witch, also, is she not?"

"People call her that," said Sidonia in a lower voice, and guardedly. (She herself did not regard her mother as anything of the kind. But there had been the ordeal of the white-hot ploughshares.)

"I need a powerful love-charm. Perhaps several, of different kinds, would be better than one. I will pay well for them."

The wife of the Holy Count Sidonia felt that she was being educated. She continued to look fixedly upward.

"Can you bring me these charms?"

"Yes. Oh, yes."

"What are they like? How quickly do they work?"

The Countess had put aside the book of devotions. She seemed to kindle—to become eager and brisk, almost like other persons.

"The kind of charm would depend upon whom it is wanted for. Some are quicker than others."

Sidonia spoke quite matter-of-factly. Charms and potions were a commodity, like bread or onions.

"I want something exceedingly strong, that will not be slow in action. It is for a young man."

A young man! Without knowing that she did so, the girl on the cushion considered this. For no particular reason the memory-picture of a face upturned to her from a seething street— half boy's, half man's, half priest's, half lover's—was summoned to her. Something prompted her, and she said :

"I must have the name of the person: It is necessary, for there are spells to be spoken if the charm is to bind and hold."

A little pause of silence, and then:

"The name is Gervais."

Sidonia was not surprised. It was as if words that were quite inevitable had been uttered. It was all inevitable; she herself spoke under compulsion, acted under compulsion. She was just a chess-piece moved over a sable board. The inarticulate sense of strong, purposeful control, which was also protective, was wonderfully comfortable. One leaned back against it as against pillows, and one's words and deeds were mechanical.

The Countess, sleek and charmingly rounded, sat with the inhuman serenity of a cat. She had not turned a hair. Naturally one spoke openly with a witch—as openly as some people spoke to a priest or a physician.

"I want these charms to-day—to-night. What will you bring me?"

The girl answered as it was given her to answer. Something was planning for her—shaping her speech. She herself sat upright on the great cushion, caressed by the feel of ladylike garments and inwardly quiet as a corpse in a coffin.

"My lady, I will go to my mother's and fetch you a liquid that can be mixed with wine, and a wax image that must be inscribed with the name you have told me and pierced with a rose thorn."

The Countess leaned a little forward.

"Do I mix this draught with the wine myself?"

"No," said Sidonia, speaking more deliberately. "I must mix it, for there are spells to be said that I could not teach you. And the person to whom you are going to offer it must enter the room where it is and remain there alone for as long as it takes to count a hundred—counting slowly—before you yourself enter. This is very important, for during that time of counting I will pierce the wax image a hundred times with the magic thorn, repeating powerful words."

(The girl had scarcely known that she knew of these things. It was herself, yet not herself—a buried person, with a memory lucid as dew and no qualms at all, released from obscure bonds by the passivity of her surface-thoughts.)

The Countess, by her very silence, appeared to be as impressed as a patient to whom a doctor has recited a medicinal formula embracing bat's tongues, moss scraped from the stones of a belfry, pulverised snail shells, and powdered bone from the scull of a man who had met a violent death. She looked with placid gravity at the witch-girl, her hands lying quiet in her lap. Sidonia looked back at her, the pupils of her extraordinary eyes seeming to have expanded until they had all but swallowed the iris. From somewhere near at hand came the thrum of plucked strings. The sunshine, thinly golden and nearly warmthless, struck through the narrow windows that were incapable of being opened. There was a smell of civet, of musk, of body-odours upon the long-dead air that was thicker than the stuffing of a feather bed and seemed body-warm by comparison with the crisp, outer chills. Here indeed was the height of luxury, of security, of cultured Christian living.

"I will pay you well for these things," said the Countess, "and if you have told the truth about them I will pay you even better afterwards. You shall stay in my service, but if you speak of me to anyone in an unseemly way I will have you tortured and burned. Being a witch, you can only live in safety under my protection."

It was spoken as smoothly as flowing honey. There was no animosity in Sabine. Providence had been more than usually benignant to send her a witch just when she needed one most.

Not a muscle of Sidonia's face changed. She sat perfectly still upon the brocade cushion of her enemy, at the feet of her enemy, in the wonderful bedchamber of her enemy. Tortured and burned? Oh, no! But the love-charms desired by Sabine to subdue her stepson should give Gervais into the arms of the outcast, the pariah. It was all working towards one end. Hell was with her—her only friend. As, without saying anything, she held out her small cupped hand for the heavy silver pieces that Sabine emptied from a sac-shaped velvet purse, she saw herself queening it in a gown of silver tissue that trailed upon the floor—unassailable, because the Young Lord was her slave. But of course Satan would remain her real—her secret—love—— Satan, who had lifted her in his strong arms when the angel rode back to Heaven.

* * * * *

Gervais was in the Street of the Martyrs. He was unarmoured, wrapped in a hooded cloak. He glanced from side to side, looking up at the rickety houses between which the cobbled laneway—eight or ten feet across—wandered like a straying dog. The wooden window-shutters were closed. Here and there a small, square window-aperture was blocked with a sheet of stretched parchment. The grass that tufted the steep roofs of thatch was mingled with tiny red, blue, and golden flowers, bird-sown. In another week, or perhaps two, they would be shrivelled by the first white rigours of winter frost. If a shutter was opened and pushed back it was to allow liquid or semi-liquid refuse to be emptied from above into the street. Hall-thawed muck was in some places nearly ankle deep, but the stench at this season was not very great. In the mid-months of summer it is probable that even the Celestial messengers flying over the town on errands of mercy or terror sheered widely away, muffling their faces in their robes perfumed with myrrh and spikenard.

The laneway, though it smelt similarly, did not look as it had done on the previous night, with an enormous amber moon rising through the frosty haze. Gervais recalled that there had been an archway at the spot where he had halted his horse. Presently he found it, and paused. Various people passed him, most of them wearing wooden shoes stuffed with straw. He would like to have questioned them, but did not know what to say. How could one inquire for a young girl in torn clothing, wonderful as an act of God, when one did not even know her baptismal name? He had been filled with a burning confidence that as soon as he reached the street where she had said she lived he should encounter her. He stood at the side of the skulking archway, becoming every moment more tormented. A bleakness of loss that was unbearable dawned and grew in him. He was baulked, and he could not open his mouth to anyone.

Two women were coming along the laneway—Catherine and Sylvane. Sylvane was half-drunk, though she walked steadily enough, her splendid, dishevelled head held as high as a queen's. As they approached the tall young man in the dark cloak, whose hood shadowed his face, Gervais cleared his throat. With a sudden access of moral courage he had determined to question them, but Sylvane forestalled him.

"Good evening, sweetheart! You're lonely, aren't you? I'm lonely, too. And I'm loving—God knows I'm loving! Give me a kiss, boy."

She swayed slightly as she stood, with her feet planted rather wide apart, one hand on her hip. An atmosphere of wine surrounded her like a tavern-halo.

Gervais, stiff in the joints from embarrassment, turned from her.

"Here! Haven't you got a civil word? God damn you? Is the black plague on me?"

Gervais walked faster. He should have made himself known to the woman, and had her grovelling at his feet; he should have questioned, with a manner of absolute authority, every shuffling person who passed by; he should have knocked at the closed doors and interrogated those who dwelt behind them by the right of his position; but he could do none of these things. It is terrible to be shy when one is twenty, and a belted knight.

What now? Though the last of the sun still gilded the topmost thatch the chill, blue dusk was emerging from nooks and crannies, and beneath a score of archways the night had already come—the night of the thanksgiving feast in the fortified dwelling of the Holy Count. He must return. To-morrow he would go to that notable house from whose opened window his girl had looked down upon him. He would not hesitate; he would ask all necessary questions, and the people of the house would answer him meekly, because he was the son of Count Arnold.

A horrible doubt as to the flesh and blood reality of the girl suddenly assailed him. Perhaps she was some faery thing that appeared and disappeared at will. He went cold at the thought, and then hot, and his teeth gritted together. "By God! I'll find her if I have to look for her in the underworld!" he said within himself.

A wall shrine showed dimly in a shadowed angle. It represented three martyrs surrounded by the symbols of their suffering, and the wooden figures had been freshly painted, so that the blue and green of their robes and the liberal scarlet of their blood was very vivid. Bunches of little waxen replicas of arms and legs hung on either side of the shrine—votive offerings from sufferers miraculously freed from rheumatic afflictions or healed of festering wounds. Going down quickly upon his knees before the three martyrs, Gervais signed himself with the cross.

"Let me find her! Bring me to her!" he implored beneath his breath.

Back in the witches' loft Sidonia, who had brought a handful of silver coins for her mother, and a sheep's liver for the cats, was groping in the bowels of the dreadful chest for the love-philtre, and for the waxen image that should be named "Gervais."

2

"Do you see that girl there? That's the witch."

"But there's a cross hung round her neck."

"The Countess must have given her that. She's going to try and make a Christian of her."

Two pages—leggy lads with the angry pimples of adolescence breaking out on face and neck—were whispering huskily. They glanced sidelong, not having the guts to stare full-faced.

"Oh, Christ! Look at the cat!" said one of them, and caught at the other's arm.

By the light of a torch thrust into an iron bracket fixed against the wall Sidonia, sitting on a wooden bench, bit keenly into the tender, meaty leg of a roast capon. A platter balanced upon her knees held a big slice of white bread soaked with gravy. She was intent—very much occupied. Nothing mattered at that moment except the meat on the capon. But a little half-grown cat, black as sin, with a rat-tail and dropped hindquarters, came slinking, and suddenly mewed —loudly, and with the shamelessness of hunger.

Where another person might have invoked the Mother of the Redeemer and come out in a cold sweat, Sidonia turned her eyes quietly upon the kitten, loosened a strip of capon meat with teeth and fingers, and dropped it upon the floor. It vanished as if by magic, and the black impet stood up on its hind legs, laying its little round forepaws against her knee.

This was too much! The pages vanished as magically as the titbit of capon had done. It takes a stout heart to support the sight of a witch-girl cosseting a familiar spirit. Doubtless the creeping cat with the unnatural cry would leap into her lap in another moment and take the shape of a marmoset. Instant retreat was the only course open to anyone save a priest.

Sidonia was alone. She had scarcely observed the two lads with their parti-coloured hose and long, hanging, scalloped sleeves of scarlet. The half-grown cat, uttering loud, blatant cries, stood up-right, with its forepaws on her knee. When she had given it the nearly-picked bone she licked her fingers delicately. It was wonderful to look and behave like a lady! Her hair, which hung loose upon her shoulders, had been thoroughly combed out. It was sleek as the plumage of a blackbird, long and heavy. She had washed her face, her neck, her hands, with water infused with cleansing herbs, and a faint, balsamic odour clung to her. Her fastidiousness might have been that of a bride.

She was alone save for the bone-gnawing cat, but on the left, beyond an arched doorway, all the chief persons of the town sat at the feast given in honour of Gervais. Flutes and fiddles sounded. Leaning a little forward, Sidonia could glimpse the tall candles, each bearing a soft yellow star, and enwreathed with evergreens as though it were Christmas. Spitted pheasants, huge, fantastic pies, baked fish garnished with relishes, together with ducks, geese, swans, and hams, had been borne past her. And now, again, she was alone.

Solitariness—ever since the first days that she could clearly remember. Daisy-pied cow pastures, with other children running and jostling together, and herself—very little and serious—left standing under a thorn-tree. "Witch-brat! Witch-brat! Oo-er! Witch-brat!" Forest hollows where running water clucked softly among stones, and leaves fell, and deer appeared like dappled visions, and small, bearded gnomes. Cobbled lanes, and the folk shrinking ever so slightly aside; only the yellow-eyed milch-goats, though unresponsive, seeming in a saturnine way to be friendly when she touched them. The loft with its fetid silence, broken sometimes by sharp, causeless rappings, and herself with her cat in her arms, staring and staring at the few red embers. As a leper of long standing must take his isolation for granted, Sidonia accepted her position without thought. On her right, behind a half-closed door, the kitchen folk, becoming merry with liquor, threw the picked leg-bones of duck and capon at each other, and smote backs, and dug humorous elbows into ribs. On her left, beyond the archway, the linen clothes and the candles lent the banquet something of the appearance of an altar during the celebration of Mass, and the smoke from the open hearth crept beneath the soot-mantled roof rafters, and the voices and laughters of fifty persons nearly drowned the noise of flute and fiddle. But where Sidonia sat, played over by the light of the one torch, there was only the draught of the passage-way and the nameless cat, that certainly did look rather like a familiar spirit as it cowered at her feet, looking up at her with lambent, grass-green eyes that asked for more food.

In the hall of the banquet the long, white-draped board was cluttered with the wreckage of many meats—disembowelled pies, bird carcasses, stripped ham-bones. The great candles guttered and ever and again their wreaths of evergreens caught fire and flared with a sudden brief spurt. The smoke that crawled beneath the roof smelt savage and of the wildwood, and there was also the odour of the strong, fire-warmed hides of the deerhounds sprawling by the hearth, with the bones that had been tossed to them between their paws.

Beneath a red canopy, at the head of the table, the Count sat, with Sabine upon his left hand and Gervais upon his right. Handsome, and of a waxen yellow hue, he kept his eyes downcast. It was almost as though the cadaver of the sanctified bishop—the town's saint—had been set upright at the feast. Inwardly the first premonitions of profound transformation that was nightly worked in him were exhibiting themselves as a nameless unease. They were like the buried, interior beginnings of decomposition in a just-dead body.

Sabine, leaning a little back in her cushioned chair, was relaxed in a happiness of faintly and evenly purring senses. She had drunk a good deal of raisin-tasting wine brought from the south, and had eaten well. God was with her, benevolent as a complaisant parent. Her only irritation was that the Count's person barred her from the sight of Gervais unless she leaned forward, which was a tax on her indolence. But Gervais would surely lie between her two arms before very long. She had paid the price of the love-philtre.

The two rows of seated guests, having drunk already nearly as much as they were able, were no longer restrained by the saintly presence sitting like a church image beneath the red canopy. Ladies sagged towards their table partners, and found the support of shoulders seasoned to carry the forged steel coats of war. Arms clipt supple waists. Knees were nudged and pinched. Humorous stories, at which the women laughed discreetly, looking sideways and simulating shame, passed from mouth to mouth. Anne, who always became markedly sedate after she had swallowed wine, sat with a rigid spine, turning her face very formally first to the man on her right and then to the man on her left. If a hand was laid on her knee she drew down her fair brows in a frown. But with Margaret the progress of the banquet had had just the opposite effect. Her dark, loose-flowing hair was dishevelled, and the bright colouring of her face was so heightened that one would have thought her cheeks were painted. The spreading stains of spilt wine marred the bleached linen. Some of the guests were still eating, using knives and fingers. Beards had been moistened with rich gravies; one man was employing a thin fish-bone as a tooth-pick; and several of the smaller dogs prowled beneath the table, snapping up the dropped fragments.

"How orderly everything is!" said the wife of a prominent townsman to her husband. "If it wasn't for the talking I could imagine that I was in church."

"Ah, we're among well-mannered people here," said the townsman, plunging his hand into the yawning cavity of a half-demolished pigeon pie. "This is a Christian household, where everything is sumptuous and seemly."

Under the dull red canopy Sabine, over whose food-soiled hands a serving boy had poured water, was drying her fingers languidly with a napkin. The tempered yellow light shed by the candles and dimmed still further by the hearth-smoke swam into a mist before her, for the southern wine was thoroughly mingled with her blood. A dwarfed hunchback with a face like a grotesque wood-carving —one of Sabine's diversions—sat on a footstool beside her. With a worried, preoccupied air, his great lower lip thrust out like a shelf, he was scratching his rough head.

The Count had not spoken for quite a considerable time. But this was nothing new. Since his conversion he had acquired the habit of monosyllables. Speech seemed unnecessary to him. He would sit for long periods so motionless that the sparrows alighted on his lap and shoulders—but always in some place where there was no likelihood of a woman's intrusion. No one could tell what he was thinking, or if he thought at all. He touched no wine, refrained from intercourse even with his lawful wife, left all business in the hands of his stewards, attended daily Mass, and was suspected of a hair-shirt. He was a saint; there was nothing further to be said or done about it.

Sabine became aware that the Count had risen to his feet. He raised his hand, and the unwearying racket of the music stopped, and with it the noise of the guests. She heard him, in one short, formal sentence, make his excuses. He bowed, turned, and she drew back her crossed feet to let him pass. He looked more like a miraculously incorrupt corpse than usual. His handsome, expressionless face was earthily sallow. The hunchback nearly tumbled off his footstool in a nervous effort to clear the way for him, and then the music, with a hysterical screech of bow-sawed strings, began again.

Across the vacant seat that was between them Sabine turned a slow, sleepy gaze of an almost infantile blueness upon Gervais.

His raiment was of a deep blood-colour. A gold chain was about his neck. He was beautiful to look at, but seemed sulky—close-lipped as his father. Gervais was tormented. He had been baulked—and by nothing more tangible than his own terror of men and women. Why had he not gone straight to the house from whose window the girl had looked down on him instead of to the Street of the Martyrs? How was he to endure the useless night that was before him? He wanted her—as a saint wants Heaven, as a hound wants meat. This want obsessed him; it was like a garment upon him. Nothing else was of the least importance. The banquet was more tedious than an unduly protracted church service. A dozen seats farther down, Hugh, his friend, was becoming playful and amorous with a little high-coloured dark girl—Margaret, one of his stepmother's favourite maidens. To such a bleak height was he raised by his spiritual and physical trouble that the sombre thought came to him, "What does Hugh know of love?"

"Gervais," said Sabine, in a voice like a dove cooing.

"Yes, madam?"

"Now that your father has left us I think you should take his seat. It is your place to preside."

"Yes, madam."

He did as she had bidden him, mechanically. She was something upon which it was always pleasant to let one's eyes rest, and she was kind also. He was not as shy with her as he was with most women.

"My darling!" purred Sabine's soul, looking at the young man from under her half-lowered auburn-lashed eyelids. It would be like Paradise to rest between his arms. She believed unshakably in the joys of Heaven, though her ideas concerning them were not exactly those of the theologians.

"Gervais, there is a matter upon which I wish to consult you—a matter that can be spoken of only in private. Will you go to my bed-chamber after the guests have risen, and wait there until I come to you? It is a matter of importance."

The young man looked towards her. It was a quick yet an abstracted glance.

"Yes. Yes, of course, madam."

He did not question her. Sometimes it had dawned even upon her unspeculative and serenely feline brain that he shrank from the intercourse of speech exactly as he shrank from the intercourse of love. But he was not of an invincible virginity, as many canonised persons were reported to have been. She knew this quite certainly. Her instincts brought her all necessary knowledge. In all essential matters she was as well informed as an animal.

A little hour-glass whose framework was of ivory—a trifle of luxury brought from the mythical coasts of the land where the grave of God lay beneath a church with cupolas of gold—stood on the board by Sabine's silver plate and goblet. Its filling of coarse, white sea-sand had half drained away. Sabine eyed it placidly. In half an hour the feast would be over and Gervais would ascend to her chamber. She turned her head aside and spoke to the serving-boy who had poured water over her hands.

"Peter, go at once and find Sidonia, the girl who was brought here to-day and who is under my protection. Tell her to immediately perform the task I have set her. Be quick, or I will have you whipped."

The boy sidled off, crab-like. The Countess' servants might regard her as pious and chastely complaisant, but they knew also that she had a temper.

Sabine turned her face again towards Gervais. It was comfortable to know that as she leaned back in the cushioned chair that was set side by side with his, the witch-girl was mingling the love-draught and speaking the necessary spells above it. A feeling of gratitude spread itself over her like the warmth of the southern wine. To-morrow, after the early Mass, she would distribute alms among the beggars of the town.

Gervais moved uneasily in his seat, stretching his legs. He wished, with irritation, that he were outside in the frosty cold, roaming the black alley-ways and trusting in the mercy of Providence to lead him, by some miracle, to love.

The long table was being cleared of its dishevelled meats and reset with dried fruits and confections. The candles were burning low. There were kissings and huggings and the little, sharp cries and squeals of women, for the majority of the guests were now more drunk than sober. The music had become fitful, for the musicians were exhausted. The banquet was nearly over.

3

SIDONIA, CARRYING A lighted candle in a candlestick of brass, climbed a spiral stair of hollow-trodden steps that turned upon itself between walls of stone. Shadows like bats, whose vague wings tremulously flickered as a flame does, followed her as she climbed. Many virgin girls would have feared the dark behind and the dark before, for the flame of the candle was a small and a weak thing, but how should a witch and the daughter of a witch fear darkness? Sidonia was not afraid. The darkness had never hurt her. Like a hunted cat, she was accustomed to obscure places. Her thought dwelt solely upon the love-draught which she was on her way to prepare—anxiously, like the thought of a housewife who is forced to carry out a difficult recipe unaided. Her lips moved as she repeated to herself various words she had memorised.

The steps of the stone stair were many. The flame of the candle shuddered, taken by seemingly causeless movements of the air. A sensation of confidence—yes, of power—spread from the centre of Sidonia's being outwards until it tingled at the tips of her fingers. A door that had been twice opened was opening for the third time in her inner self. The love-draught would constrain like the cords of death, and the ritual of the waxen image would set an unbreakable seal upon these cords. She was strong. A power that could loose or bind tingled to her finger-tips.

There was a feeling of presences about her—form and movement—that almost broke through upon her physical sight. Fiery coils, constricting, serpent-headed, that enwound her, beautifully, terribly, as she climbed. Leopard-shapes, that lifted unblinking eyes of beryl to her. (She had never seen a leopard, or even heard of one, but when the door that was within her opened all manner of things came through it, and she knew then, for her buried mind was wise as the mind of the earth—her mother, and the mother of us all.) Beckoning arms. Women-shapes whose gaping breasts revealed a burning skull in the place of a heart—symbol of dire fascination that only death can terminate. The quick-beating, rose-coloured wings of beautiful flying vipers. Either she saw these things, or knew, by reason of an inner sight, that they were there. She was not afraid. These crowding presences were a part of her strength. Shaken by the stairway draughts—or perhaps by the striving wings and varied movements—the candle-flame fluttered and bent backward.

The head of the stair, and the light of the candle weakly illuminating for a short distance a stone gallery. Sidonia paused to find her half-lost breath. She felt no fatigue. She was caught up into an unhuman serenity, as when she had faced the would be witch-harriers in the lane nine hours earlier—or was it nine years?

Nothing moved in the hollow gallery of naked stone save the swirl of half-guessed creatures that bore her company, but there was a sound—a sound between a muffled hinge-creak and a sigh. Sidonia, looking towards this sound, saw a portion of the solid wall, in height and shape like an upright coffin, turn slowly inward upon itself, disclosing an oblong of utter dark, opaque-seeming as a door of coal.

She was neither startled nor amazed. She stood, with the candle in her hand, looking—knowing and yet not knowing—who it was that was about to appear. A tall darkness detached itself from the oblong of darkness, and the Master, standing a pace or two forward from the opened wall, confronted the girl in complete silence.

He was black-clad from head to foot; masked as before. The light of the candle touched his strongly-moulded chin, his jaw, and the line of his lips. His height seemed to be more than that of a man.

The silence endured. Sidonia was moved to speak, but she did not know whether she uttered the word "Master——" in her mind or with her breath.

A hand came upon her shoulder, and from the grip of it a prickling, fluidic force flowed downward through her body—or so she thought. Her limbs became rigid, and she trembled, though not from fear or any distress. Was he speaking to her?

But surely not with words! She felt his will pass, like a subtle current, into her mind, her heart. She was his—one with him, as lover with lover.

"You are mine, Sidonia."

"Ah! yes!"

But in the gallery no one had spoken, and only for a few moments had the girl with the candle paused where the secret doorway gaped black as coal. With another dim creak and a sigh of air it softly closed again. Satan, after that handful of timeless moments, had withdrawn himself once more from his neophyte. Or—to phrase it otherwise—the dark self of the Holy Count, subconsciously in touch with the unstable and feverish girl-waif whom he had marked for a mistress, had been led by a whim of instinct to set in motion the turning wall-stone of the gallery, had seen, touched, and now retreated, for the night with its various business was before him. The following night—the night of All Souls—was set apart for the mad nuptials of the little witch-bred virgin. Usually the dark self of the Count was discreet as a dog fox, but on those occasions when the folk of his own household had glimpsed him in his secret comings and goings they had simply accepted him as an apparition of the Devil—come, doubtless to wrestle with the saint who had banished his Countess from his bed, and whose stuffed crocodile was the last relic of his former wickedness.

Sidonia, shielding her guttering candle with one hand, went forward again. She also had business to attend to. Satan was her guardian—her lover. In spirit he was with her always. To-morrow night he would take her fully to himself as an actual husband. These thoughts—these convictions—held no shrinking quality. There was not even a grimness in them. They were triumphant, warm, and comfortable. Sidonia had never known protection—scarcely shelter. She had never known love, though the passionate blood of her father was in her body, and she had embraced trees, laying her cheek against the cool smoothness of the bark, and had lain prostrate to sink her face in wild violets, moistening lips and lashes with the dew of them, her heart melting in the flame of its own unspent fondness. But now she was sustained by an upholding arm. She was no longer alone; she was guided and desired.

The narrow-bodied leopards slunk at her side, lifting towards her their flattened, snakish heads. The floating serpent-coils embraced her as she moved. The arms beckoned, the hearts shaped like skulls of fire burned with a dull red flame, and the rosy, reptilian wings beat multitudinously, like the wings of doves. Yet to the sight of any ordinary christened person there was only a young girl moving decorously in an empty passage that was like a cave of stone.

The gallery turned, and now, on the one side, there were two doors of oak—the door of the Countess' bed-chamber, and of the bed-chamber of her favourite maids. A little farther on the gallery ended in three stone steps, above which was another door. Sidonia mounted these steps, and lifted the door latch and entered a straightened turret room. It had been given to her for her own use, having stayed empty for a long period, as it was believed to be haunted by a dwarf with the body of a frog who attempted to strangle persons sleeping there.

The turret room, illuminated by the candle which the girl had placed upon a three-legged stool, contained a wooden bed, set sidelong to the wall, and a chest that faced it. Between these the floor was sparsely strewn with rushes.

Sidonia knelt by the chest, and raised the lid, and took from it the things she needed. It held besides only the velvet cloak, folded with care, a comb, and another linen shift—necessary gifts of the Countess. All about her the faintly yellow-lit obscurity was crowded with life and movement.

Like a somnambulist the girl rose from her knees, took up the candle, and descended again into the gallery. Opening the heavy door of the Countess' chamber, which turned on quiet hinges, she entered the musky and stagnant semi-warmth that lay beyond it.

The great bed bulked altar-like. Moving carefully, she lit from her own the several candles that were set about the chamber. They burned with a bland brilliance, almost overcoming the moonlight that filtered inward through the two slit-shaped windows—a mingling of argent and soft gold.

Upon a small table covered with a cloth stood the wine-cup. It was of silver, set with limped ovals of crystal—tall, and ornate as a chalice, and more than half filled with a dark wine. On a bench that ran beneath the windows lay the Countess' book of devotions, a basket of silks and wools, a hand mirror, and an ivory skull—a pious reminder of mortality.

The witch's daughter withdrew the stopper from a phial of glass—a portion of the legacy her mother had received from the wise-woman who had sheltered her, and initiated her, and then died. (A legacy borne in bundles when the lamed fugitive and her girl-child fled into the shaggy waste-lands like pursued animals.) Standing in the light of the candles, she inverted the phial, carefully, above the silver and crystal cup of wine. Thick drops of a liquid that might have been venous blood fell from it sluggishly, gout by gout. Sidonia's lips moved. She was repeating a string of meaningless words—corruptions of very ancient Greek and Hebrew names of power. Eros, Aphrodite, Demeter, and Asmodeus were all invoked in this parrot-like patter, though the girl knew nothing whatever of such persons. An evanescent, blood-red flame flickered in the hollow of the wine-cup as the thick drops fell. A panther cowered at Sidonia's feet like a great, sleek-sided, lascivious cat. Woman-shapes writhed and eddied about her as smoke does, and there was a vague stir, as of shifting coils, athwart the open spaces of the floor. A group of taller forms, lofty as the chamber's roof of stone, loomed more dimly—known of rather than seen, even with the sight of the mind. They were unclothed, and crowned with coronas. One carried a bow, one cherished a dove between her breasts, one held wheat-ears, and one was horned like a young goat. Power tingled through Sidonia, giving her a sensation of rigidity, and yet, at the same time, of a sort of leashed swiftness. Her faith in the force of the love-charm was absolute—an unbroken circle. Through it she would conquer and triumph. Wonders and energies were about her, almost articulate. Their fires bathed her. They merged with her.

(Actually the liquid bottled in the phial was a herbal decoction calculated temporarily to whip the senses. A strong wine, unmingled, might, with some constitutions, be nearly as potent.)

Now it was the turn of the waxen image. Sidonia was a priestess —a celebrant of implacable rituals. She moved in the deep bloodglow of that ancient passion upon whose anvils unbreakable fetters are forged. She was an enslaver, a riveter of chains, a symbol of the powers that are omnipresent, invisible, and pitiless. The scanty hems of her dress dragged with a dry rustle over the dusty, fleaharbouring rushes. She appeared slighter and smaller even than she was—there, in the vague largeness of the sparsely-furnished chamber, whose thick air was fetid and civet-scented. It had been the Countess' instructions that, when the wine was properly bespelled, the witch-girl should slip like a shadow to her own turret room, and in that seclusion—having observed through the doorchink the approach of the Young Lord—should pierce and repierce the image of wax, addressing it by name. And Sidonia, planning calmly, had said, "Yes," and "Yes," and paid no more attention than a duck pays to water. Something told her that there was too much light. If the Young Lord should suddenly enter and observe her business with the image things might not be as well as they would be otherwise. Moving without haste, like an acolyte in a sanctuary, she blew out all the candles save two that were set on a pair of wall-brackets jutting from the untapestried space, between the window-slits. Then, standing with bent head behind the table of the wine-cup, she stabbed with a black and withered rose-thorn the little waxen figure of a naked man.

"Gervais——" "Gervais——" "Gervais——" With every stab of the thorn she whispered the name of the person whose heart should suffer the thrust of an unmerciful love. The chamber was plunged now into semi-dusk. The outline of the great bed had become shadowy. Sidonia's own whispering voice, repeating again and again the name of the young man she had glimpsed but once (to her knowledge), grew and grew upon her consciousness. It assumed a sort of bleak reality She became aware that she was alone in the half-darkness of the Countess' bed-chamber. The door within herself, from which such a jostling medley issued, was being again drawn to. But her confidence—perfect as the belief of hypnotism or as the faith of an ecstatic saint—remained. She was the favoured of Satan, with power to loose or bind. But she was also Sidonia the waif, without a friend in the world except the Devil—a world of lustful bullies, drunken men-at-arms, smooth women with cat-like claws of cruelty, street-folk with blank or hostile faces, whips, prisons—and always, in the threatening and sombre background, the heavy smoke rolling from burning faggots.

"Gervais——" "Gervais——" She must have pricked the image twenty or thirty times. At any moment now someone might enter. Someone—— It came to her—for the first time with vividness —that the Young Lord was a flesh and blood person—a man—a knight—to whom she must yield her body in exchange for his body and soul. A shrinking flashed through her—the purely instinctive recoil of a girl. She was suddenly afraid, though she did not question for an instant that it must be so. The thought came to her, "If only the approaching person were he—my demon lover!" The eyes of her inner sight misted, and a swift, passionate relaxing of the tight-strung nerves passed over her. "Ah, Satan——"

Steps in the gallery without—the tread of man.

Sidonia, giving the involuntary little jump of a thief caught touching, dropped thorn and image. She was afraid to bend and grope for them. Her lips were dry, and they flinched, for there was a nervous trembling that she was unable to control. She was alone.

The steps were right at hand. They seemed to pause at the threshold, and then a faint crackle of rushes. Out of the deep shadows that masked the doorway a figure was advancing, rather slowly.

The moment had come. Sidonia lifted the wine-cup between her two hands. She moved forward. Her head was bent a trifle, and she caught her underlip sharply between her teeth before she spoke.

"Sir, will you be pleased to drink? It—it is the Countess' wish. She will be with you presently."

Her voice was not steady. It sounded small and odd. Some distance behind her the two lonely candles burned. They shed no light whatever upon her lowered face. She was just a creature of insignificant outline, the dragging hems of whose raiment rustled, and whose combed hair caught the faintest halo from the weak radiance at her back.

Gervais halted as soon as the girl spoke her first word. He was surprised. He had expected to find the chamber empty. This girl was strange to him—or appeared to be. He could not see her clearly, for there was not much light. He would have to drink the wine, of course—good manners obliging him to do so, though he did not require it. There was nothing to be said. As usual in the face of an unexpected woman, he was tongue-tied.

The girl was within a foot of him now, and had paused also. He was aware of a vague, balsamic odour, bearing the spirit to beds of trodden herbs at the edge of a pine-forest. The thought crossed his mind, "This woman has sweetened herself as notable and delicate harlots are said to do." He took the chalice-like cup from her hands in complete silence and drank.

Sidonia was conscious only of her own suspense. She stood, as it were, in a pause of nothingness between action and action. The height, the fair build, the dim face of the Young Lord—who had remained as dumb as a corpse walking—were reflected in her mind as in an unthinkable mirror. She merely waited.

Gervais, bound by the rules of courtesy, drank as deeply as he was able, then gave the cup back into the hands of the girl. He passed his tongue over his lips, for there had been a peculiar flavour, and the aftertaste was not quite pleasant. For how long should he stand where he was, like a fool? Would the girl go or remain? How soon would the Countess enter?

When the cup was returned to her—still in silence—Sidonia stayed stock-still for a long moment, and then mechanically turned about, going back towards the two candles, and set it carefully upon the table that was covered altar-fashion with a white cloth. Moving still like a sleep-walker, she passed behind the table and turned, raising her face. The light of the candles dwelt on her, and the eerie, greenish silver of the filtered moonlight was an impalpable nimbus —a witch-halo. She stood with her arms at her sides, the stag-eyes of her dark as death and without any apparent flicker of the lids.

Gervais had followed with his eyes the subdued, forest-movements of the dim girl because she was immediately before him and there was nothing else to attract his rather uncomfortable attention. When she turned slowly to face him, looking towards him, but without seeming to see him, it was several moments before the significance of what he saw leapt from his brain to his heart. Black hair, combed very smooth, framing a face that seemed to be nothing but an unutterable, dark, fixed gaze, child-like, deer-like, spell-like. Black hair falling like midnight rain to the girl's narrowly sloping hips, that were girdled with a white, silken cord. Magic. Miracle. Desire.

Was this reality? Was the girl of the forest—the girl of the carved window—actually here, in the Countess' bed-chamber? The thought of faery flashed across his mind. Yet she had seemed flesh, blood, and bone when she straddled his horse, steadied between his arms. His heart had begun to beat heavily, as though he were being armed for a single combat on which the fate of a city might depend. He felt the wine that he had just drunk tingling like a myriad hot arrows in his blood. He desired terribly, yet his spirit trembled like the hand of a nervous lad outstretched to touch some forbidden thing.

Moving with precaution, as though he were a hunter afraid of scaring an elusive quarry, he went slowly forward.

It seemed to Sidonia that this approach was towards her soul rather than towards her body. She was passive. She believed. She waited.

The candles guttered in some stealthy draught. There was the dry scuttle of a rat. The rushes crisped under the feet of Gervais, but the quiet was an actual presence, like the stillness that dwells in the obscurity of a church.

The young man was within hand-reach of the motionless girl. Sidonia saw him—yet scarcely saw him. She was a victim—an enslaver; terrified, yet triumphant; quailingly alive, yet numb as a person in a condition of self-hypnotism. As if obedient to some impulse not her own, she moved the merest half-pace towards him.

The whole thing was unreal—a speechless but impassioned dream. Gervais lifted his hand, and it came, like the light, tentative touch of a fowler on a snared bird, upon the girl's shoulder. Flesh and blood! With a sharp indrawing of breath that was like a gasp he caught her suddenly in his arms, and a sensation of fire went over him from head to foot. She was yielding, supple-spined, balsam-scented, subtly warm, as a living body should be. A physical thrill struck through him with a honeyed poignancy that was almost unbearable. His arms, infused with a quivering strength, pressed her to him. Her lips were as cold as when he had touched them in the Street of the Martyrs, and they trembled. His own lips, that trembled also, pressed them, and suddenly they parted, and it seemed to him that the girl's soul, like an unsteady flame, fluttered against his own.

Sidonia's knees slackened under her. There was a feeling as of riven walls, broken floodgates. The angel from Heaven had returned! It was an incredible knowledge, instantaneous as lightning and coming, like lightning, from God knows where. But it was too much. A sob caught her throat like a hand. "Oh, God! What have I done? Forgive me? I worship you. I am your servant. Say that you forgive me!"

Gervais spoke with the incoherence of words that jostled each other, hurried by passion and penitence. He was still holding the girl pressed to him, and the spur of the drug-mingled wine, through some slight, additional goad, was, as a matter of fact, quite superfluous. "I left you in the street of the Martyrs because I—I feared to hurt you. This morning I saw you lean from a window, and you threw a rose to me. As soon as I could do so I went again to the Street of the Martyrs to seek for you, but I—I did not even know your name. So I prayed to the martyrs that I might find you. I adore you! You are my saint!"

Both were trembling, though the manner of Gervais' hold upon Sidonia was as strong as the hold of the will on life. Her angel from the highest Heaven was, by the words of his own mouth, the Young Lord—the Young Lord whom she had been appointed by Satan to enthral—whom, by the witch-philtre and the ritual of the waxen image, she had enthralled. Witch-spells bound him to her, witch-drugs were mingled with his blood; the very fervour that set him a-quiver was an artificial flame fanned by the bellows of the devils that help witches. Oh, it was unbearable! She could not! She would not! Her struggling soul was inarticulate; it fought blindly, like an animal in a net.

"I beg— Oh! I beg—let me go!"

Immediately she stood released, her hair dishevelled. Gervais, as pale as herself, his nostrils widened like a hound's, was looking at her with the eyes of a wounded man.

"This is not love—it's not love! You left me in the Street of the Martyrs—you didn't love me then! Let me go now!"

She was in a passion of anguish. Emotions that had swept her forward like waves dragged her back like the terrible force of the ebb. She had forgotten the Countess as completely as the events of the day before yesterday. Nothing existed save herself and the angel who had deserted her—who was Gervais, the Young Lord. With a swift sideways movement of her body she slipped past him, making for the doorway like a hare for the thickets.

"Don't leave me like this—for Christ's sake!

(Oh, he was witch-bound!)

He was after her, but she had reached the murky threshold. An approaching light leavened the gloom. Someone bearing a candle was coming from the head of the unseen stairs towards the turning where the gallery bent like an elbow.

Wild as a soul just torn from its body, and scarcely aware of the coming candle-light that made darkness visible, Sidonia fled cat-footed, and ran up the three steps, and melted into the blackness of the haunted turret, whose door stood half-open.

Gervais was mid-way between the door of the great bed-chamber and the turrets high threshold when his shadow, cast forward by a light at his back, sprawled suddenly before him.

"Gervais!" said the honeyed voice of Sabine. And he turned.

4

INWARDLY HE WAS furious—distracted between the rage and worship of love. He had forgotten Sabine as completely as Sidonia had. To his sight, as he reluctantly faced her, she might have been a nightmare hag. She was the last person whom he wanted to see.

Sabine shielded the candle-flame with her curved palm. Her soft shoulders and bosom broke plumply from the flesh-colour and silver of her festival gown, and her auburn hair, combed straight back from her unlined forehead, was still crammed into its silver net, in which it rested upon the nape of her neck. Gervais was a trifle pale, she thought. Poor lad! No doubt the spell that was being at that moment perfected in the unlighted turret room was having an uneasy effect upon him. What was he doing in the gallery? Ah, well, it was a matter of no importance. Everything that was of importance would be consummated presently.

"I have been detained," she said, lying pleasantly. "I will speak with you now, Gervais."

"Yes, madam."

He wanted to break into passionate questions. Who was this girl? What was her name? How did she come here, and when? But he remained like a tongue-tied boy, bound with invisible fetters against which the sinews of his spirit strained almost to the point of physical anguish. Rigid, he followed Sabine into the great bed-chamber, pausing at a word from her to push to the weighty, sound-muffling door. It was as though he dosed the door upon his own desires. "Oh, to hell with you!" he said within himself, addressing his stepmother.

Sabine was experiencing a species of suave thrills—the sort of satisfaction a prosperous person might feel if they were safe in Heaven at last, with the gate shut. The small quantity of liquid in the wine-cup was puzzling, but there must, she supposed, be some occult reason for it. Perhaps a lesser draught possessed a more concentrated potency.

To Gervais it was like the grotesque repetition that occurs in some sorts of dreaming—the dim, arras-hung room, the two candles, the woman coming towards him with the silver cup. Was this unreal—or was it the other that had been illusion?

He drank like an automaton, knowing beforehand the curious aftertaste that would linger in his mouth. A certain amount of sediment contained in the love-philtre was mingled with the lees of the wine. Gervais had already drunk a good deal, and now, suddenly, his head swam. The pair of candle-flames became four, and it was only by a conscious steadying of his sight that he was able to reduce them to two again. The sensation of bodily passion, temporarily blurred, reasserted itself, and it was as though, in a swimming haze, the touch and sight of the nameless girl teasingly, divinely, encompassed him.

Sabine, who had seated herself in her cushioned chair, looked up at him, standing a couple of feet away from her. Beneath her feline tranquillity she was expectant. Would he go down on his knee, fumble for her hand, and kiss it? He was pale. He did not look at her, but past her towards the lighted candles. What span of time should suffice for the philtre to do its work upon the blood of the young man?

"This matter I wished to speak of concerns your father—and myself."

No answer. But Gervais, turning his head slowly, looked towards her now. From head to foot he was in deep-red raiment, girt with a costly swordbelt, and with a heavy, sacred medal suspended from the gold chain about his neck.

"Your father, as you know, has withdrawn himself from all the pleasures of a man; he has become a saint of God. As a wife I have no duties to fulfil. I have thought for some time of entering a convent."

(Such an idea had never crossed her mind, but it was all the same; a spiritual decision of this sort should spur the action of the philtre.)

"I—I am sorry, madam."

Gervais' response was purely mechanical. He was bemused —held in a little revolving world of his desires. The candle-flames increased from two to four; decreased again; in fact, waxed and waned like tongues of yellow moon-fire. He knew, subconsciously, that something had been said at which he ought to express regret.

Sabine rose from her chair. She came softly close; she laid her hands against the shoulders of the young man and lifted her face to him.

"What is there for me in the world, Gervais? I feel that God calls me."

Oh, but the touch of him was good! Now—now to have his arms go about her. They were alone; there would be no intrusion. Providence Itself could not have arranged matters better.

To Gervais, in the swimming state of his senses, the automatic impulse that had prompted him to speak prompted him now to enclasp the body that was almost in contact with his own. But this was not the girl of faery, with the unbound black hair of maidenhood. Oh, Mother of God! It was Sabine, his father's wife! What was he about to do?

The shock of it half-sobered him. A confused panic seized him. He had enough sense left to know that he was drunk—drunk and fevered. He must go—at once—and with as little self-betrayal as possible.

"I am sorry."

He stepped back from her steadily enough, though something seemed to be chasing itself inside his head like a kitten pursuing its own tail. In some people—self-conscious and sensitive—liquor intensifies dignity; and it was with the carriage and manner of an emperor that Gervais turned and made slowly towards the door —carefully, for he was absurdly anxious to walk in a straight line, as though his chance of salvation and his honour as a knight depended on it. He was spoken to by name—once, twice—but he did not reply. With some difficulty he found the iron ring of the door, and tugged it open. Everything was black before his eyes, for the gallery was in pitch darkness.

Sabine stood alone. Her eyes were humid; her lower lip, which seemed fuller than usual, for it was a trifle out-thrust, was moist as a small, fresh wound. He would return. A suave glow suffused her. God was good.

Her faith in the love-draught was as implicit as Sidonia's. Gervais was visibly in the toils of the witch-net. Presently he would return. She freed her hair from its captivity, passed a comb through it, and began to divest herself of her garments. She had seen to it that neither Anne nor Margaret would attend upon her this night. She got quickly between the covers of the great bed. As the feathers billowed up about her she crossed herself, repeating the Latin night prayers she had learned in childhood. Presently Gervais would return. All was well with the world. She felt just sufficiently drowsy to be deliciously comfortable. Her certainties, which were also her expectancies, lulled even as they glowingly warmed her. Her forget-me-not eyes, love-humid, closed. Her head, sunk in the feather pillows, was aureoled with auburn hair.

* * * * *

When Gervais was received by the dense and cold darkness of the gallery he reeled a trifle, for everything substantial seemed to have fallen away from him. He knew that he was drunk. What should he do? Find the girl of faery—— He groped. Everything swam. Everything was as blind as a bat. His hand encountered the churchyard coldness of a wall of stone, and he felt his way slowly along it, trying to steady himself. The girl had said that he did not love her, but that was untrue. He loved her—body and soul. He was ready to worship her in both flesh and spirit—flesh and spirit——

The death-cold wall appeared to be interminable, and he was impatient to find love. But he was drunk! The disgrace of it over-whelmed him like a seventh wave. He wanted to sob, but stiffened himself instead, endeavouring to preserve a normal balance. But the darkness rocked.

The iron ring-handle of a door! Her door, it must be. He gripped it like a drowning man, swaying on his feet, then, lurching, pushed against it, and it grated open a little way.

There was obscurity here also, but it was not eyeless. Before him, high up, a ruby cross shone with a dull glimmer: a cross that leaned slantingly athwart the shoulder of a crouching, pale-fleeced lamb—the Lamb of God! A musty incense-odour appealed to his muddled senses. He had entered the chapel-like oratory of the Holy Count, where, on occasions, Mass was celebrated for the house-hold.

He stood swaying, looking up at the narrow, sacred window that the moonlight caused to glimmer dully. He was unworthy to find love, for love was holy—holy as the Lamb of God. The feeling of disgrace and of self-shame was too great to be borne standing up-right. His knees bent, and in a moment more he was prone on his face on the stone pavement of the oratory, his forehead resting against his bent arm. Fiery wheels seemed to be turning on either side of him, though there was no sight to his eyes. Unworthy desire passed over him like successive ripples of flame, and he groaned like a young monk wrestling with temptation. After a while came numbness, begotten by the cold about him, the cold beneath him, the heavy wine, and the drug. Face downward on the stones he slept, breathing audibly.

Perhaps an hour passed, or a little more. The long, prone figure, with its forehead resting on its arm, moved. The head lifted. There was a stir, an inarticulate sound like that which a heavy sleeper utters when abruptly awakened by a call. Gervais, sitting upright, and chafing his limbs instinctively with the palms of his hands, was as dazed as a person who has died and come to life again. But someone had called him—he knew that as certainly as that he was himself and no one else. The feeling of urgency was strong upon him. He was wanted. He got to his feet. He ached, and his head felt bruised and weighty. The delirium of the drugged wine had passed from him, leaving him stunned. But he knew that he was wanted.

Taking his dim way, slowly, to the threshold of the oratory, he groped from its lighter dark into the utter blackness that lay beyond. He was steady enough on his feet now, but quite automatic in his movements. He did not think; his head throbbed as though it had been struck with a hammer. His instinctive groping had almost immediately encountered the wall of the gallery, and he moved along it. A closed door was passed, and then another. His foot struck a stone step. There were three steps. He mounted them slowly, and his outstretched hand pushed inward an unlatched door —the door of the turret room that had been allotted to the witch's daughter.

5

WHEN SIDONIA, FLEEING from love, slipped past its half-open door into the haunted turret room, she did not check her breathless self until halted by the farther wall. Then she faced about, standing with her back against it like a creature at bay. She was keyed up to abuse, to repudiate; to fight, if need be, like a dog-cornered cat.

The candle-light in the gallery was visible, indirectly, through the door opening. She heard voices. The light disappeared. There was silence.

She continued to stand with her back to the wall, her hands clenched into fists, incredulous; pierced and transpierced with intolerable disappointment. This void—this dark nothing—was the very last condition she could bear. Her whole being screamed for conflict.

There was a sound in the gallery. Steps. But the sound receded and was gradually swallowed by the muffling silence. Someone had come out from the great bed-chamber and had turned about, going from her. She was deserted for the second time.

Leaving the wall, she moved to the side of the bed. It was ancient, narrow, and chest-like, with carved panels. She dropped to her knees beside it, burrowed her head hard against the in-tucked coverings, and beat upon the panels with her fists, as though they raised a barrier between herself and her very soul. She wanted to tear herself—to scream. Her fury was wordless; outside all reason; too passionate for any definite shape of thought. It was like rolling, fiery smoke. Her body writhed. She ground her forehead into the dented bed-covers and her fists hammered softly, desperately, against the worm-eaten panels. Even black magic—the ritual of the waxen image and the strength of the philtre—was not powerful enough to overcome the invincible indifference that had tasted her mouth and left her in the Street of the Martyrs; that had seemed to thaw for a matter of moments when the tall horse, caparisoned in white and silver, had been checked by the crowd beneath the windows of the master goldsmith's house; that had, within the hour, ignored her utterly in the great bed-chamber until whipped by the

witch-drug to a brief, quivering spasm of passion. She hated him—
the Young Lord, the angel—as she had never, in all her short,
savage life, hated woman, man, or malevolent, inanimate object.
And he had kissed her for the second time—there—in Sabine's
chamber, and she—she had parted her lips for him.

She ground her brow with a sort of fury into the dented place in
the bed-coverings and moaned.

"Oh, Satan, Satan——"

It was involuntary. She muttered the name of the Devil when in
any torment as other folk called upon God.

A stillness dropped on her like a sudden cloak. Her body relaxed.
She found herself drawing quiet breaths that deepened and deepened, becoming slower and more rhythmic with every inspiration.
Her emotion, sharp as death, was deadened. Slumped down by the
bedside, with her head against it, her breast breathed like a heavy
sleeper's.

* * * * *

Someone was speaking to her.

"Child, my power dwells in you, as the flame dwells in the cup
of a lamp."

She lifted her lowered eyelids—or seemed to—and was not
astonished at what she saw, though, in the very nature of things, she
should have been. A seated woman confronted her whose marvellous body was subjected to changes as rapid as a play of light. Her
waist was cinctured with a thin girdle of lovely live serpents, that
slid and shimmered continually. Her golden hair was now an actual
sun-flame that haloed her with intolerable brilliance, now a cataract
of yellow blossoms, and now honey-pale silken plaits that touched
the ground and were interwoven with every jewel known to man.
She sat within a chair of living rock, whose high bases were curiously sculptured. Sidonia, standing before this enthroned woman,
felt delicious warmths caress her, as with tangible fingers.

"You have named me," said the woman. "I stood with you when
you mingled the juice of my herbs with the wine that is also mine.
All power lies between my hands, and in my lap. You are my child;
no man shall withstand your strength, for your strength is drawn
from me."

Sidonia shuddered under a sensation that seemed to slacken her
knees and yet flowed through her like a tide of immortal vigour.

The woman, compact of a myriad sense-tangling, changing beauties that throbbed like fire or fever, assumed the proportions of a giantess. Sidonia's sight darkened. As in a nightmare which is yet more strange than unpleasant she saw, vaguely, the sculptures upon the base of the chair of rock—now become life-size—quicken to complex movement, and they were a frieze of sentient creatures all striving in the relentless coupling of love. She appeared to be sinking, but she was not afraid. Whatever the nature of the abyss, it was a warm darkness that encompassed her—warmer than the charity of christened folk. She yielded herself to it.

* * * * *

Sidonia shivered. She straightened her crumpled little body, lifting her head from the dented bed covers. A hint of the moon's light stole through a high window-slit. It was deathly cold. In the almost-darkness the girl rose up. There was no more clenching of hands or spasmodic movements like those of an animal at bay. She stripped her dark gown downward from the shoulders, leaving herself in her linen shift, then climbed up into the bed. But she did not lay herself down in it. (It was hard, like a pallet, though the pillow was stuffed with feathers.) She sat upright looking towards the door, that was unlatched, as it had been from the first.

"Whoever you call is bound to come to you," said a shrill, un-human voice, that spoke more within her than without.

"I know that," said Sidonia, answering within herself. And she was utterly sure.

She knew also, without turning her face, that an enormous frog with an old man's head squatted on top of the wooden chest. There was other company as well. A young woman who had committed suicide by drowning herself, because the man she desired repudiated her, stood close to the bed. Sidonia had known this woman by sight. Scarcely a month had elapsed since her body, denied all religious rites, had been buried ignominiously where two roads crossed, with a stake driven through it.

"Call—call to him!" urged the suicide softly, but with a husky eagerness.

A something, half man half goat, was near the bed foot. It had pricked ears, little horns, and its yellow eyes were phosphorescent. These—and whatever else there was also—were all friendly. Almost everything had, from the first, been friendly to Sidonia, except men and women.

"Call to him!" whispered the suicide, though there was no sound, even of a whisper, in the turret room.

Sidonia's lips formed a name. There, in the solitude, in the warmthless dimness, sitting up in the hard, narrow, ancient bed, she spoke in silence over and over again:

"Gervais—Gervais———"

He would come to her—he must. All power was hers. She was calm, her pulses quiet and steady. Her mind was as unreflective as a sable pool in a forest, set round with deep enchanted fern. She was alone, yet not alone.

Minutes passed. Her lips still moved without sound. She was a will—an affirmation of faith—no more.

Footsteps—approaching down the gallery—slow, but unwavering. No thrill set her nerves a-tingle. She had known that it must be so. She was the favoured of Satan; the child of the—the woman in the throne-chair of living rock.

A foot struck against one of her threshold-steps. The door moved gratingly. A tall, dark figure, with one arm outstretched as though groping, had come deliberately into the turret room.

And the room was empty now, save for the girl sitting up in her white shift in the strait bed.

This girl looked towards the person that had entered. She did not speak or move. The sinking moon, glancing more directly in through the one window-slit as it declined, made a wan vagueness in the obscurity. The suicide, the faun, the strangling frog-dwarf, and God knows what others, had withdrawn themselves, perhaps into the buried consciousness of the witch-girl, where the portal of a teeming world stood always ajar.

* * * * *

Gervais' outstretched arm dropped. He stood stock-still. He could see dimly, for there was a hint of moonlight. There was a bed —not much wider than a coffin—with posts and wooden canopy, set sidelong to the wall, and a narrow whiteness sitting upright in it —a whiteness over which black tresses fell. This was the turret room, and in its ancient bed the girl of faery sat up straight as a little spear and looked at him!

His heart began to hammer as it had done in Sabine's chamber when candle-light and moon-mist revealed the twice-seen face that had driven him mad. He had been bestial; he had been drunken; he had almost embraced his father's wife, and now, through the operation of mysterious mercy, he was led blindfolded straight to this small room as to the shrine of a saint. He was utterly unworthy, but an angel (his guardian angel, maybe) had roused him and brought him to this threshold through the dark. He moved forward a couple of hesitant steps, divided between awe and a delight that quailed like terror.

"I—I thought a voice called me."

(It was an absurd manner in which to excuse the entering of her bed-chamber at middle night, but Gervais was beyond self-consciousness; he spoke simply, as a soul before the tribunal of God.)

"I called."

The two words were uttered in a low voice that was cool as dew; the slim, white shape in the bed had spoken.

Gervais moved again; he was at the bedside. As naturally as though it were the communion rail before a church altar, he went down on his knees.

"You called to me. You have pardoned me?"

"Yes."

He put out his hands, and they touched her knees, that were small and childish even beneath the bed-coverings. She leaned towards him. Her hands came upon his shoulders. She kissed him upon the mouth.

Gervais' arms were about her, strong as a wrestler's, convulsive. As she lifted her face from his he pillowed his head, with a great shuddering sigh, against her breast, and so remained.

What was it? What inexplicable thing had occurred in her heart —her soul? Sidonia herself was shuddering strongly. She wanted to sob, to utter little wounded moans. Her heart seemed to expand; and then to break in a warm gush of blood. A numbness of the mind and senses melted as ice melts in spring. She was tremulous, frightened, hungry, anguished, and translated to some seventh heaven far above the stars. Oh, all her short life had waited—panted—for this head that pressed itself against the soft salience of her scarcely-hidden breasts. She craved to mother it with the fierce tenderness of a tigress-creature; she melted towards it until her whole being seemed nothing but soft fire; her eyes swam with tears; she was ready to live or die indifferently for this other life—the first that had sought shelter between her fragile arms. She had come into her heritage.

Time passed over them—a soundless stream of moments. Sidonia's arms were tight about Gervais, even as his imprisoned her. Again and again her quick lips dwelt against his hair. It was ecstasy,

bland as that of a mother who suckles her first-born, and as passionate.

"My darling!" A murmurous whisper that cooed, mother-
fashion, dove-fashion.

Gervais lifted his head. Wordlessly his mouth and the mouth of
his saint became one. The pulses of each trembled towards the
other. Love, like a double flame, burned in them, shuddering like
the wind-taken flame of a candle, for both were ignorant concerning
it. But the girl was wiser than the young man.

"I worship you. You are holier to me than the Mother of God."

"No, no. Oh, my darling, get up off your knees! Gervais, you
shan't kneel in the bitter cold!"

His name, which she had repeated so often in her invocations,
was as natural on her tongue as though she had been wedded to him
for a dozen years.

He was seated sideways on the bed's edge now, and Sidonia,
embraced by his arms, clung close to him.

"What is your name, my saint?"

"Sidonia."

They kissed again, clasping each other with a nervous strength
that quivered.

"I worship you!" said Gervais unsteadily, and his voice had
deepened; there was a huskiness in it.

The girl's inner self trembled like a tear. But she was not afraid.
Under her hard-pressed cheek, as she clung against him with lowered head, she felt the rapid beating of his heart. There was no
thought in her—only emotion.

"Sidonia—Sidonia——"

All denial was dead in her. She was a woman and he was her
man, and she loved him without forethought or afterthought. His
heart was upon her heart now, and it seemed to her that it was the
weight of love itself that burdened her. She was mute, utterly passive, her eyes aswim with tears and her breast breathless.

"I must not harm you. To-morrow the priest shall marry us."

A silence followed. Nothing stirred in the darkened turret room.
"Marriage?" repeated Sidonia's inner self, like a person wakening.
"Marriage?" Such a word had never risen above the horizon of her
mind. She was the witch's daughter; she might be outraged, ravished, devil-mated, or give herself freely for love, but priest's ritual
could have no part nor lot in her. And this man who lay in her arms
as never man had lain was a christened knight, who knelt in
churches, and who, at his death, would enter into the kingdom of the

ancient, severe, and patriarchal God, unless, through a union of body and spirit with herself, he was drawn down into the red-lit halls of hell. The pulse of her life halted like the feet of a traveller who checks himself at the very lip of an abyss. The divine warmth that had held her was replaced by a spreading coldness. She—Sidonia—was the Satan-baited trap set in the path of the Young Lord, and should she once yield all of herself to him he would fall immediately beneath the power of her Master, and the night would claim him for its own. She saw herself suddenly, as it were, with wide-open eyes—sealed to the Master, moving among strange associates, a witch, with the powers of a witch, whether she would or no. Why, this very love that gave the weight of him to her young breast was the work of spell and philtre—as she had known in Sabine's chamber. Then, this knowledge had goaded her to a passion of anger against him; now, it flooded her with a passion of pain. Oh, it was she that was trapped! It seemed to her that her soul struggled like a small bird between the hands of the Master. She uttered a little involuntary moan.

"What is it, darling? Have I grieved you? I should not be here, but I swear by the Mother of God you shall remain as sacred to me as the sacrament of the altar. Oh, Sidonia, there is no heaven save on your breast!"

His mouth sought hers again, and murmured speech was lost in the silence of a kiss. He knew that he should rise up from where he was and return to his own place, but the strength to do so seemed slain in him.

So the dark minutes passed, like floating leaves carried onward by the stream of time. And in the sixty seconds of each minute's span the girl lived through a decade of conflict. How could she relinquish her man—her happiness? How could she drag him with her own arms down into the pit? How could she (oh, most impossible of all!) writhe free from the Master's grip—she who had yielded him her lips and leaned on the thought of him, who had been delivered from a witch's womb, who had invoked the spirits of the air, who had cast a spell over the hostile townsfolk—and upon the Young Lord, the knight of God?

"Do you love me, Sidonia?"

"I do—I do!" And her small, cold hand, that fluttered like a bird's wing, caressed his hair.

Then the floor rushes whispered at the threshold, and someone spoke sharply in the gloom.

6

THE SOUL OF Sabine uncurled from sleep much like a cat that tenses soft limbs, and spreads luxurious claws, and yawns pink-mouthed. For some moments the body of Sabine lay quiescent, aware only of comfort, and then a tingle of expectancy quivered through it— unsatisfied expectancy.

The forget-me-not eyes of the Countess opened. They encountered a sickly dusk, for one candle had burnt right down in its socket and the other was low. At least an hour had passed—and she was still alone.

A dawning conviction of something out of joint in the general scheme of the universe spread disquietingly over her. Mother of God! If there was no infallibility in the liberally-paid-for craft of witches what vehicle could one repose faith in? Not in relics of the saints, or water from miraculous springs, or even in the benevolent power of the Father. The uncertainty of all things was borne in upon her, and with it the first tremor of panic she had ever felt.

Drawing herself upright in the great bed, she looked towards the dying candle. All was still—no step, no rustle of movement. A surge of dull anger like a foamless, lifting wave—against God, Gervais, and the young witch—submerged the channels of her thought. The whole purpose of her nature had set tide-like towards her stepson.

Turning back the covers, she stood upon her bare soles at the bed's side, and quickly slipped on the linen shift she had discarded. Then thrust her naked feet into her pointed slipper-shoes of silver tissue and went quickly to the closed door. It was the blind, seeking instinct of the huntress.

Standing upon the threshold of her chamber, Sabine looked out into the gallery. There was only a thick, death-cold darkness there, that seemed as though it could never yield a footfall. She turned her face towards the turret room. The faintest glimmer of a lighter dark dawned upon her cat-sighted eyes, and she became aware that the witch's door stood open, and that beyond it there was a shadow of moonlight.

As a disappointed patient might seek the physician —very justly angry, yet still hoping against hope—Sabine, unmindful of chills, ghosts, and discretion, moved towards the grey moon-shadow that dwelt vaguely at the gallery's upper end. Her feet were noiseless. Her loosened hair lay upon her shoulders like the tresses of a maiden. One image only was before her; one desire urged her like a spiritual spur—Gervais.

She came to the three steps. The door had been pushed right inward, and the doorway opening glimmered grey as dew. She was ready to threaten the witch with exposure and the various tortures that were reserved for the Devil's own. She had been liberal in every way, and the girl had cheated her with a worthless drug. Perhaps—if the little dark hell-creature were sufficiently frightened —a spell possessing real power might yet be worked.

A voice—a man's voice, very low-pitched, but audible in the utter silence of the night.

Another voice answering—a woman's.

There were two in the turret room. Was the witch-girl communing with a male familiar, or Sabine was before all things feminine—felinely so. To the anger that had drawn her forward there was now added curiosity. She mounted the steps as though shod with velvet, but the dry, strewn rushes whispered at the threshold, and, knowing herself discovered, she said sharply "Sidonia!"

A moment of breath-held quiet, and then movement. "Oh, the hussy!" said Sabine's inner self, sharp and rasping as any shrew.

"Sidonia, what wantonness is this?"

No answer for some seconds, and then, out of the sight-muffling twilight:

"Madam, this maiden shall become my wife to-morrow."

Sabine's hand went to her heart; her fingers clutched at the linen fabric that covered her bosom as a drowning person clutches at blades of grass. Gervais! Her soft-fleshed body stiffened as though a knife had been driven into her. She had been despoiled—wholly and absolutely! Her treasure had been filched from her by a brazen slut! She had been fooled, cajoled—stripped of her joy so that this gutter-witch might wear it as a garment! Her nostrils dilated, and there was a feeling of constriction in her throat—the gripping, hysterical rage of a red-haired woman.

"Your wife! Gervais! would you wed with hell? Would you take the bastard daughter of a devil? This girl is a witch, whose damned soul I had thought to save through charity. She shall burn for this!"

Her voice was shrill with hysteria. It climbed so high that it almost cracked. It was like some-thing brittle and lethally acute.

"What are you saying?"

Was that Gervais' voice—abrupt to roughness, deeper-toned than she had ever heard it?

"She shall burn! Oh, God! Oh, God!"

"You are mad! This girl is pure. I have no right to be with her in this manner, but I have not dishonoured her. I have told you—she shall be my wife."

"Oh! Oh!" screamed Sabine, as though red-hot irons had been applied to her flesh. She was beside herself; it was no simulated frenzy. She stumbled down the threshold steps, tripping on the hem of her long shift, wavered some distance along the gallery, and began to shriek as if she were being stabbed to death. The dreadful cries, duplicated by echoes, would have waked the seven sleepers.

In the turret room Sidonia, who had sprung out on to the floor, was clipt by the arms of Gervais.

"She has gone mad. You shall not be frightened, my darling!"

"Oh, Gervais, you are more to me than all that is in the world! Never doubt it!"

They were going to take her from him—and it must be so. Oh, the strength of him—the strength of his arms about her! Her man!

"Gervais, never doubt that I love you!"

Muffled shouts were answering the cries in the gallery now. The witch's daughter—the quarry—knew that the hunt was up. But there was no space for terror in her heart; the anguish of love was its sole furnishing. Her cheek touched the coldness of the sacred medal that lay on Gervais' breast.

Torchlight wildly reddened the long tunnel of the gallery. A rabble of menservants and men-at-arms came jostling up the stairway. The Countess, leaning against the wall like a stabbed woman, found fresh voice to greet them.

"The witch—the witch I sought to befriend—she has bespelled your master's son! She would suck his blood, and deliver him body and soul into the hands of Satan! The witch! The vampire! Oh! Oh!"

She paused to allow her exhausted lungs to fill. Her throat was dry as parchment—ready to crack. The men and lads gaped at her like a party of ghost-seers, and the several torches fumed the arched roof of stone with wispy, resinous smoke.

"An angel came to me in a dream and roused me, and I left my bed and went to the turret room—the room of the witch. And your master's son was there. He is under her spell; his soul is already chained to her; but I command you—in the name of God!—that you tear her from him. Only her death will set him free!"

Her red-golden head fell back against the wall. Her eyes closed. Anne and Margaret, who had followed the rush of menfolk up the stair, scurried to her with little sharp cries. Their arms supported her. Both were dishevelled—Margaret flushed like fever, and Anne ague-pale. It had been a night of licence below stairs. Margaret, seated upon the knees of Hugh, had received boisterous love-lessons. He would have followed her when this present cry of alarm was raised only that his legs failed him, for the spiced wine had gone to them. Anne, frigid even in a love-scuffle, when she had drunk more than she should, was becoming deathly sick when the first shriek drifted—a mere thread of sound—into the feasting-hall. To her two handmaids the Countess seemed a swooning saint, chaste as Lucretia. They upheld her between them, their eyes wide as those of startled deer, incoherent words upon their lips. And the Countess moved her head weakly from side to side, and moaned.

The light of the torches illuminated the gallery to its farther end, where three steps led up to a doorway. Every man of those who had come up the stair was acquainted with the turret room—the haunted turret where no one slept. It was lightless, and appeared tenantless, though they knew by the mouth of their Countess that it was not. Was sulphureous smoke about to issue from it, mixed with blue flame? Or a familiar in the shape of a dwarfed crocodile? They were all men with the stomachs of fighters—more or less; callous, shockheaded, habitually blasphemous as the kitchen guard of Lucifer, but they crossed themselves now with the earnestness of children and advanced slowly, holding their torches well up.

"Stop!" The command came hollowly down the gallery. Someone was standing in the doorway of the witch's lair—the Young Lord. He appeared taller than usual, and his stripped sword was in his right hand.

"There is no witch here. My father's wife has dreamed an evil dream that has bewildered her. Go back whence you came."

He spoke with authority. The torch-bearing men had halted at the first word. They looked at him in uncertainty, and at the blade of the long, straight, double-edged sword, whose point rested upon the stone threshold. They knew that a young witch slept that night under the protection of the Countess. And then again, what business had brought the Count's son to the turret room.

At Gervais' voice Sabine reopened her eyes, and she stiffened in the arms of her two girls.

"He's bewitched! I told you so! The vampire-wanton has englamoured him. Drag her out! As soon as the soul is torn from her body his own soul will be free. An angel of God enlightened me!"

Her exhausted utterance, harshly shrill, was endowed with a sort of vital desperation. The torches wavered as the men stirred. The smoke that filled the gallery was eye-smarting, and set several coughing.

"By God! I'll kill the first man who tries to enter here!"

Bewitched or not, it was evident to the stupidest that Gervais meant what he said. The men hesitated. Violence and caution trembled, balanced against each other. It was a moment when the smell of as yet unshed blood was on the air. And then, in the witch's doorway, the Young Lord stood no longer alone, for a girl was with him.

When Gervais, with a last quick pressure of his hands upon her arms, turned from her to the threshold, stripping the scabbard from his sword, Sidonia remained passive for a couple of slow breaths. The pain in her heart had spent itself like a crashing wave, and now it was as if a brief and merciful death had stilled all of her that had, within an hour, so loved and suffered. But her mind was clear as a sorcerer's crystal. There should be no struggle to obtain her, for Gervais might suffer injury. Neither should any lay hands on her at all; she knew that she could pass through the midst of them and—be snatched from their sight. Gervais should not be forced to witness her slaying; that would hurt his soul as sword-points could harm his body. Moving quickly, she raised the lid of the chest, took out the cloak of velvet, and folded it about her. She heard the shrill urging of the Countess and the loud, abrupt voice of Gervais. The jumping, lurid light shed by flaring wood beat against her sight. She went forward until she stood in the doorway beside the man whom she had held in her arms, but she did not touch him. Looking straight before her, and seeing only the unsteady firelight that threatened but could not terrify because she had suffered too much to have any fear left, she descended the threshold steps and went barefooted directly towards the men of the Countess' household.

There was a silence in the gallery like that of momentarily held breath. Sabine, her mouth open to cry out again, remained dumb, for she was really amazed. The men gaped. This little figure of a dark-haired girl, close-wrapped in azure and argent, and coming towards them as though she were the only living creature in the world—this was the witch. They had visioned something that would scream and curse and claw. The fixed midnight eyes of this girl did not appear to see them. She held herself like a king's daughter. In some indescribable way she was—alone.

"Sidonia!"

Gervais was down the steps already, sword in hand. He was quite as bewildered as Sabine, though from a different standpoint. The young girl did not turn her head at his voice; she did not appear to have heard him. But at this naming of the trouble-causer Sabine found her tongue.

"Do not permit him to follow her! She will draw him to some dreadful death—to his damnation!"

The foremost of the men-at-arms had already sheered aside to allow the barefooted witch-maiden a clear passage. One or two said afterwards that a cold wind went with her. She had known that they could lay no hand upon her; perhaps it was the breath of this bleak faith that they felt. But they closed up quickly enough about Gervais, swords out to beat down his.

"Sidonia!" he called again. And then, "Let me pass!"

They had not harmed her, and he was unwilling to turn his point against his father's men. She was going down the gallery into the bat-like shadows.

"Stand back instantly! Let me pass!"

"God save his soul!" exclaimed Sabine faintly, and let her relaxing weight come so heavily upon the strength of Margaret that the poor girl staggered and nearly gave at the knees.

Steel clattered athwart steel; Gervais' short patience was exhausted. They were half a dozen against one, though intent only on beating aside his blade, for he was the Young Lord. It was a lively scuffle at the gallery's red-lit end. Anne and Margaret, fifteen paces from it, were both speechless—the one from the shock of sobering excitement and the other from sheer breathlessness due to the weight of the Countess, who was apparently in a half-swoon, and whom she supported with difficulty.

There was a sharp, wordless sound from a man whose wrist had been smartly sword-bitten, and his weapon dropped. The ring of opposition broke; actually, the guts of none of them were in this dubious, semi-deadly game. Gervais, pallid with wrath and with his black hair dishevelled, was down the gallery like a slipped hound. It was empty.

V. THE BLACK MASS

1

"SIDONIA! SIDONIA!" HER name, twice-uttered, was to the girl as the cry of the ancient Orpheus to the lost Eurydice, the captive of Hades—the cry of life to irrevocable death. Her feet were not stayed; she looked straight forward into the dark ahead, and death and night possessed her heart. Behind her there was the clatter of crossed steel; Gervais was endeavouring to cut his way to her through the barrier of his father's men. But he must not touch her again—never again.

She was at the turn of the gallery. All was black, yet not so utterly black that she could not take her way swiftly. She had put out one hand that she might keep by the wall, and the tips of her fingers brushed along the evenness of the stone. She had no plan, only a faith that was cold and actual as the invisible flagging beneath her feet. Automatic once more, she was borne along without question like a corpse on a deep current. Her travelling finger-tips encountered a minute pit—the merest pock-mark in the face of the wall, and just deep enough to receive the top of a seeking forefinger. As at a spoken word she paused. "Press! Press!" said an unuttered voice within her—the voice of her submerged self, that knew so much, and was wise, also, with the undivulged knowledge of others. Her forefinger fitted itself to the tiny pit, and pressed inward. Something yielded. There was a faint sound between a muffled hinge-creak and a sigh. An odour of dead air stole outward, and there was the sense of a void.

"The Master's magic door has opened for you," said Sidonia's submerged self. "You have found it because his knowledge is your knowledge. Be quick!"

And the girl groped forward into the gape of the secret entrance that smelt like a cellar that has been sealed for twenty years. "Shut the wall behind you," prompted her other self, and her fingers, assured by the faith that grants eyeless sight, sought for the pit of the inner door-spring, and found it, and with another soft sigh the tall, coffin-shaped stone that had swung inward closed gently, door-fashion, and there was nothing but a blindness that pressed upon the eyes like weights, close as a womb—and cold.

She was safe—from love and hate. Assuredly the Master stretched out the arm of his protection above his own! All the warmth of her life lay slain in her. She was incapable of amazement. Anything might happen, as in the sequence of a dream but it could not hold any real significance, for there was no hope.

Putting out her hands, she felt the walls of the place. With mechanical caution she moved, for her submerged self watched over her always heedfully, though her real self was careless with the despair of pain. For a few paces the way was level, and then her bare foot found the lip of a step. It was the first of a great number. In utter blindness she descended, her palms pressed to the stonework. The air was long-dead. The silence was like that of the grave, and so tangible that one could almost listen to it. Very little more than the width of a person's body was the secret stair. Yet in a manner, it was populous. Fears, agonies, passions—they thronged impalpably, squirmed underfoot, or clung like flattened fungi to the scarce-parted walls. Stabbed men had been dragged by the heels down this hidden way; women who had betrayed their lords had sought with frantic hands to stay their hustled descent to a death of thirst and suffocation in some sealed-up niche—clutching at the smooth masonry like a cat drowning in a well; paramours, refugees, and assassins had footed it swiftly up and down the rough-hewn steps —all the illicit traffic of a hundred years. Sidonia sensed it.

Enfolding her like a sable sheath was the known, yet the unknown. "I fear!" whispered the stifling silence. "I burn!" "I suffer!" "I bleed!" "I thirst!" The struggling wings of crowding sorrows and passions fanned the girl's loose-hanging hair. She knew that she was not alone in her anguish—whose heavy blow had so recently fallen that the wound had not yet begun to yield blood. She had company, and she understood it without consciously understanding.

The steps ended. The strait passage—unseen but felt— continued, curving like a worm. Had she traversed a mile? It was all the same to her. Again—and then again—her travelling hands encountered surfaces of metal, nail studded. Who could say what might lie behind these ancient and merciless doors, secret as the grave? Skeletons, fully clad, manacled; the long, tarnished hair of the women still adhering to scalps that were like shrivelled parchment? Or, if the legend of the town was to be believed, some dreadful, shapeless incubus, offspring of a Countess dead and excommunicated for nearly a century who had had commerce with non-human lovers? The witch's daughter did not know. Always she went forward, and voiceless voices whispered, and pleaded, and babbled like racked creatures in a delirium.

A step—a series of steps—leading upwards. A trap-door. It was not very difficult to lift. Ah! This darkness, indirectly star-leavened, was day-like after the blindness it replaced. And the smell of the frosty air, keen as a knife-edge, was like water outpoured for thirst. Sidonia saw. She breathed. The shapes of obscure things were immediately before her, a roof was over them, and beyond was the night whose moon had set. Climbing upward and out by way of the trap-door, she skirted the barrier that vaguely upreared itself.

Under a sharp-pitched, shingled roof the old, very hallowed, and miracle-working Calvary fronted a cobbled space on which a multitude of cold stars looked down. Above it rose the outer wall of the Count's massive fortress-dwelling. The crucified Christ nailed to His cross was flanked by wooden figures of the Virgin and St. John, and before this nearly life-size tableau of anguish a tribute of flowers was always laid in their season, and candles, stuck upright in their own melted wax, burned there on high festival days. Now all was dim. The anxious flame of worship had died down to an indistinguishable spark, that would rekindle when the first passers-by in the morning greyness knelt in a faith as limpid as the diamond drops of melting frost, and yet as vital as their own coarse-flavoured breath made palpable by the cold. Yet beneath the roof of the Calvary something moved. Surely no midnight worshipper daring sacrilege to lay clinging hands upon the sacred, carven group?

Sidonia recognised her surroundings. She had paused by the figure of St. John, having come from behind it, where, in the little space unvisited by any person, lay the entrance to the hidden way. The cold was bitter. No life stirred under the stars. She looked at the shape of the Crucified, of a bleached whiteness against the dark wood of the cross. Its attitude of suffering, as in the forest, woke a dull sympathy in her. She went right up to it and touched its chill, immobile contours. It, also, was a thing of pain.

The clap-clap of stumbling wooden shoes sounded with a dreadful loudness. Sidonia drew a step away from the cross and faced the human sound. The pallor of the shift that clad her from throat to ankles showed ghostly, for the cloak had opened. There was a faint scream. The clap-clap of the clumsy shoes quickened. They slipped and clattered; they were trying to run. Gradually the noise faded into the muffling night.

In a few hours' time, when the daily business of the churches was resumed, a dishevelled, beggarly young woman, dissolved in tears would kneel at the priest's feet, confessing to a wanton's life, just entered upon, and how the Holy Virgin herself, white as silver, had appeared to her at the miracle-working Calvary and snatched her soul from damnation.

As the frosty, lifeless silence settled back Sidonia drew the velvet cloak about her. She was so exhausted that she could have lain down where she was, on the little platform of the Calvary, to which a couple of steps led up. Everything—within, without—was black and cold. Her feet were numb; there was no feeling in them. But her heart was no longer numb, and in her misery her eyes brimmed with tears. "Gervais! Gervais!" her spirit whimpered. It was finished—everything was finished. She put up her hands to her face and sobbed like a child whose one toy is broken. Nothing stirred. Nothing approached her. The night had neither arms nor bosom. After some time had passed she went down the two steps before the Calvary and began to cross the dim space of cobble-stones upon which the mouths of several lane-like streets opened. In all the world there was no place for her save her mother's lair—and that only until the hue and cry should start, as it must now. But the loft above the yard pertaining to the Thieves' Kitchen was still home. Should she fear to traverse the midnight ways of the town —she who had plumbed the extremest depths, and who was lost so utterly that even the veriest lecher would let her be, as though she were indeed a damned soul wandering the dark earth?

How far-off were the stars seen between the house-tops! As remote as those glimpsed, possibly, by the inhabitants of hell.

2

SIDONIA WAS IN Heaven. There was no mistake about it; an amazing profusion of flowers—lilies and roses—grew waist-high, and the path she followed was paved with golden flagstones. How beautiful was the sward where the spangling daisies twinkled like tiny stars! Perhaps they were stars, for Heaven was above the sky. Gervais walked beside her, dressed in crimson, with his gold chain about his neck. They were far above the world, and death, and it would be always midsummer here. An old man sat on a gilt chair among the flowers, and she knew that He was God. He smiled as pleasantly at her as a venerable pedlar who had once given her a sugared apple by the wayside when she was quite small. This pleased her very much.

"We're man and wife now," said Gervais. "God Himself has married us, Sidonia."

He put his arms about her, and she slid her own arms round his neck. She held him as tightly as she was able; nothing, even in Heaven mattered at all save him. He was her treasure. They would lie in a house built entirely of gems, upon a gilded bed with a feather mattress. Yet the gold flags of the path were very cold to the soles of her feet. She had no shoes on, and that was neither right nor fitting in such a place. Oh! how cold the path was! Ugh!

Where was Heaven? Sidonia drew up her knees, for as she lay on her side on the thin litter of straw her naked feet had been in contact with a broken crock wherein bundles of dried herbs were kept. The velvet cloak was over her. A feeble, ash-grey twilight struggled with dusk beneath the rafters of the loft. There was no comfort in the fetid air, for the charcoal hearth was fireless.

The girl raised herself, drawing her numbed feet under her. She had slept for some hours. When, half-dead with the fatigue of despair, she had dragged herself up into the loft, all had been black and silent. But that was nothing. She had found her bed of straw, huddled herself in the rich cloak, shivered, lost consciousness—and dreamed. Now it was morning. The dim mound that was her mother was a motionless, low hummock in the shadows. Neither of the cats was visible. Charcoal ash lay thick on the cold hearth. Without particularly seeing anything, Sidonia contemplated all that there was to see much as a person in a condemned cell, waking in the greyness of his last dawn, might regard his surroundings. She had come to an ending. Through spells and magic Gervais was bound to her as though an invisible chain stretched between them, yet should she yield to the passion of love she had induced in him her arms would drag him down from his high place in the light of day— down—and down—— She must not! Because she loved him! And presently, in any case, the hue and cry of the witch-hunt would be raised. But they should not take her and burn her! She had a flashing, vivid picture-thought of gloating enemy faces; of Sabine, pale and auburn and composed; of Gervais, restrained by force, and suffering. No! She was not a hunted cat—a palpitating hare! She could take her life in her own two hands, and—and fling it away.

The heart in her young, shaken body gave a throb, and then quietened until it almost seemed to cease. Yes, death was the only door left; she had known it last night when the men-at-arms came to drag her from Gervais. But she would open it herself. This certainty gave her a feeling that was nearly happiness. And Gervais loved her. A thrill shot through her, arrowy, fire-golden. She had pillowed his head, she had held him between her arms—her man! But never again. Never! Her eyes filled in an instant with tears, brimmed, and two crawled slowly down her face. Death——

She got up. The ashen light had strengthened a little. The cobwebs, heavy with dust, that mantled the rafters were plain to see. It had not entered Sidonia's mind to make an ending here, in the place that was her home. Unconsciously she was quite determined that even the cold flesh and bone of her should not be at the mercy of her enemies' eyes and hands. She would disappear, as though the earth beneath her feet had opened and she had been drawn into mystery. There was a sort of victory in this. But what of her mother? When the witch-hunters came—as they must, and soon—the big, helpless woman, abject as a rabbit in the face of fear, would be a flaccid prey. And then the stake, and the fired faggots—— No! They should not! The beasts! The devils! Her mother was far less to Sidonia than her tawny cat, but she was pitiful—she had always the instinct to defend, to rescue. She could not leave Lame Lisa to the mercy of men.

Her thought roved, yet always returned to the same place, for there was only the one door. She was quite calm; she had gone far beyond all ordinary sources of horror, and saw things stark—as stark as the circumstance that was arrayed against her. She looked at her hands, and wondered how much strength there was in them. It should not be difficult to smother a person in their sleep. And if they did not wake there would be no suffering at all, nor any fear. Moving carefully she approached the dim, mounded shape that was bedded upon rags. Then it was that her eyes discovered Gib, the black cat, whose fur showed never a hair of white. He squatted on the floor, drawn closely together, with protruding, furry elbows, and his pale-green eyes were fixed as though he were keeping sinister guard upon a rat-hole. Sidonia, in her linen shift, stood beside the patchwork quilt that covered her mother. She was about to do the thing that must be done if men's justice was to be evaded. She bent down, and with extreme caution drew the quilt a little back.

Her mother's long, waxen face looked up at her—yes, looked, for the bluish eyelids only partially masked the strangely stagnant eyes. And the jaw had dropped, leaving a slightly opened mouth. The fungus-pale skin was unlined, as though the wrinkles had been pressed out. The face had the vacant but pathetically tranquil look of that of a sickly sleeping child.

Sidonia gazed earnestly for a number of moments before she understood. Then she slowly straightened herself, and a feeling of relief that was profound and astonished dawned in her. Some mercy, after all, dwelt in the structure of things. Lame Lisa had died in sleep, gently as a babe might, and one arduousness, at least, was smoothed from her daughter's darkening path. She pulled the patchwork coverlet forward so that the dead face was quite hidden. Everything had become simpler. She felt lightened. Gib still kept his vigil, staring unwinkingly. One would have thought that he was waiting to pounce upon the soul when it should venture, mouse-like, into the open. But Lame Lisa's self was probably fluttering at that moment in the free air, like a silly, dazed little bird whose cage door has been left unlatched.

The grey half-light proclaimed a heavy dawn already well established. Sidonia was combing out her hair and plaiting it. Then she slipped her feet into her wooden shoes, reclasped the velvet cloak about her throat, and shrouded all in a length of poor black stuff, that enwrapped her, hooding her head. She was ready.

The subdued, querying yowl of a cat whose mind and soul is troubled came from the brooding gloam beyond the hearth. Tib, who had been abroad all night, had returned to the loft by some grovelling entrance-hole known only to himself. Out of the shad-

ows he came, slinking with low-hung body, staring phosphores-
cent-eyed, uttering his questioning yowl.

"Tib!" said the girl in a voice that had no more substance than a
ghost has.

He lifted his square, scarred head towards her, his whiskers
cobwebby, and yowled again.

She could not leave him. Gib was self-sufficient; in some subtle
way contemptuous of all things. He had no heart; he seemed to
know far too much and to be cynical about it. On him she could turn
her back without a qualm. But Tib was her foster-child, and he
understood what had taken place—what was about to take place—
and he was unhappy.

She stooped and lifted him. He was heavy, and smelt rank. She
tucked him, babe-fashion, into a fold of her black shroud, holding
him on her left arm. He struggled.

"Tib must be a good boy! Be still!"

He obeyed her. They were in sympathy, like mother and child.
From a kitten, hardly bigger than a rat, he had been under her hands.
In his own way he knew as much as Gib did. His passive weight
dragged at her arm, and she appeared to be cradling an infant of two
months old. She looked once towards what had been her mother—a
look of relief. The black cat watched by it, saturnine, preoccupied
with some concentration that must remain nameless to others.

To raise the trap-door and descend the ladder. shod and burdened as she was, was a matter of difficulty. Only the tethered
horses observed her. The yard was empty. A soft, dull greyness was
uniform overhead. The air was raw, and moisture was out on everything like the cold sweat upon the limbs of a person prostrate with
wasting sickness. Sidonia's wooden shoes made clumsy sounds
upon the cobbles—clat-clat! clat-clat! She went as quickly as she
could, hurrying to find that which otherwise would surely overtake
her in her own despite.

In the Street of the Martyrs hooded women, young and old, went
plodding with subdued intentness to attend Mass for the dead, for it
was All Souls' Day. Sidonia, also in the cowled black of mourning,
was an unnoticed figure—some widowed young creature, babe on
arm. No candle would flicker before any saint in effigy or upon any
altar for her dead. To whom should she pray—the witch's daughter,
the Satan-sealed? Already was she herself almost a sharer in that
impenetrable mystery before whose veil the altar-candles guttered
like sickly yellow flowers. Presently a rain of women's tears would
fall to assuage the fires of Purgatory in which husband, lover, or son

shuddered and scorched. But the fire that burnt before the inner sight of the witch's daughter was upon the nearer side of the death-veil. What flames of penance or of damnation should she fear for whom the actual pitch-soaked faggots were, perhaps, already piled in the market place? So the Christian women plodded towards the anxious Masses of All Souls' Day, and Sidonia, carrying her cat, towards the city gate.

At the arched portal of the town there was some congestion, for countryfolk with their little laden asses were coming in. The great wooden doors, iron-studded, that were closed in time of danger, were set fully open, as usual. The men on guard chaffed with the peasants or genially insulted them. An ass brayed.

Sidonia found herself halted, if only for a matter of minutes. Others were in the same case. At her side two women were talking, one high-stomached, wide-faced, with light hair and tired, acqui-escent eyes, the other sharp and dark.

"They'll burn her if they can find her," said the dark one.

"Yes, they'll burn her."

"But they should torture her first! They cut off the breasts of a gipsy-witch in the forest last year, and nipped her with hot pincers."

"Yes, they did."

"Sending the Young Lord stark mad and then vanishing like a breath on a mirror! She ought to be roasted in a cage over a slow fire with a dozen cats!"

"Yes."

Tib, swaddled, hidden from sight and sustained by the frail arm of his bearer, struggled again.

"Be still!" said the girl, in a whisper that was urgent and savage. Her heart seemed to shake her body, but her feeling was of tension, not of fear. "Sending the Young Lord stark mad." Oh, her darling, her darling! But her death should restore him, for then the chain would be broken. A numbness came on her again—the merciful deadening whenever her thought turned to him that had held her since her slow tears of the dawn. The two gossips were no longer at her side. The arch of the gateway, like a dark mouth, waited. Others were passing under it, and now she herself. The downward-pointing spikes of the raised portcullis were like a row of triangular fangs above her head.

"Hey, sister! Are you on your way to find the young one's fa-ther?" said a guardsman.

"She won't! I'll bet he's had his fun and skipped," said another.

The girl bent her covered head a trifle lower, hugging the heavy tom-cat.

Soft, puddled, hoof-chopped ground underfoot. Vacant air. Blurred vistas. Crows descending upon a great rubbish-heap where lay the body of a dead goat. The town, like a strait, high-walled prison of obscene tortures, was behind; before was liberty—to find a self-chosen death.

Sidonia kept straight on, skirting the rubbish-heap, whose stench was subdued by the motionless, moist air. Beneath the low, grey sky one would have said that no wind would ever again unfurl its wings. Fine veils of ashen vapour with a bluish tinge dimmed every distance, and the boundary of every distance was the forest.

Folk moved sparsely upon the self-made, rutted road. The small black figure of the girl turned aside, going over waste land towards a tract of trees—the nearest forest-fringe.

Sidonia stood still. She looked slowly all about her. She breathed the dead-leaf smell, which is like stale incense. A leaf, yellow as gold, fell flickering without a sound. Neither doors nor raftered roof had this vague, beautiful, heartless home, that was aloof yet without hostility. It was sad, serene; giving out, like a perfume, the stagnant odour of mortality. The cat, as she bent to set him down, sprang convulsively from her arms. He gave a little yowl, and with flattened ears ran straight into the coverts, vanishing as though the earth had indeed swallowed him. He was freed from the menace of pelted stones, from the curses and shudderings of the citizens who named him "witch's familiar," and from the agonies of the bonfire into which, as the Devil's beast, he might be tossed to cap some general rejoicing.

Now the girl was as completely alone as a person should be who has come to the end of life. She stripped the black shroud from herself, and was revealed in the mantle of azure and argent. She withdrew her feet from the wooden shoes, for they hampered her, and the grass and sodden leaves were grateful. This unbreathing, lovely solitude, peopled with the stems of trees and dreaming of death, drew her into its dream. Sharp-cut thoughts were blunted. One was lonely, yet hemmed in—surrounded. None spoke, yet the quiet was a thing to be listened to. A weight like an unsubstantial hand pressed down upon one's heart, closing the wounds that had oozed blood.

"Death, death," softly repeated Sidonia's thought and she knew where death waited. She moved, treading the sound-muffling leaf-drifts with small, cold, naked feet. The wiry bracken brushed her.

Fallen trunks, as she penetrated deeper, lay athwart her path, coated with green-black moss, but she skirted them, for there was no need for haste now. Two days before she had adventured in just such a golden dimness, seeking for love. And a faint, horrid scream had tingled to her ears. Silence now. No! Hush! Listen! A wraith of string music, elusive as a wisp of vapour, drifted through the mist of trees—a lovers' air, lilting, whining. Somewhere a fiddler, having set his back towards the town, followed a faint path through the wild, turning as he went the wheel-like wooden bow that chafed the strings of his vielle. The love-search had found a voice of pain, but the death-search a wandering tune.

Sidonia had paused, listening for quite a while—indeed, until there was nothing but the in-pressing silence. Slowly she went on again, the passage of her feet muffled utterly. Her thought, held in a stillness like that of the spellbound wild-wood, was neither happy nor unhappy.

Three or four charcoal burners, unkempt as bears, their brows shaded by monkish hoods, caught a hint of blue and silver through the thinning veils of gold. They stood at gaze, staring as rough, bovine animals might. The dog that was with them did not bark; it also looked. The figure of blue and silver, half a glade away, came into clearer view. A pale profile, steadfast and unearthly wan, was vaguely seen. There were no small sounds, as of a moving creature. The figure passed on into the closer places of the trees, and was as a wisp of smoke that is, and then is not.

"What woman was that?" said one.

"She was a fairy."

"Perhaps she was a saint, or the wife of God."

"There are no such folk in the forest. It was a fairy that passed."

An increasing gloom encompassed Sidonia. Evergreens multiplied; the underfoot became harsher; and there were outcroppings of lichenous rock. The slope of the ground was downward, and she followed it, knowing what she should find. She had eaten nothing since the previous evening, and had suffered love, desperation, despair, and the deadening calm that lies beyond these things. Now she began to be aware of company. Little men, active as ants, scurried without noise among the stones and the writhed tree-roots. They wore russet-red, and had white beards and pointed ears. There were stirrings and movements in the evergreens—a sense of nameless life.

"Live! Live!" said an eager, throaty whisper at the girl's ear. "Seize love. You have it! Enjoy it to the utmost, and I will enjoy it with you. Why do you starve yourself and me? Remember his breast on yours, and the sweet stifling of your heart. Are you going to forgo that weight of happiness for ever? Return to him; he is yours to use as you will. Sister, sister."

She knew that this was the passionate and love-abused young woman who had committed suicide, and a wave of sympathetic feeling swept over her. It was honeyed, muscle-relaxing, imperative. As one who has been earnestly spoken to pauses to consider the matter, her feet were stayed, and she stood still upon a little slope of rock, the dying fern close about her, the green-black of the evergreens walling her in, and one silver-birch sapling like a motionless fountain-spray of scattered gold. Love! Passion! The half-formed, glowing thoughts that swam up into her mind were like a feast of luxuries outspread before famine, and she was aware of her own starvation of the heart and of the senses. She shivered. The dark tree-masses, like enclosing cavern walls, the fern, the rusty briars, the moist, low-hung, sunless, windless sky—it was a shaggy solitude, damp-smelling, strewn with thorns and the blunt teeth of stones; yet for the girl it crept and stirred and whispered with life. Shadowy figures of women ventured forward, were half met by hairy, goat-legged men, who skipped and pranced silently, retreated, were pursued, and the shrubs shook with amorous rustlings. Everywhere, like a vague tremor, there seemed to be the movement of love.

"Live! Live! Take him into your arms, and bind him to you as with fetters. I starve if you starve. Sister, sister——"

Sidonia covered her face with her hands and dropped to her knees upon the shelving rock. She crouched lower, until she was bent upon herself, like a creature in an ecstasy of grief.

"I want him! I want him! I love him!" her heart wailed, and all the blood in her body clamoured with a desperate incoherence, as women babble upon the rack—clamoured to live, to love.

"I will go back! I want him! I want love!"

She could go back. They would not burn her if she found her way to him first, and the arm of the Young Lord's protection was thrown about her as his priest-wedded wife. He would wed her—a witch—because he had been bespelled by a philtre, and spoken charms, and the power of the Master, whose promised paramour she was. No! No! The price was too high—his soul, and all the pride that had carried her through her life and was the very energy that nerved her love. Yet her spirit grovelled in the agony of its choice, for to die was to leave him.

Everything remained unchanged—the leaden air, the windless evergreens, the unflickering sprays of yellow leaves. Little whimpering sounds came from the girl who lay now upon her face. They might have been uttered by a beaten puppy, yet they were horribly poignant. After some time had passed she lifted herself. She was haggard, with the ghastly wanness of the olive-skinned, her eyes were heavy with the salt of tears, and the pupils of them dilated, as though she had taken the witch's drug, belladonna. She looked around her like a person menaced—beleaguered, and then went on down the slope, hastily, tripping sometimes, putting out her hands to help herself. She must find death—oh, quickly! They were like a cloud about her—the things that whispered, urged, and displayed blatant, passionate enticements. Faces leaned towards her with swimming eyes; genial composite creatures, half voluptuous, half grotesque, dragged themselves parallel with the way of her feet. Exquisite male bodies, but with legs that terminated in cleft hoofs, advanced towards her. With a sort of terror she discovered that they had the eyes and features of Gervais, but they vanished before they were actually within hand-reach. Gervais! Gervais! Oh, for his sake she must find death quickly! She hurried like one whose life is threatened, blundering, bruising her feet. Her heart hammered. The slope was rougher, steeper. The trees and shrubs stood back. At the foot of the short descent an oval pool, black and thick-looking as pitch, lay in a ring of reeds. It was supposed to be bottomless, and the whole locality haunted by evil spirits. Many suicides had leapt into its opaqueness to await the Day of Judgment in the unknown depth. No God-fearing Christian willingly approached this place.

The girl, whose long hair had come unplaited and hung about her eyes, descended the slope like a fugitive. Trembling in all her muscles, she reached the margin of the pool and a great, flat-topped stone that overhung it. Here she stood, catching her breath again, mechanically putting back her hair. Looking down upon the water, whose surface was motionless as a sheet of onyx, it appeared of a brownish black. In some places a thick, grass-green scum lay far out upon the face of the pool. Sidonia knew that the water would be deathly cold. She wondered how far she would sink down through it —slowly, slowly, unable evermore to breathe. And then what? Nothing presented itself to her mind save that she was quitting Gervais for ever—because she loved him.

"He will be fettered by the arms of his step-mother," said a voice at her ear.

"No!" she ejaculated, speaking aloud, and a faint echo of her own voice came back to her. He would not! The woman was his senior by a decade of years, and the love-charms she had purchased had been put to another use. Oh, they were trying to hold her back from death—all of them! But she had only to take a couple of short steps and she would die—for his sake. One of these steps she took. She was at the verge of the slab of stone that overhung the unplumbed pool shelf-wise. Shapes rose like steam out of the water, upon whose dark surface there was no faintest spreading ripple-ring. They turned their dead yet living eyes upon Sidonia, and seemed without utterance to forbid her. Hands touched and caressed her, and something like an ingratiating animal rubbed itself back and forth against her ankles. There was a loud crashing on the broken slope behind her, and the stone on which she stood seemed to vibrate. She pictured a troop of the lusty, hoofed men who had the eyes and features of Gervais plunging down towards her to drag her back into the passion of life, terrifying in its delight. But she would leap from the stone before they could reach her!

"Sidonia! Sidonia!"

They were calling to her with the voice of Gervais. She must leap quickly. Oh, the dead things that rose like an emanation from the water! Her cold fingers were knotted together, and her knees trembled. She was unable to force her muscles to obey her, and there was a sensation of nausea.

"Sidonia!"

How close they were! There was a thunderous noise behind her. She must leap now! She tried to gather herself for it, swaying as if about to faint, though she did not know it. And at that moment something like the impact of a thunderbolt occurred. She was caught from her feet—snatched up as by the arm of a violent giant. There was tempestuous movement—the slipping ring of a reined-back horse's sliding, iron-shod hoofs.

She was in the cruel grip of Gervais, the Young Lord, whose dark-brown stallion, lathered and half mad, pawed backward from the deadly foothold of the flat-topped stone.

3

THE CRAZED HORSE slithered, found soft foothold again, reared heavily, and finally was pulled to a standstill, sweating and shuddering. The girl, who had clung with blind, animal instinct to the rider, relaxed suddenly and burst into tears.

"Oh! Oh!" she sobbed. Life can sometimes be as shattering a thing as death.

"You were going to jump into that accursed water! Why would you rob me of happiness? Why did you leave me? My God! Am I utterly hateful, Sidonia?"

Gervais was bareheaded, pale, and wild-looking as a boy just roused from a nightmare. He was habited as he had been the night before, his sword belted about him. His whole appearance, and that of his horse, suggested a bearer of desperate news breaking at a gallop from some city of disaster.

Sidonia did not answer. Twisting a little in his arms, she turned fully to him, clasping him convulsively about the neck and pressing her face against his breast.

"Why did you go from me last night? They could not have harmed you. They dare not I searched for you until daybreak. Then I took this horse and scoured the town. No one knew anything; they were as stupid as sheep! So I rode out into the forest, for it was there that I first saw you. I prayed to God, and to the Three Martyrs, and immediately afterward I spoke with some charcoal burners, who told me they had seen a fairy woman. And so I found you. Why did you leave me, Sidonia?"

The last question was put with a passion that must and would be answered.

"Because I love you."

"It cannot be so! You were about to find death. Death's arms are dearer to you than mine!"

Oh! he must not believe that she did not love him! It was monstrous; it seemed to shake the very foundations of reality! She lifted her face from his breast, and her colourless lips sought his with the eagerness of a little hungry animal. Mouth joined with mouth.

"My saint!" said Gervais thickly.

The horse moved under them, lowering its head towards the coarse grass that here grew reed-mixed. Drawing the reins taut, Gervais disengaged himself, sprang to the ground, and then lifted the drooping girl from the saddle. He let the reins go slack again on the horse's neck, abandoning them, and himself climbed a short way up the slope, burdened as he was, to where a hollow bank made a semi-cave above a drift of leaves.

Sidonia, lying like a wounded thing upon dead leaves that were yellow and russet, clung to the young man who lay beside her. He was the god to whom she should render no worship of the body; the child to whom she must refuse her breast. Life—not death—had overtaken her, and life was far more to be feared, because it was so deadly sweet.

"My saint! My saint!" said Gervais, and he leaned over her, his eyes looking down into hers with a sort of tension that was dumb yet articulate. He seemed to hold himself back, as one fears to touch suddenly, or to oppress in any way, a person just returning from faintness.

"I am no saint!" said Sidonia, speaking with a miserable vehemence.

"Whatever you are, I worship you."

She put her hands up then, and they touched his hair. She must speak now; death would have been easier.

"Gervais—I am the daughter of a witch—and they call me a witch also."

A silence—but scarcely more than moment-long.

"No matter where you came from—no matter what name they give you—you are holy, and wonderful, and—and most dear, Sidonia. To-day a priest shall marry us."

"No! No! We must not marry You would lose your soul. You do not understand!"

"How should I lose my soul if I mix it with yours? Your soul is pure as God's Mother!"

They lay still at that, and Sidonia's body seemed to dissolve into air, leaving only her real self, whose beating pulse was love. Then, as the bodily senses became actual again, she was aware of the leaves beneath her, of the dull grey light that lay upon her eyes, of the ivy-fringe that dripped from the penthouse of the sheltering hollow bank above. Her whole nature fused and melted towards her man, glowing and malleable. Yet she must not—she dare not—

yield. Balanced between agony and rapture, she did not know whether she was in heaven or in hell.

"Do you love me, Sidonia?"

"Yes—yes! I would die for you!"

"Then give me your love."

"I have given it. My body I must not give you, for it would bring you damnation."

"Sidonia!" He spoke her name as if she had uttered a blasphemy.

They were silent for a little while, each conscious of the beating heart of the other.

"Even if there were truth in what you say—even if your love should condemn my soul to eternal torment—I would still grasp it! You are more to me than my salvation."

A throb—half of triumph, half of a sort of horror—struck through the girl. It seemed to her that the weight upon her was no longer love, but fate. She was stilled. Her real self caught back its breath, and then began to breathe steadily and deeply like a person in a trance. The fever-fire of passion died along her nerves, and she spoke softly.

"I must not wrong you. I think I am a witch; I have power sometimes. I do not call it; it comes to me. To-night I am bound by a promise to meet the Master, and others. I think the Master is Satan. Do you still love me, Gervais?"

But at the very centre of herself she knew what his answer would be.

"I love you, now and for ever!" (Oh, he was so boyish, even when he was most the man!) "You are my saint, though you may have passed through the midst of devils! No matter what chains may bind you, I'll break them, Sidonia. All hell is not strong enough to hold you from me! By God! I'll go with you to the Devil's meeting-place tonight, and—and free you, if I have to strangle Satan with my own hands!"

The girl's arms tightened convulsively about him.

"No. There is danger! You shall not lose Heaven for me!"

"You are my Heaven," said the young man.

At that Sidonia's eyes closed quickly, and then opened, tear-suffused, and her throat was constricted by a desire to sob. He would go with her; he would dare hell; she could not prevent it. And the tiny, poignant flicker of hope was painful as a stab. Her breast was shaken, and she began uncontrollably to weep. Then the burden of love—the burden of fate—lightened, and Gervais drew apart, and lifted himself, and drew the girl up also, so that her head, with its leaf-mixed tresses, was against his shoulder. And they stayed so, looking out from the shallow half-cave into the still, grey air.

"When I have delivered you from the power of Satan I will marry you in the Church of St. Saviour," said Gervais. He made the statement quite simply. In the clarity and singleness of his faith, if in nothing else, he was the knight-errant of the wandering ballad-singer's tales.

"No, Gervais, no. Your God hates me. You—you should have let me jump into the deep water."

But her tearful voice had no conviction in it.

"Sidonia, you shall not speak like that. Stretch out your arm, my saint."

She did so—a thin arm that quivered. He had drawn his dagger —the brief steel with which a knight administered the *coup de grâce* to a fallen foe. He pricked his own left wrist smartly, and then barely grazed the skin of hers. The girl winced, for she was unstrung. Gervais allowed the thick drops of his blood to fall where her blood thinly started from the graze, and her outstretched, quivering wrist was laced with red.

"We are betrothed. I have mixed my life with yours. Nothing can separate us now."

Then the girl understood the significance of what he had done. Her heart paused. She felt fear and joy. This was a solemn, an irrevocable rite of lovers. Under a mutual impulse they enclasped and kissed each other—slowly, sacredly, like bride and bridegroom. Such a rite was as binding as a marriage; each felt already wedded to the other.

Sidonia did not speak; she had no words. Her life was no longer a thing apart, like a strange, enchanted tree, where no bird alights. They huddled in the shallow half-cave, finding infinite, magical, unimagined blisses in the mere nearness that was mute, and keyed to a kind of tension.

Beneath them the great dark pool slept, keeping its secrets till the Day of Judgment. Not a reed was stirred; not a leaf fell. The evergreens were motionless as masses of malachite. The black-brown horse fed with a slight cropping sound, its broad red leather bridle and red saddle embossed with gold, eye-snaring as a patch of blood on strewn rushes.

After a longish while they began to speak to each other. Sidonia made little statements about herself, her dead mother, her cat, her lonely thoughts concerning this and that subject. But she did not say that she had at first mistaken him for an angel; she felt ashamed.

And she said nothing whatever of Sabine. That knowledge was like a poisonous toad that should be buried under a large stone—a stone that it could never lift. Gervais spoke of himself—brief, desultory things. They were like the confidences of a schoolboy. But to Sidonia they might have been the utterances of God Himself. She had never before mingled herself in this manner with another human being, and, like a fly that has slipped suddenly into honey, the sweetness submerged her until her soul was breathless.

They took no account of time. For all practical purposes they might have been in eternity, which is timeless. The motionless grey air was unchanged; the horse grazed. They were betrothed; they were no longer two, but one. Yet Satan must be overcome, and the marriage-words of the priest spoken in the Church of St. Saviour before each found full joy in the other. Sidonia realised this. Yes, Satan, her Master, must be overcome.

At some time after the sunless noon had come and gone unmarked, a half-grown child of forest nomad folk—a girl clad only in a tattered petticoat, with wild hair and her little bare, pointed buds of breasts as brown as a leaf—came straying down into the hollow, silent-footed as a fawn, and without fear. Her people were pagan, kin to the spirits and devils of the wild, so Christians said. She was carrying food, and bit at an apple as she came. Sidonia and young Gervais remembered that they were hungry. The forest-girl looked at them with serious, inscrutable eyes; she was grave, unamazed, remote. When Gervais offered her a gold coin she clasped her hand upon it without any change of expression, and gave in return black bread, goats' cheese, and apples. Still like a small, wild animal, she disappeared as silently and leisurely as she had come.

The Young Lord and the witch's daughter, sitting close in the coarse grass and laughing a little with each other, knee touching knee and shoulder leaning to shoulder, shared the cheese, the bread, and the apples. Both had never before been so happy—nor even imagined such happiness. They might have been in Paradise; their souls seemed to them golden, and each was more than a miracle to the other. After they had eaten, Gervais stretched his fine length, and pillowed his head upon Sidonia's knees. Her face assumed the look of the Madonna—rapt, brooding, soft with a divine anxiety. And time passed like grey water that does not appear to flow.

The heaviness of the air darkened imperceptibly. It seemed to thicken. One shuddered suddenly without knowing why. The horse, that for some time had ceased to graze, blew a tremulous, snorting breath through its nostrils, as though it sensed the presence of wolves.

"The night is coming," said Gervais, and he rose to his feet, drawing the witch's daughter with him. They were dazed, and could scarcely have said for how long or how short a time they had been in this place. A certain starkness of reality was returning to them. Gervais remembered the Devil, whom he must presently encounter, and the arm that he had put about the girl stiffened. They stood breast to breast, and Sidonia, on an impulse, slid both her arms about his neck and locked them there, straining up towards him, for he was much taller than she.

"Leave me!" she said breathlessly. "Let me die as I meant to! You shall not fight with the Master for me! You shall not wed me. I love you too much!"

Passion shook her, physically pressing her to him, spiritually striving to rend her from him.

"We are one; our blood has already mixed. Nothing shall separate us!"

They held to each other in silence. Sidonia began to tremble convulsively. Reaction was upon her. Her man could have taken her and broken her in pieces if he would. But Satan must first be overcome.

The clinging moment of danger passed. The girl was lifted to the saddle, upon which she sat sideways, holding to the pommel and the mane, and Gervais took the bridle leading the horse.

"Where?" he said, looking up at her in the twilight. He had not asked before.

"The crypt of the Church of St. Saviour. I—I have been told how to enter it."

It was like death to confess these things. The knowledge that she had—even though it was half against her will—desired the Master was fiery torment to Sidonia now. The torturer's heated pincers could hardly have inflicted a greater hurt to her body than her own thoughts did to her soul.

The ascent of the slope was precarious, the dark stallion scrambling heavily. Sidonia was forced to change her position, and sat astride, her bare feet in the looped stirrup leathers, for she could not reach the stirrups. But when the slope was topped, and some stony and broken ground traversed, they came on a faint forest path that the man, the girl, and the horse each knew instinctively led back to the open land that was before the town. Here Gervais himself vaulted into the saddle, and the horse, doubly burdened, took its way slowly through the fog-like dusk, that was made still blinder by the innumerable yellowing leaves, and that smelt of incense, and death, and a chilling damp.

Neither of the two that the hairy-fetlocked stallion bore forward spoke. The heaviness of fate pressed down on them like the weight of the featureless night that dropped ever lower and lower towards the earth. Sidonia was quiescent. There was nothing to be done save that which she was passively about to do; nothing could be altered. She leaned back against the breast of love with half-closed eyes. Their muffled progress was like a drifting passage through some limbo.

When the forest yielded to treeless land the whole world was blind and dark. Only the jumping flames of a fire-basket set on the battlements sixty feet above the town's one gate pulsed like an auburn star. As the stallion, bearing man and girl, trod slowly through the short tunnel-opening above which the toothed portcullis hung, the light of torches fell across their faces and the men-at-arms stared as though at an apparition. All knew that the Young Lord had ridden like a madman from the town that morning because the witch-maiden—the vampire—had vanished, taking with her his wits and his peace of mind. They were awestruck, aware of more gooseflesh than the chill of the night was responsible for standing out upon their skins. A dreadful happening was taking place, here, in the very stronghold of the Holy Count.

Hollowly the stallion's hoofs rang on the uneven street stones. All was dark, save for the yellow will-o'-the-wisp glimmer of a carried lantern, where some law-abiding person hastened home. The empty market was a lighter darkness, and above it the great, two-towered church rose like a sombre cliff. Gervais halted the horse where the market cross upreared itself dimly. He dismounted, laid his strong, careful hands upon the girl, and lifted her to the ground.

"Show me the way," he said. It was the first time he had spoken for a very long while.

Sidonia's hand had caught his instinctively. His was warm, hers cold.

"No," she said in a half whisper. "Leave me. I love you——"

His fingers tightened upon hers. "Our blood has mingled. You are my wife."

She moved a hesitant step towards the looming bulk of the church, and he moved with her. It had to be.

4

DARKER THAN THE blind night, the cathedral, massive as a stronghold, upreared its two-towered front. Its innumerable petrified
devils were hidden by the darkness and its rows of saints. None
could see how a stone Eve tempted a stone Adam above its principal door, or how, set above these two, the Son of God stretched
forward his out-turned palms, a stony crown upon His brows. The
carved fleurs-de-lys of the pinnacles, the mutely barking gargoyles,
the niched angels, all were blotted out. One of the tall doors of the
double portal, beautifully, though now invisibly, overlaid with foliage of hammered iron, was ajar. Its mercy-knocker—a ring of iron
held in the mouth of a jutting lion's head—was within easy hand-
reach of a man of ordinary height. Time and again, a fugitive, with
the stripped swords of vengeance-seekers close upon him, had
grasped that ring, and felt his slackened knees give under him,
knowing that on the very edge of death he had found the sure protection of the Church.

Where the high door stood slightly open the faintest rumour of
buried light was whispered out into the dark. Going carefully and
softly, one passed, by the grace of a narrow favour, from the night
without into the night within.

"Where is the Chapel of the Resurrection?" asked Sidonia in a
whisper. She had paused. The intangible yet real weight of awe that
had fallen so heavily upon her on the previous morning during High
Mass lay again, yoke-wise, across the shoulders of her soul. The
darkness was that of a close wood of giant, immemorial tree-trunks,
or of a sunless cavern of pillared stalactites, unimaginably lofty. But
at the far end of the vista a red spark glowed—the undying lamp of
the sanctuary that advertised the presence of God—and nearer, but
to one side, a galaxy of candle-stars, soft and butter-yellow, revealed the coffin-shaped shrine of the town's saint, its sheeted
glass, its enamelled goldwork. There were hints of unseen movement—the shuffle of a foot, the lisping drag of garments. But they
were furtive as night sounds in a forest. The silence of the place was
solid as its stones.

The young man did not speak. They went forward about twenty paces. The red spark was immediately before them, but so far removed. Gervais knelt, and the girl with him. She was expectant of sudden and terrible happenings. Oh, surely his God would protect him! She tried to turn her thought to this God, but her mind was benumbed. It was impossible to think of herself save as an outcast —hell's daughter by adoption—yet Gervais was about to free her from the Master, and draw her, as by main force, within the pale of the christened. She fixed her eyes on the distant ruby spark, knowing nothing of its significance. It was like a very small flower of fire. The stones were cold under her knees. She knew that Gervais was praying.

Before the miracle-working shrine that was illuminated by many candles the Countess Sabine knelt on a velvet cushion. Her joined hands were pressed palm to palm, and her lips moved. Her forget-me-not eyes, with their light auburn lashes, were fixed on the sharp, dry profile of the divinely mummified saint.

"Send him back to me!" prayed Sabine. "Grant that he may not find the witch—that he may never find her! Give me his love! I will distribute silver to the poor. I promise a wreath of pearls to crown your coffin. Bring him back to me to-morrow! Preserve his soul from the witch!"

She was more in earnest than she had ever been in her life. She would have pledged any jewel—anything that might possibly please him—to the enshrined saint if he would become active on her behalf. Her whole nature was merged into her petition, which she repeated over and over again. And at the back of her mind the thought of another witch—some old and ugly woman—simmered like water that is about to boil. She had heard tell of an infallible charm—a cake containing certain loathsome yet intimate ingredients baked by the witch-wife upon a board laid on the naked loins of the would-be lover, and then sent to the beloved. If he tasted it, his passionate subjugation was certain. She would not fear the blistering heat as the little fire of charcoal ate downward through the wood.

"Preserve his soul! Give me his love!" she prayed, her eyes fixed with child-like earnestness upon the coffin-shrine.

Far down the solemn cavern of the church, near the grave portal, whose height suggested entering archangels rather than men, the Chapel of the Resurrection showed vaguely, like a grotto of gloom. Sidonia, hand-linked with Gervais, approached it. The girl had something of a cat's faculty of sight in the dark; she knew that there should be a doorway here, to the right-hand side. Ah! A low-statured blackness upon blackness, arched and rounded. It was she who led Gervais now. Blindly, gripping each other's fingers, they began to descend a straightened flight of steps.

It was slow work. Gervais kept one hand against the wall, and his stern grip of her checked even the careful rate of the girl's faltering descent. With an intake of the breath Sidonia paused. Her outstretched, nervous finger-tips had encountered a barrier.

"What is it?" asked Gervais in a whisper.

"A door. It will be opened if I knock in a certain way."

She was aware that he felt for his sword, and loosened it. They stood close, side by side, on a step of the blind stair. What was behind this unseen door? All hell, perhaps. So Gervais thought. He had spiritually braced himself; he was ready. But who could say what the outcome would be, though he was a christened knight with Heaven on his side? His arm pressed the girl quickly to him. They clove to each other there in the dark. Their embrace had a convulsive, nervous energy. Each was so terribly afraid of losing the other.

Two low knocks, and then a third—hesitant knuckles against solid wood. The girl's heart stood still; for the first time she was afraid of hell. The young man, with a fumbling quickness, unsheathed his sword.

For some eternal moments—nothing. Then, simultaneously, they both knew that the door had opened. A pulse of indirect light, very feeble, beat unsteadily in the murkiness ahead. It was of the colour of fire. Sidonia caught Gervais' free hand again, and it was she who moved first. The steps had ended; the stone-flagged underfoot was level. So much was certain; the rest was an impenetrable and crushing shadow, as of the nether world, revealed but not illumined by the hidden fire-pulse. A swarm of enigmatic creatures might move beneath the cloak of this shadow, or it might be void as a tomb. There was nothing to prove or disprove it either way. Gervais visioned crawling skeletons, toad-bodied incubi, composite things with the heads of wild boars. Sidonia's mind was empty of all such; it held only the figure of the Master—a shape of strong dread and horrid fascination. There was a thick, cold vault-smell, and a sense of walls.

The vague shadows of a pair of squat, heavy, branching pillars were thrown uncertainly backward by the light of a brace of torches thrust into iron wall-sockets, one upon either side of the main vault of the crypt. At the dim threshold of this vault, where the tunnel-passage they had followed entered it at right angles, the two paused.

The passage wall still screened them from the partly-shattered darkness of the vault. A soft, whispering sound of steps came from the hollow gloom behind —the gloom from which they had come. Instantly Sidonia drew aside until she was pressed right against the wall, drawing Gervais with her. They stayed so, silent, still holding each other's hands.

A smallish figure, muffled, hooded like a monk, passed within a few steps of the witch's daughter and her man. And as it passed it gave a little husky cough—a purely human sound, and feminine. Then the eerie stillness, dead and crushing as the oppression of a tomb, was re-established, and nothing moved save the throbbing pulse of the two unseen flames.

"Gervais," said Sidonia, in the ghost of a whisper.

"Yes?"

"I will go where the light is—where the woman who passed us has gone. I will go alone. Yes! I must! I do not think—I do not think that the Master is with them yet, and if they see you they will know that you are the Young Lord, and they will all scatter, and the Master will not come. You must remain here till I call. Oh, Gervais, promise me!"

"You will call?"

"Yes! When—when the Master comes, Gervais. You will accomplish nothing if they see you now!"

It was reasonable, but he was reluctant. The girl had all a mother's desire to shield her man from who knew what unworthy sights. Love had opened wide the eyes of her spirit, and that which had seemed to her merely feverish was now unclean. She could not endure that Gervais should mix himself with such things for more than a moment.

"Come to me when I call!"

She drew her hand from his, laid the palm of it quickly against his breast, and whisked away from him where the shadow-ghosts of the two stunted pillars wavered.

The central vault of the crypt was low-browed, as though the weight of the soaring sun and moon-anointed stones above it had crushed it inward. Against its side walls was the debris of broken coffins, from which oozed ancient bones, and even a skull or two; the mortal remnant of a spear-shattering man or of a satin-trailing woman. Between the pair of pillars at the vault's upper end rose a low stone tomb, flat topped, and behind it, from pillar to pillar, a curtain had been stretched, black and shaggy, for it was of the hides of goats. Above the centre of this curtain, propped up in some manner from behind, was a great, hair-bearded wooden replica of a he-goat's head. The painted muzzle seemed to leer saturninely, and the painted white and red eyes to blink as the two firelights played athwart it. The head, the curtain, and the tomb had the appearance of a strange sanctuary—a strange altar. In utter silence, all facing the altar-tomb, the congregation knelt upon the stony floor of the vault; that was filmed with the dust of death. There were about twenty of them. '

Sidonia, after her first dozen steps, had paused. She was just behind the rearmost kneelers. She alone stood erect beneath the lowering roof that upheld the weight of the great church above. The silence was leaden, peculiar. There were none of the little noises that attend a Mass-gathering, save at the moment of the Elevation. Like a person from whom the power of the will has been abruptly withdrawn, Sidonia remained motionless, looking towards the goat's head, that seemed to wink its eyes at her.

Nothing happened. It was like the immobility of a dream in which all the muscles are strengthless, and one cannot even draw breath. She thought of Gervais, waiting out of sight behind the angle of the wall with his sword bared to slay the Devil. But there was no Devil.

The black, joined goat-skins behind the altar-tomb parted, and someone tall and sombre stepped through them—evidently from some concealed platform—and stood upon the tomb's square, flat top. It was a man, sable-habited from head to foot, cloaked, hooded, masked. The Master!

He spread out his arms in a gesture more rigid and commanding than that of a priest. There was a whisper of movement as all the kneelers bent forward. A little muscular shudder had passed over Sidonia at the moment when the goat-skins parted. All the skin of her body and every hair-fine nerve was aware of the Master. The gaze of her eyes could no more have turned itself from him than famine can look aside from food. She was terribly afraid.

Soundlessly the man in black leapt from the tomb to the vault's floor. Sidonia wanted to turn; she wanted to cry out, as she had promised Gervais. But she stood like a stock, and her throat was rigid. She could not save herself; she could not utter a sound. Fear, and the fascination of it, backed by an absolute and dreadful faith, had hypnotised her. She saw the homage rendered by the kneelers as one by one they approached the Master, still upon their knees. It was the traditional feudal worship paid to Satan by his neophytes—nameless, devoid of the last shred of shame. She continued to look,

though she craved to cover her eyes with her hands. But it was
beyond her power to lift them. The Master seemed to assume unhuman proportions. Antlers crowned him; his black garb was metallic; his hands resembled long eagle-talons; his cloak was the
darkness of half-opened bat-pinions. The confused, composite Satanic conceptions of the worshippers appeared as actual forms to the
fixed, half-clairvoyant gaze of the witch's daughter. And she was
aware of a swarm of other presences—in fact, the flickering vault of
the crypt was overcrowded. All had paid homage save she alone—
she, the only one who stood erect. And now the central figure was
turned squarely towards her, and stretched out his arm. She must
obey. He was the Master. Her soul was in his hands, like a little
bird. She moved, going towards him like a sleep-walker, on bare,
quiet feet. There was no help for her, either from Heaven or from
earth. Dully she was conscious of being clipped in the unbroken
circle of complete and shadowless despair.

Faces were lifted to her as she moved—strange faces, with some
unhuman, avid stamp upon them. Haggish women, de-sexed by
age; neurotic youths with the pulpy mouths of girls, epileptic,
kennel-bred; distorted men, discards from the human rubbish-heaps
of the lusty yet festering little forest city; young women wantonly
animal. As a person under torture sees a countenance through a
quivering mist, she recognised Violane, the goldsmith's girl. She
was within hand-reach of the Master now. She heard her name,
though she did not know whether he had spoken it aloud or not.
Wildly she desired to plead, to repudiate, to scream with what
strength she had. But she was impotent. The Master's long, nervous
hands came upon her with a peculiar suggestion of energy. In a
flash the splendid cloak of blue and silver was ripped from her,
leaving her in her shift. Then the linen, strongly clutched and
wrenched asunder, slid instantly downward from the narrow
shoulders, and in a moment lay in a pale fold about the girl's feet.
Like a sallow statue, boyish-loined, and with meagre lines, Sidonia
was revealed. Her arms hung straight at her sides. There was no
quick attempt to bend down upon herself or shield her bosom with
her palms. Her face was like a young, haggard death-mask, with
great, dreadful, fascinated eyes. When the Master lifted her,
catching her beneath the knees and shoulders, her head fell back as
though she had fainted, and the long black hair of her swept nearly
to the pavement.

Indeed, it appeared to Sidonia that she died at that moment. But
death brought no cessation of consciousness. It was as though the

living spirit were chained to a body that it could no longer control or defend—that might be the passive prey of beasts or worms.

Upon the flat top of the altar-tomb the girl was laid at full length. She resembled a corpse, though her eyes were open. The mineral coldness was like a bed of smooth fire beneath her; her spirit winced violently, but not her flesh. Lying so, unable to turn her head as she was unable to lift her hand, she could see nothing save the painted wooden goat-mask that out-thrust itself above her, played over by the broken firelight.

* * * * *

A space of time in which one might count a hundred, not counting too quickly, had surely elapsed since his Sidonia slipped from him, promising to call to him as soon as she was face to face with the Devil—so it seemed to Gervais. The tension of such waiting was intolerable. The void of silence was in itself a dreadful thing. He would have welcomed the hiss of serpents, the scrape of scales, hoarse croaks and leathery wing-rustles. One cannot thrust one's sword into the maw of nothingness. The only light being the doubtful reflection of some unseen, reddish flame, it was hardly more than a sinister twilight. The beating of the young man's heart imitated the hoofstrokes of a hurrying horse. He was aware of sweat that pricked out upon him. There must be an end to this! The fear that Sidonia—his woman—had melted again into the unseen world rowelled him like a spur. He signed himself hurriedly with the cross, invoked St. Michael, the conqueror of Lucifer, beneath his breath, and moved from the wall against which he had stood for a century of moments.

His hunter's tread was noiseless. At the side of the nearest pillar he paused, standing close to it. He saw, at the farther end of the vault, the goatskin curtain, the wooden goat's head, the altar-tomb, with a sable-cloaked and hooded figure standing before it. He saw the sparse circle of the kneeling congregation. He saw what appeared to be a woman's naked corpse laid out upon the altar-tomb. Where was Sidonia? Where was the Devil? He had expected—he hardly knew, what, but not this fantastic decorum, this semblance of sanctuary, priest and altar. He looked, holding himself perfectly still, his mind groping desperately and to no purpose.

The priest-figure turned to face the kneelers—a tall, masked man. But was he a man? Gervais felt the skin of his flesh wince and shiver. He desired to make the sign of the cross again, but thought it better to remain unstirring. The priest-figure spread out its arms, and all the kneelers abased themselves. Where was Sidonia? God in Heaven! where was Sidonia? Some black-furred thing—seemingly a cat, leg-trussed, and hooded to prevent it mewing—that had been laid upon the woman on the tomb was lifted solemnly towards the goat-head, while the kneelers bent until their foreheads touched the floor. Gervais grew rigid as his own sword. So terrible was the unuttered sacrilege that he half expected the thick-set pillars to tremble, and the low, vaulted roof to crack across.

"Ecce Agnus Dei——*"* They were the sonorous Latin words familiar to all Christians. Spoken deeply, they vibrated like the note of a jarred bell.

The soul of Gervais became cold, and then hot as fire. Only Satan would dare such a blasphemy. And he—he must defend the honour of God! He took a quick, forward step.

"God is dead!"

The loud, thrilling voice carried a savage and incommunicable triumph. It was like a blow. Immediately noise broke loose—screaming cackles of hysterical laughter; animal-like sounds; whoops; shouted words, senseless or obscene; sharp female shrieks, suggesting devil-possession. The emotional tension had snapped with the suddenness of an overstretched bowstring. With an epileptic instability the twenty or more devil-worshippers had lapsed from unnatural passivity to unnatural frenzy. A beldame with straggling, grey-shot hair beat the breast that she had exposed, shuffling her feet like a dancing bear. A full-bodied girl was casting her garments this way and that, as though they scorched her. One of the gnarled gutter-men—a hunchback—mauled another girl, who whimpered as a baby does, prostrate on the death-dusted floor. A youth spun round and round like a top, with extended arms, his glazed eyes ecstatic, his teeth bared. Some were imitating the antics of goats or dogs, and one woman, still upon her knees, threw herself from side to side, rolling her eyeballs dreadfully and frothing at the mouth. It was like a mad-house—a low vaulted dungeon for the violently insane. Delirium!

Gervais had halted. He was amazed, confused, as though a swarm of imps had flown into his face. It was the welter of a wallowing-stye, the capers of the moonstruck, an outrageous nightmare. Fiends had certainly entered into the bodies of these people —tormenting fiends, unhuman, scarcely even animal. Yet there was release, and an insensate joy.

Sword in hand, he looked beneath frowning brows to right and left, and then at the altar-tomb. It was tenantless. Satan had lifted the woman who had been herself the living altar. She was grappled to him starkly, but appeared boneless as a corpse that has not yet begun to stiffen. Her very long black hair fell like a ravelled veil. There was a strange, dreadful cry—such as might have come from the lips and throat of a dead creature galvanised from without—the cry of a trapped soul.

Sidonia! Blood of Christ! It was she—therein the arms of Satan! Gervais' mind and spirit and energy fused in one dark, blood-red flame. His woman—in the arms of hell!

His sword was up. He lunged forward like a crazy hound. But the Devil saw him—and doubtless feared the might of God that clothed his shoulders. He released the girl, who fell like a sack of rubbish, and sprang backward.

"Put out the torches!" The loud words echoed hollowly beneath the roof. They were peremptory, as a command of Lucifer should be.

Now came a mad scuffle, squeals, showering sparks, smoke— darkness. But before the darkness dropped smothering sight, the sword of Gervais had found the body of Satan. There was a groan, deep and shuddering—surely more vibrant than that of any mere human being—and then nothingness, save for the fugitive glow of a few stamped embers. The spell had been broken. The young man, blinded as much by the suddenness as by the actual night, stood stock-still, and the fingers of his left hand, with a killer's instinct, felt along the blade of his sword. It was wet—the Devil's blood! He experienced a triumph that lifted him for an instant to the height of the mailed and helmeted archangels, and his teeth gritted. But where was Sidonia?

All about him there were noises, like the scurrying of rats. The darkness was quick as a carcass riddled with maggots. He had no fears; he had defeated Satan, even as the winged Michael himself. Remembering that the girl had fallen to the floor, he stooped and groped very carefully. After a few moments his hand touched a woman's shoulder and the long, scattered hair of her head. Sheathing his sword as hastily and awkwardly as he had unsheathed it, he gathered the inert, unseen body up into his arms. It seemed pulseless. Yet it, and the soul within it, was redeemed from hell. She was all his now—his to wed with the sacred church rites that would tie them as unbreakably to each other in the golden, eternal groves of Paradise as in the fortified house of his father. He hugged the easy weight of her to him, and had the novel sensation of desiring to crush it utterly from sheer savage tenderness. Somehow, with the help of the saints who were undoubtedly with him, he must find his way out of this death-place to the upper world.

He turned, and began to move in the direction where he felt the door and the stair should be found, but with the utmost caution for fear of encountering a pillar, or some vaguer obstacle. There were shufflings, scrapings, rustles, and he heard a smothered squeal that could only have come from the lips of a woman. His foot struck something that rolled—a skull. A laboured breathing, like that of a wounded animal, sounded very near, and then, as he groped on, he lost it. Several times he met the implacable surface of walls, which he followed, hoping to find the turning that led to the stair. The rat-like sounds of stifled panic and dispersion had all ceased. He found himself cursing mechanically, in a whisper, and then, recalling the circumstances, prayed instead (also in a whisper) to the Three Martyrs. Immediately they responded, for the smell of the mouldy air subtly altered, and he knew that the stair-door was open and the curving flight of steps was before him. The Three Martyrs were leading him, he was sure of that. So in this confidence he passed through the unseen doorway, and mounted the unseen stair, a step at a time. The burden in his arms had become very heavy.

At last—the first murky glimmer of returning sight, as when life begins to grely leaven the darkness of death for a person climbing upward out of the prison of the underworld. Gervais became aware of the stair-walls, of the arched, doorless doorway where the steps ended. At the top of the flight he staggered, pausing. The cold, motionless, heavy-brooding dusk of the great church was like broad day after the horror of the dark from which he had come. Everything was as unchanged as the windless heart of a forest. The blasphemies, the madness, the grapple of Hell and Heaven in the crypt, might have been buried a hundred miles underground, or have taken place a hundred years off. Like a bed of daffodils, the yellow candle-stars surrounding the saint's shrine bloomed serene, softly bright and remote. Beyond them, suspended by invisible chains, glowed the dull, living ruby of the sanctuary lamp. As naturally as a knight, exhausted but victorious, turns towards his waiting overlord, Gervais approached the sanctuary. He wanted to kneel, to lay the girl—his redeemed love —upon the step that led to the high altar. Her nakedness at that moment meant as little to him as it would have done to Adam. The only reality in the world was his victory over Satan.

The lighted shrine was upon his left and partly hidden by the great shaft of a column as he came nearer to the sanctuary, whose lamp was a low-hung ember in the murk.

Something—someone—lay on the church's pavement at full length, supported by downturned palms, the head cast back, in the attitude of a speared wolf whose hindquarters are paralysed, and who lifts his bloody muzzle skyward as he endeavours to drag himself into the coverts.

Gervais halted. He looked—he recognised. His heart sprang in him, and all the blood in his body was again dark fire. Here, before Christ's altar, like a dying beast, was Satan—Satan, who had already tasted his sword! He shifted his grip of the girl's slight, sagging body so that her feet touched the ground, and he held her against him in the hollow of one arm. This left his sword-hand free. Whipping a cross-hilted dagger from his belt—the weapon of the *coup de grâce* with which he had pricked his wrist and Sidonia's —he put it to his lips, thereby invoking the Crucified, and stooped to strike.

A loud and terrible cry went dwindling roofward. It seemed a shocking and lonely thing in the solemnity of height and space. Immediately it was taken up eerily, and feebly repeated in several places, for various echoes nested beneath the vaulting of the cavern-church. Even as the high echoes spoke there was the scuffle and subdued clatter of feet. Who would have thought that there were so many folk within the cathedral?

Gervais stood up straightly now, the sagging girl held to him, her head dropped forward as though her neck were broken. The dagger was in his hand. It was wet to the hilt. Had he indeed slain Satan —or at least one of his lieutenants? He did not know, but the soul of him lifted itself like a winged conqueror with its foot set upon the crushed skull of the dragon. Blurred light was approaching —candles plucked from the candle-stands that surrounded the shrine. Gervais recognised the liveries of several of his father's retainers—the escort of the pious Countess, who for the last hour had been at her prayers before the incorruptible saint. There was a cluster of men and women of all classes, too, for on this night of the Feast of the Dead many prayed, kneeling or prostrate, upon the dim, stony pavement of God.

The little flame-tongues of the uplifted candles revealed the Young Lord, the hanging head of the girl, and the long-limbed, sombre thing at his feet, that twitched and half-moved in the very act of dying. There was a simultaneous gasp. The candle-bearers and the rest checked as though their hearts had actually stopped beating, forbidding an advance. Gervais looked at them and beyond them with eyes that seemed, in the tremulous light, to glitter.

There came a woman's scream, like a harpy's for sharpness. Sabine, elemental in her curiosities as any rag-picker's tousle-haired slut, had risen instantly from her stiffened knees at the sound of the knife-cry and the frightened scurry of feet. Violence of any kind was a sweetness in her nostrils, though she appeared so placid. She was incapable of understanding why anyone should flinch from blood unless it was their own. She had come well forward between two of the candle-bearers, her nun-like head-dress of starched linen, so fine that it was semi-transparent, pure as December snow, and revealing a low frontlet of pearls.

"Gervais! Oh, sirs, he is bespelled! Look at the witch!"

And at that moment the girl Sidonia, reviving, lifted her dropped head and moaned, and shuddered, and slid a convulsive arm about the neck of her supporter. Gervais raised the wetted dagger.

"Hear, all of you! By the power of Christ I have overcome Satan —or one of his chief ministers. This girl is freed from him. She is God's ward, and my betrothed wife. See for yourselves!"

He was so big with triumph, so outside and above his reticences, his quick, sensitive awkwardness of the spirit, that he was almost another person—a stranger to them.

They hesitated for a breath, their eyes staring, and then moved as with one impulse—Sabine with the foremost, her mouth half-open.

The light of the several candles fell fully upon what was to be seen.

"Oh-h-h!" screamed Sabine again, but with a different note. This was genuine; all the soul she had had suffered a strong shock. "Oh-h-h! God save us!"

"Angels defend us!" said a man's deep, hoarse voice, that quivered as though his throat-muscles were convulsed.

The black mask of the Master was gone, and Arnold, the Holy Count, twisted half over upon his back, lay his length on the church flags, with a froth of blood bubbling at his lips.

"The Count!"

Sabine, the stripped, savage woman staring at death, leaned forward, her two hands clutching at the skirt of her robe, which she had lifted instinctively as if to save its hems from blood.

"The Count!"—the muffled outcry of a dozen persons, aghast as sinners drawn from their graves to face the general Judgment.

For the first time since he had struck the death-blow Gervais looked down. There were several moments of silence, in which everything seemed arrested.

"It's not so. It cannot be so! This is trickery! I struck a blasphemer—a minister of Satan. Satan is trying to bewilder me."

His head was up. His voice went out with a violence that was like that of furious anger.

"He is bewitched! Sirs, the witch-girl has brought him to the slaying of his own father!"

Sabine saw light. Already she was reviving, for her mind and brain were resilient as a beggarwoman's. Like a flash it came to her that the incorrupt saint was, perhaps, about to answer her prayers.

There was a sort of groan—the utterance of a horror that still paralysed the witnesses.

"You are deceived, I tell you! All of you! Cannot you understand? It is trickery—a devilish illusion that will vanish! This is not my father!"

"Oh, hear him!" moaned Sabine. "Oh, my son—my son!" She swayed forward, sank to her knees, and collapsed, with one arm flung across the black-clad body beneath which a puddle—dark in the candle-light—was widening.

The Count moved. His eyelids flickered and opened. He appeared to be trying to speak.

"God be merciful——"

It was only a movement of the lips where the bubbled froth was streaked with scarlet. The Count's day-self would never have formed such words, for, held in the trance of its passionless, inhuman rectitude, it knew no need of mercy; nor would his night-self have formed them, save as a blasphemy. His strange, lightish eyes, of the same shade of violet-grey as his son's, stared upward, as the soul looks from the obscene pits of its betrayals to the far mountains of its hope. Far, far above his stony-pillowed head the spring of the unseen roof-arches were embellished with carved angel-faces and beast-faces, but higher yet, above the hollow, sky-forbidding roof, the yearning spires stretched a-tiptoe towards the wonder of the unknown.

The Count's eyes filmed. The lids quivered, and came half down over them. His lower jaw slackened suddenly, as though a muscle had been cut.

"Seize him! He is his father's murderer!"

One of the foremost candle-bearers, a big-built fellow with greying hair who wore the Count's livery, shot out an arm towards Gervais.

"Seize him! Murderer!"—an outbreak of cries, whose echoes in the spaciousness flew hither and thither like the ghosts of bats. Mysteriously, what was almost a throng had gathered, and the great church was filled with dim, agitated sounds that drew towards the one centre. Only the tiny, sombre, red flower of the sanctuary lamp burned unshaken. Some inner peace, untouchable, dwelt within itself with brooding wings. More lights approached. Gervais had not moved from his place. His face was haggard. He had been staring clown at the dead man, and now looked up, under drawn brows, at those who appeared to waver in the wavering illumination, and who were pressed together, ready to launch themselves upon him. He had the appearance of one dream-struck.

There was a unanimous movement. "Seize him!"

But Sabine flung herself upright, kneeling erect by the body, not grovelling beside it. She spread out her arms. There was blood on her pure head-dress and on her hands. Her blue eyes were those of a wounded and pleading child, pitifully melting as any saint's.

"No, No! Oh, sirs, hear me! Here, at his slain father's side, I tell you this! Take the woman—burn her—torture the wicked spirit that lives in her and my son will be set free. Take her; it is the will of God!"

She appeared inspired—a creature as holy, even in her grief, as had been the dead Count himself.

"It is the will of God! The witch! The witch!"

Men, women, priests, retainers, pages, beggar-folk cried out together. The lights swayed as one jostled another in the curious shuffle and shifting of a gathering that is about to lunge.

And then Sidonia, casting back her small head for a moment against the shoulder of the Young Lord, looked into the light of the candles and into the blurred faces of those who held them. Then, with a sudden wrench, she was free of the arm that had sustained her. She lurched forward, bare as Eve save for the lank tresses that were black as sin. Her hands went out as if seeking—clutching. Her knees sagged. But she had taken three or four steps towards the pack of christened people—her enemies since birth—before she pitched face downward to the pavement, falling right at the feet of the Count's lusty servants, of the priests, of the pious women hysterical with fear and hate. It was the final surrender. Sacrifice——

Behind her a violent scuffle shocked the grim, sacred dignity of the church, as half a dozen men flung themselves upon Gervais to disarm him. He fought like a man possessed. Perhaps the fallen girl heard the struggle. But her long struggle was over. She was a fetter, whose only good is that it can be broken.

VI. THE MIRACLE

1

NIGHT—— HOW LONG had the night endured—how long would it endure? But there could be no morning, with its upspringing of the heart and golden arrows of light out of the East. At times it was difficult for Sidonia to realise that she was not already dead. She was blind, for the palpable blackness pressed its fingers upon her eyes. She was cold as an uncoffined corpse thrown into a trench in the ground must surely be. A weight lay on her breast, for what air there was was in itself a sort of suffocation; it resembled a fetid fluid, long stagnant. She was deaf, for no sound came to the ears. Yet she was aware of the harsh and vilely sodden litter that her body pressed, and of the thick stench, in which dankness and the sickly taint of decay were mingled with the odour of ancient excrements. And then her mind was stirring—like a hurt thing fumbling to lick its wounds and sores. She wished that she could quieten it, but that was impossible, and its feverish movements increased.

Death—— This rotting dark was timeless, yet—sometime —those who had cast her where she was would draw her forth, and that—that would be death.

She raised herself suddenly half-upright upon the mat of reeking straw with which the place was bedded down. Fire! Her naked body began to shudder, and the teeth chattered in her head. The blackness was flame-painted—long, hot flames that shot up and thickened.

"No!" she said out loud. "Oh, no—no!"

Her own voice fell extraordinarily upon her hearing. It was like some other person's—some person in great distress. It silenced her. She sat up on the pad of straw with her arms crossed over her breast to still her shivering. Events, scenes, crowded in upon her madly, as though she were drowning. She saw the high cavern of the cathedral's interior, the candle-lit faces, the gigantic palls of shadow. She heard the cries. And she had torn herself from the Young Lord to go to her enemies, and then had fallen. She had a blurred remembrance, that was like a dream of sickness, of torches, harsh hands, and a shock that had partly stunned. That must have been when they cast her from above into the place where she now was. How many hours had elapsed since then—or was it only a short while?

She sat shivering. The stench had substance; it was almost a physical being that enveloped octopus-fashion. The dark was solid also.

Fire——

"No! No!" her spirit screamed. But she kept her lips closed. She had an impulse to throw herself face downward, and twist, and clutch. But the sensed vileness that was beneath her—like moist grave-rubbish—exerted its horror even over the spasm of her fear. For a livid, timeless instant—hell's eternity on a pin-point—she touched the very bottom of terror's pit, and her heart seemed to burst asunder like that of the condemned wretch who is being pressed to death beneath heaped iron weights. Then a spreading numbness—— The convulsive shivering died away, and the spasmodic chattering of the teeth. It was as though the nerves along which suffering travels had been overstretched with such swift violence that they had relaxed utterly, never to be so stretched again. And the numbness strengthened and deepened—if such can be said of a nullity.

Sidonia knew that she would burn. It was inevitable— fore-ordained. It was right and fitting; it would free Gervais. "For this was I born; for this came I into the world." She had no knowledge of the saying, uttered in a land far to the East, and long before her conception and her birth, but the spirit of it was within her own stilled breast, whose breathing had become slow and regular. "For this was I born——" She was a thing apart; a forest herb whose very sap of life is the venom of death. She loved Gervais; she must burn——

The squeal of a rat—the first sound since her own low outcry —stabbed the soundlessness that pressed weightily in upon the ears. There was a quick, furtive rustle, that yet seemed very loud. Rats larger than half-grown kittens were found in such prison-pits at this. They were ravenous, savage, packed with amazing strength and energy. Condemned persons left overlong, and weakened by the wounds of torture, had been attacked by them—some said overwhelmed and completely devoured.

Sidonia heard the squeal and the rustle, and they meant nothing to her—nothing. She sat in the darkness on the felted straw-pad, and now and again the great rats shrieked and scuttled.

"For this was I born——" An inexpressible peace was settling upon her. It was like a night-blue cloud, profound as the abyss in which the stars were suspended after the manner of small silver lamps, profounder than the depths she had visioned when she soared upward on the winged black horse. And then a species of withdrawal—a gradual detachment, as of self from self. Was she rising? Was she outside her meagre, motionless body as well as within it? Oh, she could see—at least with the eyes of the risen self, that seemed to stand erect, treading as if upon swansdown. Wonderful flowers were growing round her, rooted in fetid slime and in dark, noisome hollows, like the water-lilies whose white, thick-petalled chalices are filled with an ineffable odour. There was a winnowing as of great wings, and shadows and rainbows passed alternately over her. Bubbles floated, rising and falling, and in each was mirrored some scene of life that stirred like a pulse, and fluc-tuated. She saw figures she recognised—men and women of the town—tiny, active, and distinct. They gesticulated, laughed, ar-gued, wept, prayed. She recognised Violane, who was lying flat on a bed with her face pressed into a feather pillow; and Sabine, who was being attired in black garments by two girls in a room where candles burned, and who leaned first on one girl and then on the other, tilting back her head as though she were about to faint. And Gervais—he was bound like a captive, and looked fully at her. She loved him, and because of this love nothing could really separate them. Indeed, he was actually with her, among the lily-flowers that drew their beauties from the slime. For she was not the witch's daughter, here, where the bubbles of life floated, and the shadows and rainbows followed each other in accordance with some rhythm that was like the recurrent beat of music. None of the creatures she had known before were with her now—serpents and leopards, sa-tyrs and composite things, aerial demons, bare idol-figures, and the passion-bound simulacra of suicides. But a marvellous, pure bird with a thin ring of golden flame about its head hovered very high above, and she thought that she could hear it singing, lark-fashion. There was no pain, there was no fear. Everything was just as it should be, and, in its inevitable flowering, lovely as summer.

She was not alone. She heard, and saw, and smelled flower-odours. She was most happy——

"Show a light here! There she is."

"Christ's wounds! She's deaf and blind. The Devil's drawn the soul out of her!"

"Has he? We'll burn what's left!"

These were like voices coming through many thicknesses, or voices heard only in the mind. Sidonia closed her eyes, shutting out all the real yet unearthly loveliness that encompassed her. She was sinking, gently. It was like a return to sleep and dreaming after an awakening of brief duration. But had it been brief?

She opened her eyes. Crude firelight fell across them. Fire—— She must burn—— She blinked, dazzled, and then looked upward.

"Good morning, witch! All here, body and soul?"

"Shut your mouth! Don't bait her. D'you see those eyes? They could put a curse on a man that all the priests in the world couldn't shift."

Above the girl's head a square opening gaped where a solid trap-door had been heaved open, two faces peered down, and a shower of lurid light was spilt into the prison-pit.

"Here, witch! Stand up and dress yourself."

Something was dropped through the aperture—a coarse smock, yellow-white. Sidonia got immediately to her feet. She slipped the smock over her head, clumsily, but with a certain tranquil deliberateness, and it clothed her to the ankles. She looked upward again. She was not aware of exhaustion, bruised flesh, or any faintness. Her body was light, and seemed insensitive as a numbed limb. Part of her was here, in the prison-pit—the slime-bed—but part of her was in the region of the slime-born lilies whose cups were filled with sweetness, and far, far above which the pure bird hovered. Simultaneously she was asleep, and dreaming strangely and darkly, and awake——

A rope came dangling through the trap-opening.

"Come up, witch!"

Obediently she gripped it with both hands, waiting.

"Christ's wounds! She acts like a lamb of God!" said one of the two above, hoarsely, to his mate.

"I don't like it. I thought one of us would have to drop into that kennel and truss her properly, and toss her up to the other."

"We're saved trouble. But she's too quiet. I'll bet she's worse than a bad one."

"She's dangerous."

They began to draw up the burdened rope. Then one, leaning forward, caught the hanging girl by the arm, and in a moment she was hauled through and sprawled on the wooden flooring like a part-drowned cat drawn from a well. Raising herself weakly, she lifted her eyes to the two men, and they crossed themselves, for in the great onyx gaze of them there appeared to be neither sight nor fear.

Only the torch lit the circular room that was above the prison-pit, but the night was over and gone, and it was already full morning of the day following the Feast of the Dead.

2

IT WAS ALREADY full morning of the day following the Feast of the Dead. A dull and sultry daylight slanted inward through the long window-slit, and the stern dusk of the room was leavened by it—leavened, but not lightened. The dun skins of deer hung, in the place of tapestry, against the stone walls. The narrow wooden bed, with its posts and roof, was in deep shadow, and also the great carved chest. In a solid chair, with crossed legs a man sat, curiously slumped. His shoulders pressed the wall behind him; his face was lifted and turned sideways towards the entering light. Thongs bound his wrists together at his back, and other thongs held him to the chair. He had been there a long while—staring into the eyeless dark that gradually greyed, until now the day had come. His wrists—though this was hidden from sight—were bloodied from the cut of the thongs where he had tugged against them. His face—a dim thing in the room's twilight—was like wet clay, for he had sweated.

For hours Gervais had suffered in the manner of persons put to the torture, whose limbs are being stretched by ropes and pulleys, and their heads compressed by iron bands until the blood trickles from ears and nostrils. It was not to be borne—it was monstrous! Yet he still endured it, and minute by minute it increased. He was aware of a kind of madness working in him. And then there were prolonged flashes of livid thought, clear as bared knives, from which the spirit winced away, yet could not really stir. He had crossed swords with the legions of hell, and—they had prevailed. The blare of their brazen trumpets was sounding over him; their spiked spears were brandished; their fantastic, horned helmets triumphed, and their vast bat-wing banners, leathern and dreadful. His father, the Count, was dead, and he himself was his slayer. How could he ever have believed that his one blade could put an end to Satan—Satan, who could change his shape as a black cloud does, and substitute living, christened flesh for his own false human semblance? No; this Satan, whose mightiness he had defied, had made of him his father's murderer, and Sidonia was to burn.

A shudder of the muscles passed over him, but he knew that he could not free himself. He had endeavoured to do so until his wrists were raw, and the sweat stood on him like water cast in his face. And then there was the strong door of the room, fast-locked on its outer side. Hell had triumphed. He was in hell. God was more remote than the white cone of a mountain peak seen from the bottom of a valley-chasm. The saints and angels had withdrawn also—a mere flight of little far-off winged things. The great pinions of the dragon flapped, and from his gullet came a visible hot stench like the scorch of burning flesh. Christ!

The bound man groaned. It was the first sound he had uttered during the long hours since midnight. He felt that he must presently become wholly mad, for the pressure about his brain was beyond the endurance of a son of woman. But that would be no deliverance for Sidonia. She was so frail, yet so tenacious and loving. She had lain in his arms; they had exchanged long kisses and mingled their blood. He had redeemed her soul and carried her naked. She was sacred. And morning had come, and in an hour perhaps, or less than that, they would burn her. Torture—fire—— His brain clouded—a dull red cloud. This was merciful. He saw the lack-lustre slant of entering light, and for the moment it held no significance. He drew a deep breath. Christ! The insupportable thing was real—real as his own life! He moved convulsively. The thongs held. Unless some man or angel freed him he must go mad!

The stillness was unbroken. There had been no sound at all since those who rendered him helpless had left him where he was. This silence was more dreadful than any outcry—the whistling, neighing, and rumbling tumult of devils, or the non-human screeching of a torture-room. It was, in itself, a protracted torture——

An hour must have passed since sunrise. The light was curiously dull——

A twisting key grated. With a creak the door opened inward, carefully. Gervais stared towards it as souls held in the fiercest fires of purgatory might turn their speechless gaze to Heaven's messenger.

The young man, Hugh, his friend, stood just within the room.

Gervais moistened his lips. "Hugh," he said.

The other came forward, slowly. He looked haggard, and it set an alien stamp on him.

"For Christ's sake release me. I've no weapon. I swear, on my honour as a knight, to make no attempt to overpower you."

His voice grated as the key had done.

Hugh did not immediately answer. He seemed to be examining with puzzled and anxious eyes, and his hand strayed to his sheathed dagger and halted there. When a man is a ghastly and public victim of witchcraft, and has fought a pack of assailants with every appearance of demoniac possession, it is disconcerting that he should speak like a normal Christian, and appear merely a sword-companion in duress. There was nothing of the Devil about Gervais, straitened and crippled—only pain.

"I—I cannot wholly free you. Not yet. But I'll cut the thongs, Gervais."

The captive uttered nothing. All the lines of his face were set and tense. Not yet. That meant that the witch-burning was still unaccomplished. He was rigid with a waiting tension that stretched nerve and muscle.

With the edge of his dagger Hugh severed the many bonds. Then he stood back a little. He was awkward, uneasy. This was quite beyond his short experience, that embraced only the thrust and skirmish of mounted warfare and rough love-play with every soft thing in petticoats. An impulse urged him to cross himself, but another impulse held him from doing so, for this was Gervais, his friend, who had just spoken as sanely as any man.

Deliberately Gervais moved—very deliberately. He was holding himself back. He did not speak. There was nothing more to be said. He had given his promise to Hugh, as one knight to another, and it could not be broken. But Hugh would leave him, locking the door again, and then—— His brain smouldered, and strength rushed back into the stiffened channels—molten strength. He passed his palms mechanically over his cramped thighs, looking down as he did so at the bloody weals where his wrists had been thong-bruised.

Hugh, who had thought of many things to say before his entrance, found himself wordless. And also he had business elsewhere —business that should lift the witch-thrall from his friend— business of great moment and gravity, and invested, likewise, with the piercing interest that attaches to a boy's first experiment in the flaying of a living cat, or the baiting of a maimed fox. He found himself at the threshold, paused, nearly spoke, retreated with abruptness, drew the door to, and locked it. He was as much in a sweat as though the Devil in the form of a maned lion had sprung out and roared at him.

Gervais came to his feet as the key turned. From the middle downward he was benumbed. A prickling of returning blood assailed his limbs. He steadied himself for an instant with his hand against the wall, then, with a movement that was between a lunge and a lurch, he was at the door. Stooping, with his ear against it, he listened—— Muffled, the sound of steps that dwindled as they withdrew came to him. He knew that the gallery was empty. He straightened, and, like an animal in a cage, paced round the room a couple of times. He must wait—wait until Hugh was beyond hearing. There might be others, but that could not be helped. Nothing should hold him—nothing could stay him now. His mind was clear, but an intense heat dwelt in it. It seemed to him that not only was he strong; he was strength itself. How, then, could they halt him? He caught up the massive chair in which he had been a bound prisoner, swung it, and crashed it against the oaken barrier. There was a thunderous splintering sound. Again—again. Then, abandoning the battered chair, he drove headlong at the door with his shoulder. Torn clean from lock and hinges, it fell outward into the gallery, filling the hollow place with noise. Two men of good weight and muscle, armed with pikes, could only with difficulty have accomplished such a thing. But Gervais loved a woman.

He had pitched forward with the door, and now picked himself up, dazed barely for the moment. No time was to be lost, though Hugh had said "Not yet." Empty-handed, his doublet ripped from shoulder to swordless sword-belt as though by a dog's teeth, he started down the gallery. Behind him there were footsteps and a cry.

Down a steep spiral stair, vague-lit by arrow-slits, through a rush-strewn hall, naked and monastic, whose open hearth was a bed of cold ashes, and so out into a cobbled court, and the strange light of a lowering day. There was pursuit behind, but not a living soul in front—not even a cur. All had gone to watch the witch-burning— dogs as well as Christians. Only a tame raven with a clipped wing half hopped, half fluttered out of the way, uttering a raucous croak. An ill omen? No! there were neither good nor evil omens when one was as resistless as a bolt from God's cross-bow.

Gervais ran like a greyhound. The hunt was up. His quarry was a girl abandoned by both Heaven and Hell, and he himself was the quarry of those who came at his heels, but he disregarded them as a spurred horse ignores the yelp of mongrels. Sidonia—— Thoughts streamed through his mind that were formless as water—or flowing blood. He drew swift, steady breath through widened nostrils, and his lips were implacable—set like a swordsman's. He neither hoped nor feared; he ran.

The town seemed purged of its inhabitants; even the cobble-stones would have left their places to see the witch-burning if they could have dislodged themselves. Yet there was a murmurous crowd-sound close at hand—the market-square—and a smell of smoke, and of pitch——

3

WHEN SIDONIA CAME out under the roof of the sky, all that surrounded her appeared strange, as though it pertained to some region
at the world's end, although she was quite incurious concerning it.
The house-fronts, whose window-shutters were thrown back, and
from whose window-openings craning faces looked down, might
have been the façades of dwellings in Cathay—they seemed so
utterly unrelated to any past experience of hope or fear.

She moved between the two scrub-bearded, leathern-tunicked
men who had drawn her from the prison-pit. Her arms were bent
behind her and fastened. Just above either elbow a cord was tied.
The men held these cords: they seemed unwilling to touch her, as if
she were carrion, or a walking leper. The morning was dull, close.
The sky was greyish, hazed over, as on certain sultry days in August
or July. And there was warmth in the windless air—leaden-heavy,
unnatural. Perspiration pricked out upon the faces of people
standing three and four deep where the laneway widened, con-
verging upon the market-square. Was this the last month of frosty
autumn—the threshold of winter?

"It's the fire of hell," said one woman to another. "Hell's closer
to us than we think."

"As close as that hell-thing they're bringing now. The breath of
the Devil goes with his mistress."

They caught their own breaths in a spasm of half-exquisite
spiritual fear, feeling that the hot gape of the dragon was opened
above them, and the flames of the pit of damnation beneath their
feet might break forth out of the suddenly cracking ground. Only
the power of the Cross, of blessed water, of Church rites, and of the
bones and miraculous flesh of saints, held back the menace from
them, as an island stems a flood.

Sidonia walked slowly. Her body was numbed and lightsome; it
did not obey her as readily as it should—it did not seem fully to
belong to her. She was aware of no fatigue, nor of any hurts of the
flesh, though from head to heel she was as much bruised as if she
had been beaten. She had a sensation of looking down upon herself

from a height. How small she was, there, between the two cord-muscled men, and the house-walls that rose up to thatch and swallows' nests. Her straight, coarse smock was open at the breast, partially revealing the spring-like bosom that had been kissed by Satan's deputy, and had borne the weight of love, and yet was virgin still. Her uncombed hair fell about her shoulders. Her face had a famine-look, and yet was serene as a dead child's, the gaze of the eyes fixed straight ahead. Yes, she saw all this concerning herself, as though she were her own spectator. She even, in an impersonal way, felt pity for herself. Fire was a grievous death for a girl of sixteen years. Fire was torture—a thing at which the senses shrieked and shrank. Something in this girl who was herself should be grovelling, demented. Poor creature! "For this was I born; for this came I into the world." The rhythm of existence, unhindered now by any struggle of the soul, pulsed through her. Winter and summer, death and life, night and day—alternating shadows and rainbows above the lily-flowers that drew their magical beauties from the slime. She was extraordinarily happy, and a song of joy came dropping downward, lark-fashion, from the radiant height where the white, haloed bird hovered. It was wonderful to know that nothing could really hurt her—nothing! She was above it all.

"Look at the eyes of her. Pray God she doesn't turn them this way! They should have blinded her and torn out her tongue before they brought her into the open. She'll put the evil look on us—yes, and curse the whole town, as soon as she feels the fire."

"She walks like a woman I once saw who had a strange spirit in her and used to go abroad in her sleep."

"She's possessed. Her familiar will jump out of her mouth in the shape of a red mouse or a toad when she begins to burn."

"Hell-cat! Devil-brat!" piped up a small child, and its mother slapped it briskly. "Do you want the witch to change you into a hedgehog?" she said in a sharp whisper. "You hold your tongue, or I'll take you indoors, and you shan't see the big fire!"

"Hell-cat! Devil-brat!" How far away the little shrill voice seemed. They had called out such words on the morning when the Young Lord entered the town. That was two days ago. Gervais—— She had renounced him, and he was with her—oh, always! She was happier than she had believed it possible for any creature to be.

"Keep back! Keep back!"

Soldiers with pikes were endeavouring to maintain a clear way to the middle of the market-square, where was the newly planted stake, the faggots, and the chains. The open space seethed with

people, all crazy to see. There was savage jostling; women with
infants at their breasts were wedged between bearded, sweating
men, and aged persons, trying to claw a way through, became
querulous or seized with palpitations. One of the wheeled stages
upon which miracle-plays were performed in public at Easter-time
had been drawn well forward to command a view of the stake. It
was set out with cushioned seats and footstools, and there, in a
semi-circle, were the town's notables—the mitred bishop, an abbot
or two, the heads of the guilds, wearing gold chains and finger-rings
of fine workmanship, and at the centre of the formal half-circle, on
a higher seat, Sabine, the widowed Countess. She was vested in
black, her head nun-like with its wide-winged crown of starched
linen. The fingers of her clasped hands were entwisted with the gold
and silver beads of a rosary. She did not appear paler than usual, but
held herself with a meek dignity, quiet and slow-breathing, that
seemed mutely to reproach Heaven for the unmerited, unparalleled
things that had befallen her.

"The saints comfort the Countess!" said an old woman to her
neighbour. "There's her man dead and her stepson bewitched, and
she as calm as God Himself."

"Such doings!" said the neighbour, high-stomached, the mother
of many. "They say the cathedral was full of devils last night. A
widower who lodges in our street was there, and a friend of his
sister told me what he saw. A thing with great ears like a donkey,
and hoofs, and a forked tail, held a bandage over the Young Lord's
eyes, so that he couldn't see what he was about, and he ran his
sword right through his father's body as he knelt at his prayers.
Then an angel came straight down from Heaven, and broke the
sword in two, and the thing with the great ears vanished, and the
naked witch turned into a white serpent and fell to the floor, and
then changed back to a woman again, and the people seized her, and
sprinkled her with holy water, and bound her."

"God save us! I was asleep in my bed through it all."

A vibration struck through the crowd. The shudder of a general
vague movement passed over it.

"Here she comes!"

There was a trample, a jostle, the squeal of children. On the steps
going up to the great doors of the cathedral people stood close with
their hands on one another's shoulders. Boys had even climbed up
the stonework, clinging to the carved kings and angels that were
nearly life-size, or to the projecting gargoyles where the leaden
waterspouts terminated. Inside the church, as everyone knew, the

dead Count lay in state, with tall candles burning at his head and feet. He was habited in purple and ermine, his hands folded on his breast over the little crystal-enclosed relic of the True Cross he habitually wore, and his face expressionless and austere in its perfect calm as a wax death-mask.

An involuntary movement of interest stirred the formal personages seated on the dais of the wheeled wooden stage. Sabine's bosom heaved. Her hands, unjewelled save for the rich beads of the entwisted rosary, tightened one upon the other. This was the moment for which she had prayed, promising gifts to the town's saint. She felt the thrill of that pure triumph which is pure joy. Her nature spread and contracted its claws like a tickled cat. God was good.

Sidonia, walking between her two gaolers, but not in contact with either, was in a very narrow and winding lane whose sides were close-pressed bodies.

"Witch! Witch!"

"God's curse on you!"

"The Devil can't save you now, my girl!"

"Satan's wife!"

"Fire for the hell-faggot!"

Women's voices, men's voices—— She recalled a clearing in the forest of autumn, and a mob of forest-folk, and an ashen-haired thing that had once been a woman clawing and screaming. She had been furious and afraid then—afraid of the fire—and fear was a garment she had discarded. It was ordained that she should pass through just such a close crowd of watching people, and that they should cry out——

A lanky, vagabond jester, unshaven, grimier than a mendicant friar, began to babble to anyone who would listen to him, turning his head from side to side.

"There she is! There she is! That's the slut that set the foul fiend on me in the forest—the same that put her spell on a whole street two days ago, and then vanished out of sight. She's a witch—she's a black witch! Her fiend nearly knocked the soul out of me."

A big, tawny-haired wench—Sylvane—who was standing near him, uttered a laugh.

"Bah! You and your soul! Your witch has lived right by my doorstep for the last half year. What do you know about that?"

Her bear-leader gave her a nudge in the side.

"Don't publish it, you fool!"

"Fool yourself!"

With them was the dark-eyed Catherine, sallower than usual, with a livid bruise on one cheek and her much-abused mouth drooping like a tired mother's. Her sick, sad, passion-weary gaze was fastened upon the oncoming girl who was so soon to burn, and her eyes filled up with tears that overbrimmed and crawled down her face. They were the only tears in all the crush of the sweating crowd.

Near the market cross, with the wheeled stage drawn to one side, a considerable space had been kept clear. Here was the stake— firmly planted, tall, and pointed like a wooden spike intended for impalement. Billets of wood were stacked up about it, forming a sort of mound from which it rose. And there was a great quantity of bound faggots, and burning coals in a fire-basket, and brands wound with tow and anointed with pitch to serve as torches, and a heap of chains. The sullen sky had become heavier than ever. There was not the feeblest movement of the dead air. It was like a pregnant morning in August—the month of thunder.

Sidonia had come to the end of her road. There was fire, and the smell of fire— She looked upon the stake and the faggots, and from the hovering height of her spirit felt again a far-off pity for herself. It was a grievous death—the sort to which a girl would be dragged with strengthless knees and chattering teeth. Yet it, like everything else, was ordained, and could not be otherwise. Serene, she looked down upon herself in her coarse death-smock.

A silence had fallen on the crowd. The condemned girl, at a word from her gaolers, mounted upon the high-piled billets of wood, and stood against the stake. She did this as simply as though it were church steps she were climbing to hear the daily Mass. Everyone in the crowd could see her now, if it were only her head and shoulders and black hair. Her wrists were unbound, and then fastened behind the stake. An iron chain was passed round her waist, tightly securing her. Immediately facing her was the tall market cross, whereon a painted Christ-figure hung. She looked straight at this figure, for it was on the level of her lifted eyes.

"She's defying God," said a tailor in a lowered voice to a shoe-maker. His pregnant wife, who was with him, felt a throb within her as the quickened child stirred abruptly. A deadly feeling overpowered her; specks swam before her eyes, and she seemed to be sinking down, down, towards hell——

Behind the Countess's cushioned seat Anne and Margaret, standing side to side, unconsciously grasped each other's hands. Margaret was pale as a clout, with eyes like a ghost-seer's that yet were avid; Anne had a sharpened, rigid look. They did not speak to each other, even in a whisper; they only gripped hands.

Along the narrow, cleared path that the condemned girl had followed came Hugh, hurrying like any page, bareheaded, sword-girt, visibly perturbed and sweating. Sabine leant forward a trifle. She knew that he had been with Gervais—Gervais, who would so soon be free—widowed of the witch-vampire. Her Gervais—— She desired to speak to him. But she must keep her lips closed.

Hugh raised his eyes to the stake, against which the chained girl now leaned her head as if she were just a little weary. He spoke quickly to her two gaolers, and to others who were with them, and then stood aside, watching. He was convinced, that Gervais' soul was about to be delivered from eternal perdition. And, also, he had never seen a woman burned before.

The faggots were piled about the heap of wood billets in such a manner as to secure an upward draught, and shavings soaked with oil were strewn between them. No time was lost now. Four torches wrapped in pitch-dipped tow were thrust simultaneously into the iron fire-basket, and burst into flame. Immediately they were applied to the faggots, and four blurred fingers of pitch-smelling smoke went up from them, and the frailer twigs crackled.

"She burns!"

One would have thought that the whole crowd spoke from a single hoarse throat.

Sabine, unknowing, had caught her lower lip between her teeth. She leaned far forward. God and Gervais were inextricably mingled in the inarticulate triumph of her heart. Margaret uttered a quick moan that might have been either of pain or excitement. She wished that Hugh were beside her; she would like to have clutched his arm, and felt it go round her body, bracing her up to him. A feverish ripple passed over the crowd. Every face strained to see. Mothers forgot the children at their bosoms, sweethearts were hand-parted, neighbours trod and elbowed each other.

"She burns!"

On the raised, step-like base of the market cross a young girl sank to her knees with a smothered scream. When her relatives drew her to her feet there was froth at her lips.

"Violane! Violane!" they said.

"She has visions," whimpered her mother. "Only the day before yesterday she was visited by a virgin from Paradise, and gave my new cloak to her. The sight of the witch has thrown her into a fit."

"Oh-h! The fire—the fire!" gasped the goldsmith's daughter, whose nerve had given way, and who had the hysterical conviction that it was she herself whom the town was burning for her traffic with devils and with the strange congregations of the Black Mass.

The crackling about the faggot-hidden foot of the stake had become louder, and thickening smoke streamed upward.

Sidonia lifted her head from where she had rested it. She heard the fire, she smelt the fire; she saw the smoke that rose about her. Her spirit, half folding its wings, dropped towards her body, which was still numb. It was like the descent of a bird that has been fluttering among high sprays of blossom. The first leaping flicker of flame thrust upward its cleft tongue. She saw it—the fire—the red fire towards which her naked feet had travelled since her birth! A strange elation was upon her, catching her up between its pinions as the black horse of her desire had done. It seemed to her that a glorious, sanguine flower, long folded in the bud, was breaking open now at last, and its petals were upcurling flames. Through the rising smoke she looked at the pallid Christ-figure, with its outspread arms, whose many wounds were painted red. She had pitied it as it hung upon the forest Calvary, she had put her arms about it in her own despair beneath the penthouse roof of the town's miraculous shrine, and now it faced her in its unchanging abandonment of pain, hidden and revealed alternately by the thick, brownish breath of her burning. Oh, but the pale body shone from head to feet like living silver, and the wounds glowed as the small red lamp in the church had done. It moved; the limbs straightened, and the head lifted. The outspread arms were opened after the manner of triumph. There was no pain here, only a consummation like her own. Her small breasts heaved, her face tilted more rigidly upward, the eyes deer-wide and wonderful.

There was a confused, hoarse murmur: "The fire has her!" "Why doesn't she scream?" "They should have tortured her first; she's in a witch's trance!" "Why don't they pour pitch on the faggots?" "She'll scream when it lays hold on her feet—she must."

The low sky had taken on a slaty tinge, and the air had darkened until all the upturned faces appeared livid as those of drowned persons. Brief sparkles of red-gold were mingled with the smoke of the burning faggots, that thickened moment by moment. Those in the forefront of the crowd nearest to the stake gaped like dead fish, or contorted their features as though they were themselves enduring torture. The crowd, with one mind, panted like a tormented animal to hear the burning girl utter her first cry. It would break the tension——

Protesting voices—a swaying cleavage of the packed mass. What was this? Heads turned. People were uncertain whether to look towards the stake or towards this obscure yet violent disturbance. The disruption continued. Some one was fighting a headlong passage through the crowd, that strove to sunder before him with squeals, outcries, and the deeper voices of jostling men.

"The Young Lord!" A score of throats uttered it. "God save us! It's the Young Lord!"

Sabine half rose. Hugh turned his head as though something had set its teeth in him, and spoke instantly to the nearest man-at-arms. Up on the wheeled stage Margaret laughed, caught hold of Anne, choked, and hid her face on the satin-clad bosom of the other girl.

Nothing could turn Gervais. He had known it, and it was so. The people of the crowd were just so many herded sheep. There was the strength of twenty in his shoulders—in his arms and hands. He saw the smoke roll upward, mixed with fiery sparks; he saw the small, dark, lifted head of Sidonia, the witch, the saint—— Ah! Would they stop him? He was at grips with a cluster of men-at-arms. But they were children in muscle measured with himself. The bones of a man's forearm cracked audibly. Another, cast heavily, lay where he had fallen, groaning. The smell of the smoke was sharp in the nostrils; the heat of the fire was palpable. The men-at-arms were ten against one—men of straw. His brain was clear—a red clearness——

"Gervais!"

Out of the smoke, out of the dragon-breath of the increasing flames that licked up almost to her feet, the girl's voice came—a clear voice, rather high-pitched, unquivering.

If a magician's word of power had been uttered, the effect could not have been more complete, more sudden. The tangle of struggling men relaxed, for the Young Lord—the madman—like an awakened sleeper who has fought with dreams, looked instantly upward, passive, his chest heaving, his bloodless face streaked with sweat, his body naked to the waist save for a few shredded tatters of dark red. Sabine was upon her feet, and the Bishop had risen also. All those within hearing of the voice from the stake were speechless —incapable of any action. What unprecedented thing was about to happen?

"Gervais! There is no pain."

And there was not, though the naked soles of her feet were set on wood that had begun to glow and smoulder beneath them, and sparks were mixed with her hair, and the hot, pouring smoke was a partial veil between her and the world of men. She saw him even though the wide, fearless eyes of her body were semi-blinded, and her spirit stooped to him and stretched out quick hands. He could not be separated from her. It only seemed to him that he could. Her hands caressed him as they had done in the turret room and in the forest solitude.

"Gervais—Gervais—I dreamed that your God had given me to you, and it is true!"

Overhead, without the least warning, there was a crashing shock of thunder that jarred the stolid, well-bedded cobblestones under-foot. The sky, from side to side, was one momentary glare, livid, grey-blue, scribbled with molten-white zigzags. A rush of icy air swept across the open, and with it a slanting flood of rain, mixed with sleet.

Of such a suddenness was the visitation from heaven that, like the blow of a divine fist, it left every creature in the market-square stunned and silly—capable only of huddling like storm-struck cattle that lower their heads and crowd close. Sabine was down in her deep-cushioned seat, crouched upon herself animal-fashion, and the two girls cowered at the back of her. Mothers dumbly shielded their children; all were pressed together in a conglomerate mass, without will or even sense; various masterless dogs slunk through the partly-opened doors of the great church to refuge, but the herd of men and women with immortal souls only swayed slightly under the savage punishment of the violet-black sky, and there was a vague, general moan. Near the centre of the market Sylvane, who was always thrown into a cringing panic by thunder, whimpered between the arms of Catherine, who turned her own face skyward to the scourging rain.

A loud hissing rose from the burning faggots that surrounded the stake. The smoke drove every way, leaving the chained victim in full view. Her eyes were closed now; her head, turned a little to one side, leaned back against the high, supporting post.

Unhindered, free of his assailants, of whom he had crippled two, the rush of the sleety rain laying its fluid whips across his bared chest and back and shoulders, Gervais was at the foot of the stake in a few strides. The drenched, fire-blackened faggots hissed at him like a nest of serpents. He set his feet on them, scrambling upward. He trod fire—fire that fought with rain. The half-burned brands broke and crumbled under him, but the smouldering billets—the core of the mound—held firm. He grasped the stake, swaying, level at last with the excommunicated—the condemned. Her eyes were closed, her wet hair clung to cheek and throat, and to the young, bruised, rain-purged bosom. The edges of her smock were charred. She appeared to know nothing of either heat or cold. Gervais was busy with the chain that had been passed twice about the girl's meagre waist. The rain descended upon them as though angels had broken down the barriers of some chill, celestial deep, and hailstones leapt like white grasshoppers about the ruined fire-heap, whose expiring breath was acrid and down-beaten smoke.

Again the thunder crashed, like a loud, departing word. The cessation of the deluge was as sudden as its onset. The sky-vault that had resembled a low roof of purple slate, rifted, and a pale sword of the sun struck downward. A transient rainbow spanned the town, and a million water-drops flashed like diamond, amethyst, and topaz. (Many people said afterward that Michael, the leader of the hosts of God, had been visible for a glorious instant, clad in the golden mail of a knight, his helmet crowned with a circlet of blazing jewels, and the sombre folds of the dragon under his feet.) In several quarters cocks crowed. The wet cobblestones glistened. On the summit of the drenched fire-heap a young man, half-naked like a vagabond, caught in his arms a wretched, nerveless girl whose feet were heat-scorched, for the chain had loosened at last, slipping downward over her narrow loins, and she yielded with it, helpless as a baby.

"A miracle!"

Who raised the cry? Some shrill-voiced woman, overwrought, soaked to the skin, sun-blinded. It was like the touch on a quick nerve.

"A miracle!" It went from mouth to mouth. It was a shout. The sodden crowd surged with a unanimous movement. They did not think; they were incapable of it; they knew.

"A miracle! The white witch! The saint of God!"

"God has saved His saint!" It was the woman who had first proclaimed the miracle. She ran forward, fell to her knees on the stony, puddled ground, and raised a pair of thin and quivering arms. Her face was lifted to the stake that rose from the fire-heap as though it were a Calvary.

"A saint? Oh, Christ! I stripped her naked once!" said Sylvane, clutching Catherine's shoulder and gazing stupidly. The long-legged jester had flopped to his knees as though he were in church.

Down from the fire-heap came Gervais, carrying his Sidonia. He was exhausted, and more than a trifle dazed. No knight-errant, surely, ever bore such an appearance. He was pitiable. He had emerged, as it were, from the seven infernal circles of the nether world—triumphant.

Scores were kneeling now. Tears ran down the faces of men and women, and many sobbed openly and loudly. They pressed round, and furtive, reverent hands were extended to touch the death-smock, the hanging arm, the blistered feet of Sidonia, the child of the hunted. Margaret was weeping hysterically against the breast of Hugh. The Bishop, assisted by his clergy, was at that moment descending from the wheeled stage to set the seal of his blessing upon the wonder that had occurred, and Sabine, preparing with small, deliberate, preening movements to follow his sodden dignity, knew with a rush of suave emotional certainty that Heaven had. summoned her to enter a religious house and become a saint herself. A notable saint—one who would never, under any circumstances, lift her eyes to a man, and who would presently acquire miraculous powers.

Cloaks and upper garments of all sorts had been spread recklessly in a thick pile, and here the Young Lord laid Sidonia down. He kept her hand between his palms, shivering himself, for he was nearly bare, and the reaction had set in. Opposite to him Catherine knelt, chafing the girl's other hand. The whole town, it seemed, hung upon Sidonia's rousing.

And Sidonia opened her strange, dark eyes, and they were happy, for she had dreamed that Tib, her yellow cat, had returned, as cats will do, to the loft above the Street of the Martyrs, and she knew that she would presently find him there. She had dreamed also of God, as once before; and He was benevolent, and had spoken kindly to her. So she drew her hand softly away from Catherine, and lifted it to touch Gervais' hair, and he stooped at once, and kissed her upon the lips.

THE END

RAMBLE HOUSE's

HARRY STEPHEN KEELER WEBWORK MYSTERIES

(RH) indicates the title is available ONLY in the RAMBLE HOUSE edition

The Ace of Spades Murder
The Affair of the Bottled Deuce (RH)
The Amazing Web
The Barking Clock
Behind That Mask
The Book with the Orange Leaves
The Bottle with the Green Wax Seal
The Box from Japan
The Case of the Canny Killer
The Case of the Crazy Corpse (RH)
The Case of the Flying Hands (RH)
The Case of the Ivory Arrow
The Case of the Jeweled Ragpicker
The Case of the Lavender Gripsack
The Case of the Mysterious Moll
The Case of the 16 Beans
The Case of the Transparent Nude (RH)
The Case of the Transposed Legs
The Case of the Two-Headed Idiot (RH)
The Case of the Two Strange Ladies
The Circus Stealers (RH)
Cleopatra's Tears
A Copy of Beowulf (RH)
The Crimson Cube (RH)
The Face of the Man From Saturn
Find the Clock
The Five Silver Buddhas
The 4th King
The Gallows Waits, My Lord! (RH)
The Green Jade Hand
Finger! Finger!
Hangman's Nights (RH)
I, Chameleon (RH)
I Killed Lincoln at 10:13! (RH)
The Iron Ring
The Man Who Changed His Skin (RH)
The Man with the Crimson Box
The Man with the Magic Eardrums
The Man with the Wooden Spectacles
The Marceau Case
The Matilda Hunter Murder
The Monocled Monster

The Murder of London Lew
The Murdered Mathematician
The Mysterious Card (RH)
The Mysterious Ivory Ball of Wong Shing Li (RH)
The Mystery of the Fiddling Cracksman
The Peacock Fan
The Photo of Lady X (RH)
The Portrait of Jirjohn Cobb
Report on Vanessa Hewstone (RH)
Riddle of the Travelling Skull
Riddle of the Wooden Parrakeet (RH)
The Scarlet Mummy (RH)
The Search for X-Y-Z
The Sharkskin Book
Sing Sing Nights
The Six From Nowhere (RH)
The Skull of the Waltzing Clown
The Spectacles of Mr. Cagliostro
Stand By—London Calling!
The Steeltown Strangler
The Stolen Gravestone (RH)
Strange Journey (RH)
The Strange Will
The Straw Hat Murders (RH)
The Street of 1000 Eyes (RH)
Thieves' Nights
Three Novellos (RH)
The Tiger Snake
The Trap (RH)
Vagabond Nights (Defrauded Yeggman)
Vagabond Nights 2 (10 Hours)
The Vanishing Gold Truck
The Voice of the Seven Sparrows
The Washington Square Enigma
When Thief Meets Thief
The White Circle (RH)
The Wonderful Scheme of Mr. Christopher Thorne
X. Jones—of Scotland Yard
Y. Cheung, Business Detective

Keeler Related Works

A To Izzard: A Harry Stephen Keeler Companion by Fender Tucker—Articles and stories about Harry, by Harry, and in his style. Included is a compleat bibliography.

Wild About Harry: Reviews of Keeler Novels—Edited by Richard Polt & Fender Tucker—22 reviews of works by Harry Stephen Keeler from *Keeler News*. A perfect introduction to the author.

The Keeler Keyhole Collection: Annotated newsletter rants from Harry Stephen Keeler, edited by Francis M. Nevins. Over 400 pages of incredibly personal Keeleriana.

Fakealoo—Pastiches of the style of Harry Stephen Keeler by selected demented members of the HSK Society. Updated every year with the new winner.

Strands of the Web: Short Stories of Harry Stephen Keeler—29 stories, just about all that Keeler wrote, are edited and introduced by Fred Cleaver.

RAMBLE HOUSE's Loon Sanctuary

A Clear Path to Cross—Sharon Knowles short mystery stories by Ed Lynskey.

A Corpse Walks in Brooklyn and Other Stories—Volume 5 in the Day Keene in the Detective Pulps series.

A Fair Californian—Novel by Olive Harper about a young woman's quest for gold — a quest that turns into something completely unexpected.

A Jimmy Starr Omnibus—Three 40s novels by Jimmy Starr.

A Niche in Time and Other Stories—Classic SF by William F. Temple.

A Shot Rang Out—Three decades of reviews and articles by today's Anthony Boucher, Jon Breen. An essential book for any mystery lover's library.

A Snark Selection—Lewis Carroll's *The Hunting of the Snark* with two Snarkian chapters by Harry Stephen Keeler—Illustrated by Gavin L. O'Keefe.

A Young Man's Heart—A forgotten early classic by Cornell Woolrich.

Alexander Laing Novels—*The Motives of Nicholas Holtz* and *Dr. Scarlett*, stories of medical mayhem and intrigue from the 30s.

An Angel in the Street—Modern hardboiled noir by Peter Genovese.

Automaton—Brilliant treatise on robotics: 1928-style! By H. Stafford Hatfield.

Away From the Here and Now—Clare Winger Harris stories, collected by Richard A. Lupoff

Beast or Man?—A 1930 novel of racism and horror by Sean M'Guire. Introduced by John Pelan.

Black Hogan Strikes Again—Australia's Peter Renwick pens a tale of the 30s outback.

Black River Falls—Suspense from the master, Ed Gorman.

Blondy's Boy Friend—A snappy 1930 story by Philip Wylie, writing as Leatrice Homesley.

Blood in a Snap—The *Finnegan's Wake* of the 21st century, by Jim Weiler.

Blood Moon—The first of the Robert Payne series by Ed Gorman.

Bogart '48—Hollywood action with Bogie by John Stanley and Kenn Davis

Butterfly Man—1930s novel by Lew Levenson about a dancer who must come to terms with his homosexuality.

Calling Lou Largo!—Two Lou Largo novels by William Ard.

Cathedral of Horror—First volume of collected stories by weird fiction writer Arthur J. Burks.

Chalk Face—Curious supernatural murder thriller by Waldo Frank.

Cornucopia of Crime—Francis M. Nevins assembled this huge collection of his writings about crime literature and the people who write it. Essential for any serious mystery library.

Corpse Without Flesh—Strange novel of forensics by George Bruce

Crimson Clown Novels—By Johnston McCulley, author of the Zorro novels, *The Crimson Clown* and *The Crimson Clown Again*.

Dago Red—22 tales of dark suspense by Bill Pronzini.

Dark Sanctuary—Weird Menace story by H. B. Gregory.

David Hume Novels—*Corpses Never Argue, Cemetery First Stop, Make Way for the Mourners, Eternity Here I Come.* 1930s British hardboiled fiction with an attitude.

David&Son: Peregrine Parentus and other tales—Collection of tales and memoirs by Avram Davidson and Ethan Davidson, some published for the first time. Introduced by Grania Davidson Davis.

Dead Man Talks Too Much—Hollywood boozer by Weed Dickenson.

Death in a Bowl—1930's murder mystery by Raoul Whitfield.

Death March of the Dancing Dolls and Other Stories—Volume Three in the Day Keene in the Detective Pulps series. Introduced by Bill Crider.

Deep Space and other Stories—A collection of SF gems by Richard A. Lupoff.

Detective Duff Unravels It—Episodic mysteries by Harvey O'Higgins.

Devil's Planet—Locked room mystery set on the planet Mars, by Manly Wade Wellman.

Dime Novels: Ramble House's 10-Cent Books—*Knife in the Dark* by Robert Leslie Bellem, *Hot Lead* and *Song of Death* by Ed Earl Repp, *A Hashish House in New York* by H.H. Kane, and five more.

Doctor Arnoldi—Tiffany Thayer's story of the death of death.

Don Diablo: Book of a Lost Film—Two-volume treatment of a western by Paul Landres, with diagrams. Intro by Francis M. Nevins.

Dope and Swastikas—Two strange novels from 1922 by Edmund Snell

Dope Tales #1—Two dope-riddled classics; *Dope Runners* by Gerald Grantham and *Death Takes the Joystick* by Phillip Condé.

Dope Tales #2—Two more narco-classics; *The Invisible Hand* by Rex Dark and *The Smokers of Hashish* by Norman Berrow.

Dope Tales #3—Two enchanting novels of opium by the master, Sax Rohmer. *Dope* and *The Yellow Claw.*

Double Hot & Double Sex—Two combos of '60s softcore sex novels by Morris Hershman.

Dr. Odin—Douglas Newton's 1933 racial potboiler comes back to life.

E. C. R. Lorac—*Black Beadle, Case in the Clinic, The Devil and the C.I.D.* and *Slippery Staircase.* Classic Golden Age murder mysteries.

E. Charles Vivian—*Evidence in Blue, Accessory After, The Lady of the Terraces* and *Ladies in the Case.*

E. R. Punshon novels—*Information Received, Crossword Mystery, Dictator's Way, Diabolic Candelabra, Music Tells All, Helen Passes By, The House of Godwinsson, The Golden Dagger, The Attending Truth, Strange Ending, Brought to Light, Dark is the Clue, Triple Quest,* and *Six Were Present*: featuring Bobby Owen.

Ed "Strangler" Lewis: Facts within a Myth—Authoritative illustrated biography of the famous American wrestler Ed Lewis, by noted historian Steve Yohe.

Evangelical Cockroach—Jack Woodford writes about writing.

Fatal Accident—Murder by automobile, a 1936 mystery by Cecil M. Wills.

Fighting Mad—Tod Robbins' 1922 novel about boxing and life.

Five Million in Cash—Gangster thriller by Tiffany Thayer writing as O. B. King.

Food for the Fungus Lady—Collection of weird stories by Ralston Shields, edited and introduced by John Pelan.

Francis M. Nevins—Three omnibus volumes of novels featuring his legal sleuth Loren Mensing and scam-artist Milo Turner: *Publish and Perish / Corrupt and Ensnare, Into the Same River Twice / Beneficiaries' Requiem* and *The 120-Hour Clock / The Ninety Million Dollar Mouse* — and the short story collection *Night Forms*.

Freaks and Fantasies—Eerie tales by Tod Robbins, collaborator of Tod Browning on the film FREAKS.

Gadsby—A lipogram (a novel without the letter E). Ernest Vincent Wright's last work, published in 1939 right before his death.

Gelett Burgess Novels—*The Master of Mysteries, The White Cat, Two O'Clock Courage, Ladies in Boxes, Find the Woman, The Heart Line, The Picaroons* and *Lady Mechante*. Recently added is A Gelett Burgess Sampler, edited by Alfred Jan. All are introduced by Richard A. Lupoff.

Geronimo—S. M. Barrett's 1905 autobiography of a noble American.

Gordon Eklund—*Second Creation, Retro Man* and *Stalking the Sun*: three volumes of the author's best short stories.

Go Forth and Multiply—Anthology of science fiction tales of repopulation, edited by Gordon Van Gelder.

Hake Talbot Novels—*Rim of the Pit, The Hangman's Handyman*. Classic locked room mysteries, with mapback covers by Gavin O'Keefe.

Hands Out of Hell and Other Stories—John H. Knox's eerie hallucinations

Hell is a City—William Ard's masterpiece.

Hollywood Dreams—A novel of Tinsel Town and the Depression by Richard O'Brien.

Homicide House—#6 in the Day Keene in the Detective Pulps series.

Hostesses in Hell and Other Stories—Russell Gray's most graphic stories

House of the Restless Dead—Strange and ominous tales by Hugh B. Cave

Inclination to Murder—1966 thriller by New Zealand's Harriet Hunter.

Invaders from the Dark—Classic werewolf tale from Greye La Spina.

J. Poindexter, Colored—Classic satirical black novel by Irvin S. Cobb.

Jack Mann Novels—Strange murder in the English countryside. *Gees' First Case, Nightmare Farm, Grey Shapes, The Ninth Life, The Glass Too Many, Her Ways Are Death, The Kleinert Case* and *Maker of Shadows*.

Jake Hardy—A lusty western tale from Wesley Tallant.

James Corbett—*Vampire of the Skies, The Ghost Plane, Murder Begets Murder* and *The Air Killer* – strange thriller novels from this singular British author.

Jim Harmon Double Novels—*Vixen Hollow/Celluloid Scandal, The Man Who Made Maniacs/Silent Siren, Ape Rape/Wanton Witch, Sex Burns Like Fire/Twist Session, Sudden Lust/Passion Strip, Sin Unlimited/Harlot Master, Twilight Girls/Sex Institution*. Written in the early 60s and never reprinted until now.

Joel Townsley Rogers Novels and Short Stories—By the author of *The Red Right Hand: Once In a Red Moon, Lady With the Dice, The Stopped Clock, Never Leave My Bed*. Also two short story collections: *Night of Horror* and *Killing Time*.

John Carstairs, Space Detective—Arboreal Sci-fi by Frank Belknap Long

John G. Brandon—*The Case of the Withered Hand, Finger-Prints Never Lie*, and *Death on Delivery*: crime thrillers by Australian author John G. Brandon.

John S. Glasby—Two collections of Glasby's Lovecraftian stories: *The Brooding City* and *Beyond the Rim*. Introduced by John Pelan.

Joseph Shallit Novels—*The Case of the Billion Dollar Body, Lady Don't Die on My Doorstep, Kiss the Killer, Yell Bloody Murder, Take Your Last Look*. One of America's best 50's authors and a favorite of author Bill Pronzini.

Keller Memento—45 short stories of the amazing and weird by Dr. David Keller.

Killer's Caress—Cary Moran's 1936 hardboiled thriller.

Knowing the Unknowable: Putting Psi to Work—Damien Broderick, PhD puts forward the valid case for evidence of Psi.

Laughing Death—1932 Yellow Peril thriller by Walter C. Brown.

League of the Grateful Dead and Other Stories—Volume One in the Day Keene in the Detective Pulps series.

Library of Death—Ghastly tale by Ronald S. L. Harding, introduced by John Pelan

Lords of the Earth—A novel of meddling dabblers in the occult invoking the ancient powers of Atlantis. J.M.A. Mills' sequel to *The Tomb of the Dark Ones*.

Mad-Doctor Merciful—Collin Brooks' unsettling novel of medical experimentation with supernatural forces.

Malcolm Jameson Novels and Short Stories—*Astonishing! Astounding!, Tarnished Bomb, The Alien Envoy and Other Stories* and *The Chariots of San Fernando and Other Stories*. All introduced and edited by John Pelan or Richard A. Lupoff.

Man Out of Hell and Other Stories—Volume II of the John H. Knox weird pulps collection.

Marblehead: A Novel of H.P. Lovecraft—A long-lost masterpiece from Richard A. Lupoff. This is the "director's cut", the long version that has never been published before.

Mark of the Laughing Death and Other Stories—Shockers from the pulps by Francis James, introduced by John Pelan.

Mark Hansom Novels—*Master of Souls, The Ghost of Gaston Revere, The Madman, The Shadow on the House, Sorcerer's Chessmen & The Wizard of Berner's Abbey*.

Max Afford Novels—*Owl of Darkness, Death's Mannikins, Blood on His Hands, The Dead Are Blind, The Sheep and the Wolves, Sinners in Paradise* and *Two Locked Room Mysteries and a Ripping Yarn* by one of Australia's finest mystery novelists.

Miles Burton novels—*A Smell of Smoke, Death Leaves No Card, Situation Vacant* and *Death Paints a Picture*.

Mr. South Burned His Mouth—Gentry Nyland's only novel: a thriller.

Molly and her Man of War— Romantic novel with a difference, by Arabella Kenealy.

Money Brawl—Two books about the writing business by Jack Woodford and H. Bedford-Jones. Introduced by Richard A. Lupoff.

More Secret Adventures of Sherlock Holmes—Gary Lovisi's second collection of tales about the unknown sides of the great detective.

Muddled Mind: Complete Works of Ed Wood, Jr.—David Hayes and Hayden Davis deconstruct the life and works of the mad, but canny, genius.

Murder among the Nudists—1934 mystery by Peter Hunt, featuring a naked Detective-Inspector going undercover in a nudist colony.

Murder in Black and White—1931 classic tennis whodunit by Evelyn Elder.

Murder in Shawnee—Two novels of the Alleghenies by John Douglas: *Shawnee Alley Fire* and *Haunts*.

Murder in Suffolk—A 1938 murder mystery novel by the mysterious 'A. Fielding.'

My Deadly Angel—1955 Cold War drama by John Chelton.

My First Time: The One Experience You Never Forget—Michael Birchwood—64 true first-person narratives of how they lost it.

My Touch Brings Death—Second volume of collected stories by Russell Gray.

Mysterious Martin, the Master of Murder—Two versions of a strange 1912 novel by Tod Robbins about a man who writes books that can kill.

Norman Berrow Novels—*The Bishop's Sword, Ghost House, Don't Go Out After Dark, Claws of the Cougar, The Smokers of Hashish, The Secret Dancer, Don't Jump Mr. Boland!, The Footprints of Satan, Fingers for Ransom, The Three Tiers of Fantasy, The Spaniard's Thumb, The Eleventh Plague, Words Have Wings, One Thrilling Night, The Lady's in Danger, It Howls at Night, The Terror in the Fog, Oil Under the Window, Murder in the Melody, The Singing Room.* This is the complete Norman Berrow library of locked-room mysteries, several of which are masterpieces.

Old Faithful and Other Stories—SF classic tales by Raymond Z. Gallun

Old Times' Sake—Short stories by James Reasoner from Mike Shayne Magazine.

One Dreadful Night—A classic mystery by Ronald S. L. Harding

Pair O' Jacks—A mystery novel and a diatribe about publishing by Jack Woodford

Pawns of Destiny—Psychological drama by Kay Seaton.

Perfect .38—Two early Timothy Dane novels by William Ard. More to come.

Prince Pax—Devilish intrigue by George Sylvester Viereck and Philip Eldridge

Prose Bowl—Futuristic satire of a world where hack writing has replaced football as our national obsession, by Bill Pronzini and Barry N. Malzberg.

Ralph Trevor novels—*Murder in Silk, Front Page Murder, Easy for the Crook, The Deputy Avenger,* etc.

Red Light—The history of legal prostitution in Shreveport Louisiana by Eric Brock. Includes wonderful photos of the houses and the ladies.

Researching American-Made Toy Soldiers—A 276-page collection of a lifetime of articles by toy soldier expert Richard O'Brien.

Reunion in Hell—Volume One of the John H. Knox series of weird stories from the pulps. Introduced by horror expert John Pelan.

Ripped from the Headlines!—The Jack the Ripper story as told in the newspaper articles in the *New York* and *London Times.*

Rough Cut & New, Improved Murder—Ed Gorman's first two novels.

R. R. Ryan Novels — *Freak Museum, The Subjugated Beast, Death of a Sadist, Echo of a Curse, Devil's Shelter* and *No Escape*. Introduced by John Pelan.

Roland Daniel Novels — *Ruby of a Thousand Dreams, The Girl in the Dark,* and *A Roland Daniel Double: The Signal and The Return of Wu Fang.*

Ruled By Radio — 1925 futuristic novel by Robert L. Hadfield & Frank E. Farncombe.

Rupert Penny Novels — *Policeman's Holiday, Policeman's Evidence, Lucky Policeman, Policeman in Armour, Sealed Room Murder, Sweet Poison, The Talkative Policeman, She had to Have Gas* and *Cut and Run* (by Martin Tanner.) Rupert Penny is the pseudonym of Australian Charles Thornett, a master of the locked room, impossible crime plot.

Sacred Locomotive Flies — Richard A. Lupoff's psychedelic SF story.

Sam — Early gay novel by Lonnie Coleman.

Sand's Game — Spectacular hardboiled noir from Ennis Willie, edited by Lynn Myers and Stephen Mertz, with contributions from Max Allan Collins, Bill Crider, Wayne Dundee, Bill Pronzini, Gary Lovisi and James Reasoner.

Sand's War — More violent fiction from the typewriter of Ennis Willie

Satan's Den Exposed — True crime in Truth or Consequences New Mexico — Award-winning journalism by the *Desert Journal.*

Satan's Secret and Selected Stories — Barnard Stacey's only novel with a selection of his best short stories.

Satans of Saturn — Novellas from the pulps by Otis Adelbert Kline and E. H. Price

Satan's Sin House and Other Stories — Horrific gore by Wayne Rogers

Second Creation — The first volume of selected short stories by Gordon Eklund.

Secrets of a Teenage Superhero — Graphic lit by Jonathan Sweet

Sex Slave — Potboiler of lust in the days of Cleopatra by Dion Leclerq, 1966.

Sideslip — 1968 SF masterpiece by Ted White and Dave Van Arnam.

Slammer Days — Two full-length prison memoirs: *Men into Beasts* (1952) by George Sylvester Viereck and *Home Away From Home* (1962) by Jack Woodford.

Star Griffin — Michael Kurland's 1987 masterpiece of SF drollery is back.

Stakeout on Millennium Drive — Award-winning Indianapolis Noir by Ian Woollen.

Strands of the Web: Short Stories of Harry Stephen Keeler — Edited and Introduced by Fred Cleaver.

Summer Camp for Corpses and Other Stories — Weird Menace tales from Arthur Leo Zagat; introduced by John Pelan.

Suzy — A collection of comic strips by Richard O'Brien and Bob Vojtko from 1970.

Tail of the Lizard King / Kaliwood — Two novellas by Adam Mudman Bezecny paying homage to the sleaze genre.

Tales of the Macabre and Ordinary — Modern twisted horror by Chris Mikul, author of the *Bizarrism* series.

Tales of Terror and Torment Vols. #1 & #2 — John Pelan selects and introduces these samplers of weird menace tales from the pulps.

Tenebrae — Ernest G. Henham's 1898 horror tale brought back.

The Crimson Butterfly — Early novel by Edmund Snell involving superstition and aberrant Lepidoptera in Borneo.

The Crimson Query — A 1929 thriller from Arlton Eadie. A perfect way to get introduced.

The Daymakers, City of the Tiger & Perchance to Wake — Three volumes of stories taken from the influential British science fiction magazine *Science Fantasy*. Compiled by John Boston & Damien Broderick.

The Devil Drives — An odd prison and lost treasure novel from 1932 by Virgil Markham.

The Devil of Pei-Ling — Herbert Asbury's 1929 tale of the occult.

The Devil's Mistress — A 1915 Scottish gothic tale by J. W. Brodie-Innes, a member of Aleister Crowley's Golden Dawn.

The Devil's Nightclub and Other Stories — John Pelan introduces some gruesome tales by Nat Schachner.

The Devil's Saint—1924 fantasy novel by Dulcie Deamer.

The Dirges of Maldoror — O'Keefe's illustrated English translation of Lautréamont's *Les Chants de Maldoror*.

The Disentanglers — Episodic intrigue at the turn of last century by Andrew Lang

The Dog Poker Code — A spoof of *The Da Vinci Code* by D. B. Smithee.

The Dumpling — Political murder from 1907 by Coulson Kernahan.

The End of It All and Other Stories — Ed Gorman selected his favorite short stories for this huge collection.

The Evil of Li-Sin — A Gerald Verner double, combining *The Menace of Li-Sin* and *The Vengeance of Li-Sin*, together with an introduction by John Pelan and an afterword and bibliography by Chris Verner.

The Fangs of Suet Pudding — A 1944 novel of the German invasion by Adams Farr

The Finger of Destiny and Other Stories — Edmund Snell's superb collection of weird stories of Borneo.

The Gold Star Line — Seaboard adventure from L.T. Meade and Robert Eustace.

The Great Boo-Boo — Curious 1892 politico-satirical fantasy by Henry S. Wilcox.

The Great Orme Terror — Horror stories by Garnett Radcliffe from the pulps

The Hairbreadth Escapes of Major Mendax — Francis Blake Crofton's 1889 boys' book.

The House That Time Forgot and Other Stories — Insane pulpitude by Robert F. Young

The House of the Vampire — 1907 poetic thriller by George S. Viereck.

The Illustrious Corpse — Murder hijinx from Tiffany Thayer

The Incredible Adventures of Rowland Hern — Intriguing 1928 impossible crimes by Nicholas Olde.

The John Dickson Carr Companion — Comprehensive reference work compiled by James E. Keirans. Indispensable resource for the Carr *aficionado*.

The Julius Caesar Murder Case — A 1935 retelling of the assassination by Wallace Irwin that's more fun than Shakespeare's version.

The Kid Was a Killer — Caryl Chessman's only novel, based on his own experiences.

The Koky Comics — A collection of all of the 1978-1981 Sunday and daily comic strips by Richard O'Brien and Mort Gerberg, in two volumes.

The Lord of Terror — 1925 mystery with master-criminal, Fantômas.

The Man who was Murdered Twice — Intriguing murder mystery by Robert H. Leitfred.

The Melamare Mystery — A classic 1929 Arsene Lupin mystery by Maurice Leblanc

The Man Who Was Secrett — Epic SF stories from John Brunner

The Man Without a Planet — Science fiction tales by Richard Wilson

The N. R. De Mexico Novels — Robert Bragg, the real N.R. de Mexico, presents *Marijuana Girl, Madman on a Drum, Private Chauffeur* in one volume.

The Night Remembers — A 1991 Jack Walsh mystery from Ed Gorman.

The One After Snelling — Kickass modern noir from Richard O'Brien.

The Organ Reader — A huge compilation of just about everything published in the 1971-1972 radical bay-area newspaper, *THE ORGAN*. A coffee table book that points out the shallowness of the coffee table mindset.

The Place of Hairy Death — Collected weird horror tales by Anthony M. Rud.

The Poker Club — Three in one! Ed Gorman's ground-breaking novel, the short story it was based upon, and the screenplay of the film made from it.

The Private Journal & Diary of John H. Surratt — The memoirs of the man who conspired to assassinate President Lincoln.

The Ramble House Coloring Book — Twenty illustrations to color in, each adapted from one of Gavin L. O'Keefe's cover designs.

The Ramble House Mapbacks — Recently revised book by Gavin L. O'Keefe with color pictures of all the Ramble House books with mapbacks.

The Secret Adventures of Sherlock Holmes — Three Sherlockian pastiches by the Brooklyn author/publisher, Gary Lovisi.

The Secret of the Morgue — Frederick G. Eberhard's 1932 mystery involving murder and forensic science with an undercurrent of the malaise that's driven by Prohibition.

The Sign of the Scorpion — A 1935 Edmund Snell tale of oriental evil.

The Silent Terror of Chu-Sheng — Yellow Peril suspense novel by Eugene Thomas.

The Singular Problem of the Stygian House-Boat — Two classic tales by John Kendrick Bangs about the denizens of Hades.

The Smiling Corpse — Philip Wylie and Bernard Bergman's odd 1935 novel.

The Sorcery Club — Classic supernatural novel by Elliott O'Donnell.

The Spider: Satan's Murder Machines — A thesis about Iron Man.

The Stench of Death: An Odoriferous Omnibus by Jack Moskovitz — Two complete novels and two novellas from 60's sleaze author, Jack Moskovitz.

The Story Writer and Other Stories — Classic SF from Richard Wilson

The Strange Thirteen — Richard B. Gamon's odd stories about Raj India.

The Technique of the Mystery Story — Carolyn Wells' tips about writing.

Victims & Villains — Intriguing Sherlockiana from Derham Groves.

Wade Wright Novels — *Echo of Fear, Death At Nostalgia Street, It Leads to Murder* and *Shadows' Edge*, a double book featuring *Shadows Don't Bleed* and *The Sharp Edge*.

Walter S. Masterman Novels — *The Green Toad, The Flying Beast, The Yellow Mistletoe, The Wrong Verdict, The Perjured Alibi, The Border Line, The Bloodhounds Bay, The Curse of Cantire, The Curse of the Reckaviles, Death Turns Traitor, The Wrong Letter, The Death Coins, The Nameless Crime, The Tangle, The Baddington Horror, The Hooded Monster*, and *The Man Without a Head*.

We Are the Dead and Other Stories — Volume Two in the Day Keene in the Detective Pulps series, introduced by Ed Gorman. When done, there may be 11 in the series.

Welsh Rarebit Tales — Charming stories from 1902 by Harle Oren Cummins

West Texas War and Other Western Stories — Western hijinks by Gary Lovisi.

What Was That?—Ghostly murder mystery from 1920 by Katharine Haviland Taylor.

What If? Volume 3 — Richard A. Lupoff introduces three decades worth of SF short stories that should have won a Hugo, but didn't.

When the Bat Man Thirsts and Other Stories — Weird tales from Frederick C. Davis.

When the Dead Walk — Gary Lovisi takes us into the zombie-infested South.

Whip Dodge: Man Hunter — Wesley Tallant's saga of a bounty hunter of the old West.

Win, Place and Die! — The first new mystery by Milt Ozaki in decades. The ultimate novel of 70s Reno.

Writer, Volumes 1, 2 & 3 — A *magnus opus* from Richard A. Lupoff summing up his life as writer.

Wyatt Blassingame — Four volumes of collected stories: *The Tongueless Horror, The Unholy Goddess, Lady of the Yellow Death* and *Mistress of Terror*.

You'll Die Laughing — Bruce Elliott's 1945 novel of murder at a practical joker's English countryside manor.

You're Not Alone: 30 Science Fiction Stories from *Cosmos Magazine*, edited by Damien Broderick.

RAMBLE HOUSE
www.ramblehouse.com
flyingspiderster@gmail.com
10329 Sheephead Drive, Vancleave MS 39565